TWILIGHT OF THE PUMPKIN MAN

Jack Beaumont

KING'S WAY PRESS

For my precious wife and children who make each day special and worth living!

TWILIGHT OF THE PUMPKIN MAN

Jack Beaumont

THE PUMPKIN MAN IS BACK...

He gazed upon the body of the young girl where she lay, splayed out on top of the bloody mattress in a bold and shocking mockery of the crucifixion. He nodded his head smiling in approval of his own brutal handiwork. Satisfied that his message would be well received by his intended audience, he remained content for now.

She looks good, he thought. *A true work of art.*

The completed work was a culmination of several hours of viciously torturing the girl, using her in every way possible; he was very satisfied with his finished product indeed. His driving, insistent physical lust had been slaked for the moment; his spiritual lust for blood never to be quenched, had at least been temporarily sated. Both cravings would return soon; the craving for bloodshed taking precedence over the lesser need for physical satisfaction. Already, he'd begun formulating plans for his next victim; dreaming of the blood that he would spill next.

This time around he was determined that things would be vastly different than in his previous attempts to conquer this town. Having been defeated twice by the citizens of Summer's Cove, and the unlikely band of heroes who arose within, he wouldn't make the same crippling mistakes again. He wouldn't betray his presence prematurely as he'd done in the past. If nothing else, his prolonged periods of interment had helped him to develop much needed patience; provided him with clarity. This time the sheep wouldn't know about the ravenous wolf in their midst…until it was far too late for all of them. He would *not* fail in his conquest again.

In the past, he'd invaded the dreams of the weak-minded as a precursor to his arrival in Summer's Cove. He wouldn't be tipping his hand early again. This time, they'd receive no such advance warnings; no such chances for an early intervention. No planting of murderous intent and ideas in the heads of his victims, no recruitment of his disciples weeks in advance. No, this time he was going to be as silent as a venomous spider before striking its prey. No threats; no warnings, no dreams, or disturbing visions. This time around, he would collect his disciples as he went about his conquest, much like the *other* had done in *His* lifetime.

He was going to go about things much smarter this time…and he was confident in, and pleased with, his superior planning. Sixteen years had passed since his last stunning defeat. He wasn't about to let a feeble old woman, or a fallen preacher, stop him. *Never again.* This most recent term of interment, spent trapped and buried in Hunter's Glen, had allowed him to think, to watch, to analyze his failures, to come up with a better plan of attack.

He was too powerful, too eternal, to be thwarted by these weak and pitiful creations of his former master. As he felt that familiar, ever present hate for these lowly, pitiful creatures flowing through him, he felt alive. He felt free! The fear and the pain that this young girl had given voice to as she suffered, bled, and finally died, had invigorated him, making him strong again after his insufferable sixteen-year nap.

He surveyed his handiwork a final time before turning to leave the room. The girl was lying on the bed completely naked, arms stretched straight out to the sides, as if reaching for either edge of the mattress, her legs extended straight down from her body, ankles overlapping each other. Her lustrous mane of long silky brown hair lay artfully arranged on the pillow upon which her head softly rested, framing each side of her unmarked, and uncommonly beautiful face. Her light blue eyes remained open and staring at the ceiling; the glaze of death dulling their once brilliant shine.

The palm of each delicate hand had been turned upward, pinned to the mattress with a sharp steak knife. He hated that he'd had to improvise, but he was left without choice, because he couldn't find any nails that were long enough to do the trick. But such was life.

It would suffice.

The girl's ankles had been crossed, and pinned together with a razor-sharp, wooden handled, carving knife that had been driven through them, and deep into the mattress below. Atop her radiant head sat the green, rough-hewn crown of thorns that he'd hastily woven together from the knockout rose bushes that graced the front of her house. Blood trailed down the sides of girl's pale face in thin streams from where the thorns had pricked the tender flesh of her scalp.

She became a nearly perfect mirror image of the crucifixion…with the exception of the missing hole in her side. Instead, a ragged, bloody, gaping hole marred the girl's chest where her heart should have been. While not an *exact* recreation of the scene that he wished to mockingly portray, it was close enough.

It would have to do.

He only wished that his fun hadn't had to end so quickly, but he had other pressing matters to attend to. He let out a long, ominous chuckle as he raised his right hand to his mouth, taking a large bite out of the girl's rapidly cooling heart.

Maybe I should go visit mother now, The Pumpkin Man thought with a sneer...

CHAPTER 1

JUNE 25TH, 2019

A WARM BREEZE FLOWED THROUGH THE AIR OF THE picturesque glen, causing the long grasses to sway gently to and fro in the wind. Birds loudly sang their cheerful afternoon songs in the large oak and pine trees lining the other side of the flowing Pumpkin Vine River. The sun hung high in the afternoon sky, overseeing this bright and cloudless day. June bugs and other insects created a low hum that could just barely be heard over the water babbling across the water-smoothed river stones. Somewhere in the distance a squirrel barked as it frolicked in the trees.

On this side of the rushing stream, the day was just as beautiful, but there was a conspicuous lack of the same signs of wildlife and activity that were abundant on the opposite side of the riverbank. Although you could hear the varied sounds of life coming from across the river, save for the babbling sound of water caressing the rocks in the stream, this side of Hunter's Glen remained eerily quiet.

The voluptuous blond girl who had parked her car at the foot of the rolling hill in the center of the glen didn't seem to notice, or to even care about, the unnatural silence of this place. She exited the driver's side door of the car, and then walked to the back door on the same side, opened it, briefly leaning in. A second later, she stepped back, allowing a young child to emerge from the car.

The girl closed the back door of the car and then leaned forward into the still open driver's side door, removing a large blanket and a small wicker picnic basket. After fetching the items, she closed the door and with her free hand she reached down, taking her son Samuel's hand, leading him up the hill toward the large, and very old, oak tree.

"Do you think Daddy will talk to me today?" Samuel asked, beaming at his mother with a wide, toothy, three-year old smile.

"Maybe," she responded. It concerned her a little that Samuel always claimed that his "Daddy" spoke to him whenever they visited Hunter's Glen. The truth was that she wasn't even sure where Samuel's father currently lived, much less why he would be "speaking" to her son from this, and *only* this, location. It was as if he were dead and his "ghost" was somehow tied to this place. This ironically, happened to be the last place that Betty had laid eyes on Samuel's father. She had heard from others that he'd fled someplace, likely towards the West Coast.

∙∙∙

She wasn't even sure why she was drawn so strongly to this place, but she felt the need to visit the glen at least once a year. Although she didn't remember all that had happened to her here, nearly four years ago, she did know that she had some sort of deep connection with this place. Her mother and her doctors had told her that something really, really bad had once happened to her here...and that Samuel's father was the cause. They were adamant that she shouldn't visit Hunter's Glen, especially alone. They said that it might trigger a chain of traumatic memories...memories that were better off forgotten. They said that visiting this place might cause her to suffer a severe panic attack, or even send her into a traumatic state of shock.

Truthfully, she didn't feel even the slightest amount of fear or trepidation upon entering Hunter's Glen for the first time since the "accident". In fact, the majestic beauty of this serene wilderness setting seemed to welcome her to itself with open arms. Each time she visited; it was as if she were home at last. As she had taken in the breathtaking views of the large oak, pine, and dogwood trees, the long and flowing grasses, and the rushing stream for the first time since the "accident"; the warmth from the sun had caressed her skin as a gentle breeze blew light kisses across her cheeks. She'd felt at home here. Safe. Not even the slightest sense of dread or apprehension had scarred her consciousness. This place was perfect. Serene. Comforting.

Since that first visit here, the summer after she left the hospital, she'd visited the glen at least once, sometimes twice each year. The first time that Samuel had mentioned his "Daddy" in Hunter's Glen was when he was just a year old. She'd left him sleeping peacefully on a plush blanket under the large oak tree at the top of the hill, while she'd trudged back down the hill to retrieve the cellphone that she'd left charging in the car.

When she came back to the child, he was sitting up. She heard him say, "Yes, da-da". At the time she hadn't thought much of it. As she was carrying Sammy down the hill on her hip that afternoon, heading back to their car, Sammy waved over her shoulder and said, "Bye da-da". While she thought it odd at the time, she hadn't been too concerned over it.

The following year, when they visited Hunter's Glen again, Samuel spoke of his father yet again. "Daddy talks to me here," he had told her at the time. Figuring that he was just exercising his vivid imagination, she still hadn't been bothered too much by the child's words. She did mention it to his pediatrician during his wellness checkup the following day.

"He's probably just making up a 'daddy' in his head to cope with not having a father figure in the home," Doctor Young said. "I wouldn't worry about it too much. Unless he starts talking about this 'daddy' all the time, or unless he seems to start becoming detached from reality in other ways. Then, we might have a problem."

"So, I shouldn't worry about it?"

"Not unless his 'daddy' starts telling him to do things. Especially things that are contrary to his character. Should his 'daddy' start telling him to act out, especially in ways that are violent or temperamental, then we might have more cause for concern. Otherwise, I would consider this very much a non-issue."

"Okay. I'll take your word for it."

Doctor Young had been her own pediatrician growing up. She'd known him for most of her life; she trusted him nearly as much as she trusted her own father. He'd said not to worry, so she'd trusted his judgment. She hadn't worried about it much over the past several years.

"Some children have imaginary friends. Your son has created an imaginary 'daddy'. It's not that uncommon," he'd reassured her, as they'd walked toward the checkout desk at the front of the practice. As the doctor handed her son's file to the receptionist, he put his firm, reassuring hand on her shoulder, in a fatherly manner. "In fact, I wouldn't be surprised at all if when you start dating, and you introduce a good man to your son, that this imaginary 'daddy' disappears rather quickly."

"Thank you, Doctor," she'd said with a grateful smile as she turned her attention to the receptionist and paid her bill. She'd taken the doctor's advice and hadn't worried about Sammy's "daddy" since that day. The only time that his "daddy" seemed to appear was when they visited Hunter's Glen... and he didn't seem to be a threat of any kind, to either herself or Samuel.

If girl had only known then how wrong she was, and how much of a threat that Samuel's "daddy" really presented, she would never have entered Hunter's Glen again, with or without her child...

JACK BEAUMONT

CHAPTER 2
HUNTER'S GLEN SEPTEMBER 19TH, 2032

Samuel and his mother pulled into Hunter's Glen on a beautiful summer-like fall day. The sun shone brightly overhead; the grasses in the fields blew back and forth in the warm, gentle breeze that flowed through the meadow. The river was making soft gurgling noises, as the water rushed over the rocks in its path, making its way toward the ocean.

Across the river birds sang their cheerful songs and unseen animals caused the brush to rustle with their passing. Somewhere in one of the large oak trees across the water a family of squirrels chittered back and forth as they played chase up, down, and around the tree. A deer crashed through the underbrush, possibly spooked by the car that had invaded the quiet meadow across the stream.

As he and his mother made their way up the hill to the huge oak tree that stood at the center of the meadow, the meadow where they had come picnicking every year since he could remember, he wondered at the quietness that always encompassed this side of the glen. Although he could hear all manner of birds, wildlife, and even insects coming from across the river, Samuel couldn't remember ever hearing, or even seeing, any signs of life in the glen proper. Not even an ant hill, or a bee buzzing by, could be found on this side of the river. It was as if life itself stopped at the point where the river ended, and the solid ground of the opposing riverbank began.

There was nothing to be heard on this side of the river. Except for the voice. His "Daddy", as he'd come to know the voice over the years. Although his mother wasn't aware of it, he still "heard" the voice that claimed to be his father each and every time that they came to visit out here. The voice was always there, just waiting for him; ready to hold a mental conversation that only they could hear. It was strange, but in a weird way also comforting, to know that the voice would be waiting to greet him when he came out here.

At the age of ten, when he finally realized that mentioning the voice to his mother seemed to deeply disturb her, he'd made a conscious decision not to let her know that he still heard it when they came to visit. The following year when they visited Hunter's Glen, he didn't say anything about hearing his "Daddy's" voice for the first time since he was able to speak. In fact, on the way home his mother had asked him directly about it.

"Did your Daddy speak to you today, honey?" she asked, intently scanning his face in the rearview mirror.

"No. I didn't hear the voice today," he lied, as he watched her reflection for any signs that she didn't believe him. His mother frowned for a second, then gave him a slight smile.

"That's good. Maybe he's moved on."

And, that was the last time he'd ever discussed the voice with her. He was glad too. When he was little, the voice of his "Daddy" had always been comforting. Fun.

Even kind and warm. Each visit here had been like visiting with a favorite uncle, or close family friend.

Until last year.

The voice had started turning darker last year. In every past visit, the voice had always filled him with a feeling of warmth and love. Last year, that abruptly changed. He thought he could detect an undercurrent of something malevolent hiding just underneath the surface facade of friendliness and warmth. It had scared him more than a little. Upon leaving Hunter's Glen, he'd been glad that he didn't have to discuss with his mother the voice, or the things that it'd said to him.

■■■

The change started when they first arrived on a warm, late summer day the prior September. As always, the voice seemed to know immediately that they'd arrived. Just like every time prior, his "Daddy" had seemed happy to know that Samuel was there. But, unlike previous visits, there seemed to be an urgency to the voice; one that had never existed before. A dark need. A deep longing. Although still friendly enough, the voice seemed to possess an undercurrent of anger and aggression bubbling just beneath the surface. It reminded him of when his mother would get mad at him for something and he could see her anger running just beneath the surface of her features, although her face remained calm.

That wasn't the worst part of it either. The worst part was the things that it had said to him that day. The questions it had asked of him. Questions that made him cringe. Questions about his mother. Questions about his girlfriend. Questions about taking revenge on the people who bullied him at school. Never before had the voice discussed topics such as violence, sex, and revenge with him. It was as if the voice were interviewing him for something. Taking measure of him…and he didn't like it. He didn't like it at all.

After a while, he tried shutting the voice out of his mind. In spite of his efforts to silence it, he was still being peppered with questions and dark suggestions in his mind. He chose to ignore them. He found that by going for a swim and getting as far away as possible from the massive oak tree, that the voice became more like hearing a distant radio program. It became diluted with "static" the further that he got away from that tree.

For the first time in his life, he felt an intense rush of relief when his mother announced that it was time to go home for the day…

CHAPTER 3
SEPTEMBER 19TH, 2032

The former Mayor of Summer's Cove awoke with a start for the third time in as many days. As the last vestiges of the terrible dream slipped from his mind, he shivered again involuntarily. He didn't know why this was happening to him. He'd never been prone to nightmares; so why was he having them now? So frequently? Especially deeply disturbing nightmares about an evil that had been laid to rest long ago?

Elton Crosby had never been a superstitious man. If anything, the exact opposite had been true for most of his life. He'd believed in neither the boogeyman, nor Gods, nor spirits, goblins, or ghouls. He'd been an avowed atheist, who regarded the religious crowd with deep disdain and contempt for most of his adult life. His stringent unbelief in anything that he couldn't see had almost been his downfall. Something major had happened sixteen years ago which had changed all of that for good. The day that he stood face to face with real, malevolent evil, and survived, had changed him forever.

Now, he attended church more than some of the people who he'd once despised for their faith. He'd also taken to wearing a small silver crucifix around his neck.

Call it faith, call it superstition, call it what you will, he'd seen something so profound that it had changed his life on many levels. He could never go back to the belief system that he'd once held so dear.

No way, he thought. *Not after what I've seen with my own eyes.*

What he'd seen had been the stuff of pure nightmares. The sort of nightmares that were usually consigned to a low-budget Hollywood film reel. But, unfortunately, it had been all too real. The blood, the violence, the death and destruction. All of it had been real, rather than the results of Hollywood special effects. Real blood running in the streets; real lives shattered forever.

The Pumpkin Man, he thought.

An ancient evil that he'd once thought of as nothing more than the hysterical delusions of a bunch of small-town hicks. *Only, he wasn't a delusion,* he sighed as he rolled out of bed. As his feet hit the floor, he took a deep breath, stretched his arms, and smiled. He could smell the savory, thick aroma of cooking bacon wafting upstairs from the kitchen. The kitchen where his now wife, Juanita Tanner-Crosby, was busy preparing breakfast.

■■■

They say that those who suffer through a traumatic event sometimes grow much closer to each other. Often closer than ever before. Tragedy had a way of forming bonds between those who shared in it. This had turned out to be very true in the case of Elton Crosby and Juanita Tanner. They'd both witnessed the final moments of the evil being known as The Pumpkin Man.

They'd also witnessed something else that no one else had reported seeing that night.

Something unexplainable. Something that had caused Elton to closely reexamine his faith, or actually his lack thereof. As Mrs. Elmira Camp had sacrificed her life to destroy The Pumpkin Man, Elton had witnessed a sight to behold. Before she fell to the ground dead, killed by the raging hellfire that had issued from The Pumpkin Man's dying mouth, Elton had witnessed a man superimposed over her features for just the briefest of moments.

It was a man who had radiated love and kindness beyond explanation. A man who had helped give Elmira the capacity to save the town from a great evil. A man who had given the elderly woman, who had not walked in years, the ability to not only walk, but also the power to defeat a monster. A man who could not be. A man who *was*. A man who Elton Crosby had always denied existed.

Yet, he must.

Elton had seen him with his own eyes and that small thing, that small miracle, had changed his life forever. So had the events in the town of Summer's Cove that fateful Halloween night. He'd never been the same. In many ways, his life was much better now. Fuller; more complete. Whole. Richer. Sweeter.

As he made his way downstairs to greet his lovely wife with a warm good morning kiss, he wondered if he should tell her about the nightmares that had started up a few days ago...

JACK BEAUMONT

CHAPTER 4
SEPTEMBER 19TH, 2032

Their annual visit to Hunter's Glen was upon him again. He still didn't really understand his mother's deep attachment to this place. Sure, it was serene and beautiful, but it wasn't the only such location in the surrounding area. Why didn't they just go to Carter's Lake, like so many of his other classmates did? Why this secluded, yet breathtakingly beautiful, location so far out in the middle of nowhere?

For the first time ever, when his mother told him that they were coming here today, he looked upon the trip with deepening dread. He hoped that the voice would be gone for real this time. But, since he knew that there was little hope that the voice had just disappeared after all of these years, he hoped and prayed that it was at least back to "normal"; as if hearing a voice speaking to you in your head could be considered as such. For the first time, he sincerely hoped that the voice wouldn't be there at all. Hearing nothing would be a vast improvement over listening to the vile things that the voice had shared with him last year.

Alas, as soon as they parked the car, approached the large oak and spread out their picnic blanket, he was eagerly greeted by the voice. Bombarded might be a better word. His dread at hearing the disembodied voice soon turned to relief instead. It seemed that his "Daddy" was in a cheerful mood. The darkness that he'd detected the year prior seemed to have fled, and the voice had taken on its normal, friendly demeanor once again.

After finishing his part of the picnic lunch, shared with his mother, he went for a swim in the river. All the while they'd eaten, he'd engaged in a cheerful mental conversation with the voice. Reflecting on that conversation now, as he swam, he felt a little silly that he'd almost been too scared to come here today. The voice possessed none of that dark edge that he remembered from last year, and the "conversation" had been light and pleasant. After about thirty minutes of swimming in the river, the combined effects of warm sunlight, a full belly, and the soothing water started making him very sleepy. While his mother was walking through the long grasses in the field by the river, seemingly lost in her own thoughts, he decided to take a quick nap underneath the big oak tree.

Not long after he lay down on the blanket that they'd spread on the ground, in the shade of the tree, when they first arrived, using his jeans and shirt as a pillow, he fell fast asleep. That's when the most horrific nightmare he'd ever experienced began. The voice was his guide on this mental trip of terror. The things that the voice showed him in the dream absolutely horrified, and disgusted him, at the same time.

The nightmare that the voice played for him in his mind's eye took place right here in Hunter's Glen. As the dream began, it became clear to Samuel that the vantage point of this graphic scene was coming from underneath this very tree, where he lay sleeping at this moment. He sensed that he was witnessing this scene through the eyes and ears of the voice inside his head.

At first the scene was very blurry, out of focus. It was as if he were gazing through a window that was covered in thick frost or heavy condensation. A few moments later, upon his vision clearing, he was startled to see a girl running away from his vantage point, as the person whose eyes he was seeing this through picked up and hurled a hefty rock, viciously sailing it through the air toward the fleeing girl's head. To Samuel's dismay, the rock caught the girl squarely in the back of the head, striking her with tremendous force, emphasized with a sickening *crack*. The solid blow, and her own momentum, throwing her forward, knocking her sprawling over the hood of a vintage red Camaro. The car was parked at the base of the hill, near the bank of the stream. The girl lay face down, spread-eagled across the hood of the car, unmoving, blood already dripping from her nasty head wound, a tiny red river running down the hood of the car, as her limp feet dangled just inches above the ground.

All the while, as he watched these horrific events playing out through someone else's eyes, Samuel felt a seething, white-hot rage. A feeling that was so intense that it literally caused him to feel nauseated, even in his deep sleep. He felt, as well as tasted, bile starting to rise in the back of his throat. He fought the strong urge to vomit as his mind recoiled from what he was seeing; yet he was unable to look away.

What came next was a horror unspeakable, as he was forced to watch as the unconscious, bleeding, and possibly dying young girl was assaulted in the worst possible ways. Samuel tried not to see what was happening, but since he was only a guest inside the head of the man doing this, he couldn't close his eyes, or even look away. Nor could he block out the terrible sounds of the assault as it took place. He was forced to watch and hear what transpired, as it happened; his sleeping body threatening to revolt, and cause him to spew the contents of his lunch.

Finally, after what seemed like an eternity had passed, the brutal assault ended. The man callously threw the girl off the hood of the car onto the ground, like an empty container that's contents had been used up. He began to open the driver's door of the Camaro. The graphic scene started to fade in Samuel's head as the man sat down behind the wheel of the car. Before the vision completely faded to black, he heard malevolent, and ominous laughter; the type of laughter that only evil could give birth to. Nothing he'd ever heard in his short life compared. It was pure evil, set to laughter.

Samuel gasped loudly, bolting upright from the rapidly departing nightmare. His body was covered in cold sweat, his stomach still feeling queasy from the overpowering rage that he'd felt in the other's mind; not to mention the traumatic scene he'd just witnessed. It had all been so real. It had been so appalling. It had been so violent… and so terribly, terribly vivid that he still felt the fear, the rage, and the nausea from the dream.

Samuel pushed up from the ground, standing on trembling legs, stretching his limbs. Slowly, the effects of the nightmare began wearing off. The nausea and the feared subsided, and he began to feel slightly better. To his surprise, he discovered that another vestige of the dream remained. He was both mortified, and embarrassed, when he noticed that he still sported a bulging stiffness in the front of his jeans.

JACK BEAUMONT

CHAPTER 5

The long car ride home from Hunter's Glen was unusually quiet. This was just fine with Samuel, as he was still trying to process the disturbing nightmare he'd been shown. He was sure that what he'd witnessed, through the eyes of another, had been more than just a dream. He couldn't determine whether what the voice had shown him was a vision of the past, or something that was destined to happen in the future. Something that had happened in Hunter's Glen once before, or something that could be stopped from happening yet.

He also found himself wondering about what had, or what would, become of the girl. Had she just been abandoned there and left to die, or had the man done something even worse before departing? She'd been tossed to the ground in front of the car. Samuel had a stomach-churning thought; *what if the man ran her over with the car to finish her off? And, if these things hadn't happened yet, was there a way that he could save her from suffering her fate?*

The silence in the car was just starting to become thick, even oppressive, when it was broken by his mother.

"What're you brooding about over there?" she asked. "You're not usually this quiet."

"Nothing," he muttered absentmindedly.

"Something's bothering you," Betty said. "I know you better than anyone else, and I know when something's wrong." She hesitated before asking, "You're not hearing the voice again are you? Be honest."

The question startled him back out of his contemplative replaying of the vision and back into the present.

"No!" he said a little too loudly, with a little too much emphasis. "No," he repeated in a more normal tone. "I was just thinking about school and stuff," he lied, hoping to convince her.

"Okay," she replied hesitantly.

He knew that his answer didn't sound very convincing, not even to his own ears. A sideways glance, using his peripheral vision, told him that his mother wasn't completely buying his answer either. She had that disappointed look on her face; the one she always got when she knew he wasn't being completely honest.

At least she's dropped it for now, he thought. The last thing he wanted to do right now was recount the details of the atrocious nightmare to his mother.

His mother had possibly decided to chalk up his surly silence during the rest of the ride home as teenage angst. The sullen moodiness that teenage boys were famous for. Whatever the reason, he was thankful for the ensuing silence during the rest of the ride home.

■■■

That night, Samuel woke three times in a cold panic. Each time, as he woke, the nightmare from earlier that day slowly faded from his mind. Each time, he heard the same ominous, malevolent laughter just as he regained consciousness.

After the third time of being awakened by the nightmare, he decided he was done trying to get any rest for the night. It was 6:AM already, not too long until he needed to get up and start getting ready for school anyway. As he left the bed to go to the bathroom, relieving his aching bladder, he thought that he heard the voice in his head beckoning for him to, "Come to me Samuel". This was strange. He'd never heard the voice outside of Hunter's Glen before.

Maybe it's my imagination, he thought.

No, it's not, the familiar voice in his head said. *I want you to come to me.*

He started to worry that something was seriously wrong with him. *Maybe I **am** going crazy,* he thought. He inspected his reflection in the bathroom mirror, looking for any visible signs of insanity.

His mother had warned him long ago not to mention the voice to anyone else. Anyone other than her. "People will get the wrong idea and they won't believe you," she'd told him as a little boy. "Or worse," she'd said, "They'll think that you're crazy."

As he finished up in the bathroom, and decided to study for his World History test for a few minutes before it was time to get ready for school, he prayed that he wasn't losing his sanity.

JACK BEAUMONT

CHAPTER 6
SEPTEMBER 19TH, 2032

The Pumpkin Man felt renewed, refreshed, and powerful once again. There was something about that child; the illegitimate offspring of William, last person whose physical body he'd inhabited. Whenever the boy and his mother came to visit, his power was renewed, restored for a short time. It was like he was a battery that needed recharging, and the boy acted like a charging station; his psychic energy providing the much-needed recharge.

That's why the girl was so strongly drawn to this place...because it was *his* will. He had implanted the desire in her mind to visit Hunter's Glen at least once every year. He had maintained a lifeline to this girl through the child that she bore. With each person he possessed, with each body he took over, he seemed to retain a part of the individual mind of the original occupant. He maintained some of their memories, some of their thoughts, some of who they were. This served as a connection between him, the boy, and the boy's mother.

He remembered when he had first inhabited Titus Anastas; the power that he had acquired through *that* connection. He gained powers that he never knew were even possible before. Once he rose again, in the body of the transient, he had lacked that same powerful connection. But now? Now he felt power like never before, whenever his "son" was near him. He knew that if he could just possess the body of his "son" that he would be more powerful than ever when he rose yet again.

That's why he'd spent the last sixteen years grooming the boy. He'd started off as the doting "Daddy"; engaging the child from an early age. Getting the boy accustomed to hearing his "voice". Making sure to keep their conversations warm and pleasant; fatherly even. With each and every visit from the boy and his mother, he inserted himself deeper and deeper into the boy's mind; reaching into his inner psyche, learning of the child's desires, his fears, even his aspirations. Planting seeds. Seeds that he carefully watered over time.

It wasn't until last year that he began pushing the boundaries, showing the boy more of the nature of his true self. As expected, the change in his demeanor had shocked, and even scared, the boy. He had known that this would happen. But, because he could read the boy's most intimate thoughts, he also knew that there was a morbid curiosity there as well; a seeking nature. He knew that he had developed something to work with.

So much for the all-powerful one. It seemed like there was a basic design flaw common to all his creations. No matter how pure his pitiful creatures thought themselves, not matter how much they tried to suppress the lingering darkness lurking inside, all of them seemed to have at least a small, dark corner hidden inside their beating hearts. Some managed to shut the darkness behind a heavily locked door in the furthermost reaches of their hearts; but none could rid themselves of the dark taint completely. Some even managed to erect a near impenetrable wall around the imposing darkness, like a concrete retaining wall holding back an earthen dam, but the darkness, while held back, still remained; silent, probing, prowling...just waiting to be tapped.

Once that outer retaining wall, or locked door, was breached, these creatures then belonged to *his* master; and by extension to himself. He was a general in his master's army, but he considered himself to be on par with the master himself. While he served the greater purpose of his master, he also thought his master was an abject fool. Rather than attacking these creatures subtly, as was the master's way, he preferred a direct, full-frontal assault. If he could harness the surging power that he felt was within reach, by procuring the boy's physical form, he might become powerful enough to challenge even the master himself.

Patience, he warned himself.

He knew that his lack of patience had laid waste to his designs in the past. Patience, therefore, was a crucial part of his plans this time. He had waited these sixteen long years for his opportunity to rise again; and he wasn't about to let impatience derail him yet again. He would possess the boy's physical form in due time. Then he would rise again; more powerful, more dangerous, and more vengeful than ever before...

JACK BEAUMONT

CHAPTER 7
SEPTEMBER 20ᵀᴴ, 2032

As Betty prepared breakfast for Samuel and herself, she couldn't help stealing glances at him, where he sat at the breakfast table, sipping his orange juice, waiting on her to finish cooking his bacon and eggs. She knew that something was bothering him, but she also knew that prying too much, too soon, would only make him more reticent to talk with her about it.

She hoped that the "voice" wasn't back again.

While Doctor Young had told her when Samuel was young that the "voice" would disappear in time, and that it shouldn't be anything to worry about, he'd also warned her that should the "voice" turn dark or violent, she might need to investigate professional therapy for Samuel. For the last six years, he'd claimed that the voice was gone. And, not once in those early years, during which he'd claimed to have heard the voice, had he ever said anything about it being anything but friendly and kind.

Why would the voice return after all this time? Don't create a problem where none exists, she told herself. This was a favorite saying of her recently departed mother, and it was advice that she tried to live by.

While she couldn't be sure that the "voice" was what was bothering Samuel, she did know that his mood had darkened considerably after their picnic lunch in Hunter's Glen. Something had occurred there to alter his usual bright and cheerful, outgoing countenance into one of quiet, pensive brooding. While it was possible that the timing of this mood shift was coincidental, she didn't really believe in coincidences.

Was it possible that he'd gotten a text, or call, from Heather and they had broken up? Maybe the timing was just coincidental to their visit? Maybe something else, unrelated, had caused his mood to sour?

She did know that he hadn't slept very well last night. She'd heard him crying out more than once in his sleep. Once, she had looked in on him and he was tossing and turning in the throes of an obvious nightmare. A second time, just as she was about to push the bedroom door open further, entering his room to wake him, he sat bolt upright in the bed, letting out a small gasp.

Instead of entering his room, possibly embarrassing him in doing so, she'd quietly closed the door that she'd opened just a crack. She went back to her bed, deciding not to intervene. She decided to wait to see if he mentioned anything about the dreams in the morning. Probably whatever he was brooding over, since yesterday afternoon, was haunting him in his sleep too.

As she studiously observed him this morning, it was clear by his appearance that sleep had been a stranger to him last night. He looked haggard and disheveled. His eyes were slightly bloodshot, bags and dark circles under them. He looked almost "sweaty". His hair was slightly unkempt; his face pale and drawn. Something was bothering him enough to keep him from sleeping soundly…and it showed in all aspects of his appearance. She hoped that soon he would trust her enough to confide in her as to what was wrong. Experience taught her that until that time came, she really couldn't do much to help him. He needed to confide in her of his own volition.

As she watched him finishing off his breakfast, she could only hope that everything was alright with him. *At least he still has his appetite,* she thought, a small smile gracing her lips. Samuel was her anchor in life. Her rock. All that she had in this world. She couldn't lose him to mental illness. She *wouldn't* lose him to mental illness. She couldn't allow the "voice", or whatever was eating at him, to steal him away from her.

She vowed to keep a very close watch on him for the next few days. She'd love to think that whatever was preoccupying his mind was nothing more than just the usual woes and worries of the teenage years, but she needed to be sure that it wasn't something more. Something evil. Something that was tugging at the back of her mind; an idea that she couldn't quite grasp; something that was there but just slightly, tantalizingly, out of reach. The word "evil" seemed to fit, but she couldn't say how for sure.

She wasn't sure why, but a sudden chill crept up her spine when she thought of that word, *"evil"*.

If she only knew…

JACK BEAUMONT

CHAPTER 8
SEPTEMBER 26ᵀᴴ, 2032

I have to go back, he thought. *I have to find out if what I saw in that nightmare was real. I have to see if I can stop it, if it hasn't already happened. I have to save the girl if I can; if not, I need to find out what happened to her.*

Samuel was thinking nonstop about the disturbing vision, for he was convinced now that that was exactly what it been. Since he and his mother had left Hunter's Glen a week ago, it had been on his mind all day, every day. Every night, his mind replayed the vision over and over in his head, although never with the same vividness and clarity with which he'd witnessed the events through the eyes of the perpetrator.

He thought that the events of that dreadful attack were to happen sometime this fall, based on what he recalled from the background of the scene. He remembered seeing the trees across the river from the car, recalling how they were nearly devoid of leaves. He remembered the crunchy leaves that littered the ground around the shining, red Camaro. He *knew* that it had to be sometime in fall when the assault took place. That meant that the attack could happen soon; if he were right, and it was a dark premonition of the future.

As Mr. Meacham, the teacher in his Chemistry 101 class, droned on and on regarding mole equations, he stared out the window of the classroom, once again mulling over what he'd seen through the eyes of the voice. He was so absorbed in his thoughts that he missed the bell when it rang to dismiss the class.

"You gonna sit there all day? Or are you coming to lunch with me, handsome?"

"Huh?" he asked, slightly confused after being jarred out of his contemplative reflection. "Oh, Heather, it's you," he mumbled, taking in his girlfriend who stood over him, as he sat at his desk.

Heather Long was the girl that most boys in the town had chased since elementary school. She was tall and shapely. Her dark, long, brown hair providing a perfect juxtaposition to her deep, strikingly blue eyes. It was a combination you didn't see in many people. Her smile lit up the room, the radiance of which made it hard to look away from her. Samuel had noticed even grown men sometimes staring at Heather when they went out to dinner, or a movie. He'd once heard her described by one of his classmates as "so pretty that it almost hurts to look at her".

"Were you expecting someone else?" she asked, flashing her million-dollar, perfect smile. "You were so deep in thought that you didn't even hear the bell ring. I don't know what you're thinking about, but it'd better be me," she playfully teased, taking his hand in hers.

"Of course, I was thinking about you. Who else would any man think of when you're around?" he replied, standing and gathering his books, pencils, and papers; shoving them hurriedly into his backpack. The couple held hands as they exited the classroom, heading down the long corridor towards the lunchroom. Samuel felt his mood being buoyed by Heather, and her infectious good nature. In the back of his mind, he still pondered how to save the girl in the vision from her fate, but he was able to maintain a semi-normal appearance and demeanor for Heather's sake, while they ate lunch together.

Briefly, he entertained the thought of telling her exactly what was on his mind. He ended up dismissing that idea rather quickly, fearing that she might think that he was some kind of pervert, or something worse. He didn't want to have to reveal to her that he'd been hearing a voice in his head for as long as he could remember. He knew that revelation would make him sound crazy for sure.

Perhaps, had he managed to share his thoughts and fears; or if he had discussed the voice, and what it had revealed to him with someone else, anyone else, many lives could have been saved...

JACK BEAUMONT

CHAPTER 9

Summer's Cove, Alabama was a town that had seen more than its share of tragedy. It was a town that had experienced not one, but two separate incidents of mass murder, and mayhem, at the hands of a diabolical menace. A specter that was part man, part demon, and one-hundred percent pure evil.

The Pumpkin Man had visited this town twice in a period of one hundred years; both times leaving death and destruction in his wake. Each time he had ultimately been defeated, but not before many people in this small town lost their lives; and not before the town itself had been nearly destroyed.

To look upon Summer's Cove was to see a small town in America that was not unlike most other small towns littering the landscape of the geographical United States. Locally owned, small businesses still occupied most of Main Street. Everyone still gave a friendly wave to everyone else as they passed by on the streets and sidewalks. Everyone knew nearly everyone else in town; and consequently most people also knew everyone else's business as well.

It was not unusual to hear friends and neighbors engaging in friendly conversation about who's moving in, who's moving out, how the crops are faring, and who's currently dating who. Friendly small talk, and the occasional friendly gossip session, was the norm in Summer's Cove. There was one subject however that most people in the town knew about but, as if by some unspoken mutual agreement, was never, ever talked about: The Pumpkin Man and the horrific events of Halloween, 2015.

In fact, the very day following the events of that tragic Halloween night, the mayor, Elton Crosby, and what had remained of the town officials and elders, made a pact not to discuss the details of exactly what had happened in Summer's Cove with anyone from the outside world. In a town meeting on the morning of November 1st, it was decided by unanimous vote that the entire town would remain silent about The Pumpkin Man. As the national news media descended upon the small burg, they had hatched a cover story that had satisfied outsider curiosity, while not making the whole town appear to be inhabited by the insane.

The "official" story they offered to State Investigators was that a chemical pesticide had infiltrated the town's water system. Those citizens who had ingested large amounts of the contaminated water had been consumed by severe hallucinations, and maniacal delusions. The chemicals caused some townspeople to react violently, even causing them to kill or maim their own neighbors and loved ones. Mass hysteria ensued, and the people involved had blamed a local mythological figure called The Pumpkin Man for their toxin induced crime sprees.

Dozens of people had been arrested for crimes committed while under the influence of the poisonous water. Several of those arrested had been deemed clinically insane upon examination by mental health professionals; and those folks had been institutionalized rather than jailed. Some of those affected had committed crimes so heinous that life sentences were handed down by juries. Still others, who hadn't committed any crimes at all, were also institutionalized under the umbrella of being a possible threat to themselves or others. Some had experienced severe breaks with reality as a result of the carnage they had witnessed. A couple of folks had committed suicide within two years of the event.

Some sixteen years later, all the surviving people involved in these acts of horror either remained in prison or were safely locked away in mental facilities across the land. A few of the accused had died in the years since. Almost all the living perpetrators still claimed that The Pumpkin Man had been to blame for their actions. Only the surviving townspeople of Summer's Cove knew the truth; and they weren't talking.

It was only behind closed doors that the events of 2015 were ever mentioned, even then the voices of those speaking were kept to a whisper, as if invoking the name of The Pumpkin Man too loudly would cause him to appear once again. While most of the townspeople were confident that he was gone forever, and would never rise again, there was still a palpable tension that arose each year as Halloween approached.

What used to be a time of year filled with happy children, decorated storefront windows, and a town festival, was now largely a time filled with memories of death and destruction. Oh, they still celebrated Halloween here, but it was with a heavier, almost reserved spirit rather than the fun-filled celebrations that took place in other towns across America. The Pumpkin Man festival no longer took place as it had in the past, for over a century. The tradition had been carried out each year in a more solemn tone for the first couple of years after 2015, but growing fear that the festival itself would draw unwanted attention, and "truth seekers", to Hunter's Glen had led to its abandonment by town leadership. Where Halloween had once been conducted with a gleeful, party-like atmosphere in Summer's Cove, it was now observed as a solemn reminder of tragedy and death.

A very small group of town elders had held secretive meetings, and maintained preventative measures aimed at keeping The Pumpkin Man in his final resting place in the years that had followed. Prayers were held over the unmarked grave each Halloween, and the burial site was routinely checked for signs of disturbance. Even those traditions had been relaxed in the last few years, as confidence that the threat was gone for good slowly grew.

It'd been sixteen long years since The Pumpkin Man had reappeared in Summer's Cove, bringing death in his wake. The town finally seemed to have recovered fully from its physical, emotional, mental, and spiritual wounds suffered at his hands. The town proper, the buildings that made up the town, had fully recovered a long time ago. The businesses which had once been burned down, blown up, or otherwise severely damaged, had all been rebuilt or repaired. The stores were all once again occupied, and local businesses were thriving.

The deep mystery surrounding the events in Summer's Cove had even had one positive side effect amongst all of the tragedy. The only silver lining in the otherwise dark and gloomy cloud hovering over the town was the fact that curiosity over the mass hysteria, and the "myth" of The Pumpkin Man, had actually brought in a bunch of new residents to Summer's Cove. Where there had once been many vacant homes languishing on the local real estate market, in the days following the tragic events, there was now not a vacant home to be found, either in Summer's Cove, or the neighboring communities. Home values had risen drastically as a result. New businesses had sprung up around the old, and the town seemed to thrive.

News media types, amateur journalists, witch hunters, paranormal activity "experts", "demonologists", and those simply possessing a morbid curiosity, had all flocked to the small town in the days following Halloween 2015. Even in spite of the justification that Elton and others had come up with to explain away the phenomenon, there existed plenty enough "evidence" to convince "paranormal experts" and conspiracy theorists that something huge was being covered up in Summer's Cove.

Altogether, for the average citizen, life in Summer's Cove had returned to pretty much what it was before The Pumpkin Man rose again. As the saying goes, life goes on.

That is...

until it doesn't...

JACK BEAUMONT

CHAPTER 10
OCTOBER 5TH, 2032

Brad Riviera jerked upright, screaming out, loudly. Beside him in bed, his wife Melissa awoke with a jolt. It took her a second to realize that it was Brad's screaming that woke her. As she sat up, she realized he was still screaming, sitting upright in bed clutching his pillow tightly in his lap. She put her arms around him, gently trying to wake him.

"Brad!" she whispered, holding him, rocking him slightly. His breathing raspy and rapid; she could feel his heart raging against his chest. "Brad, calm down. Come on. Shhh. It's okay," she cooed, trying to soothe him. Finally, he turned to look at her, eyes wide with fear and panic. As his breathing began to calm, she could feel him shivering and trembling in her arms. His tension slowly began evaporating, his body relaxing, as he leaned into her loving embrace.

What kind of dream could cause him to be this upset? she wondered silently to herself. *Brad's not afraid of anything that I know of. He's the bravest man I've ever known.*

Brad Riviera was somewhat of a minor celebrity; owning his own paranormal investigations company called "Ghosts, Ghouls, and Demons Inc." for the last twenty years. He appeared as a regular guest on the hit television show *Ghost Hunters,* and had been interviewed by many paranormal publications, magazines, and websites, before landing his own television show. He'd spent the night in places that gave Melissa the creeps just thinking about. Old prisons, sanitariums, and hotels that people claimed were haunted was his specialty. Some of these places didn't look safe to spend the night inside of, ghosts or not.

She'd never seen anything that had scared the man in all the years that she'd known him. Not even things that would have made some men quake in their boots, whimpering for their mothers. The closest she'd witnessed him to actually being moderately afraid was the night that they'd first met; over fifteen years ago.

She'd won a contest to be a guest "hunter" during a televised event, in which Brad and his crew would be spending a long and dark night in Eastern State Penitentiary. They were attempting to discover what kind of paranormal activity they might record. She had to admit, she was intimidated by the place as soon as she entered its rusty, foreboding gates. She could feel a palpable tension in the air, much as she did around other supposedly haunted places that had featured the most credible reports of paranormal activity. She was a little scared of this place. So much torture, so much pain had happened within these boundaries. So many spirits crying out for release; the remnants of the men who were once housed here. She could almost feel the heavy spirit activity thick in the air; like an unseen electrical field.

Ever since a small girl, she'd maintained a fascination with ghosts and haunted places. She had loved reading ghost stories with her father; dreaming of visiting real haunted houses when she was little. While Eastern State Penitentiary wasn't a house, it was supposedly the most haunted prison in the United States, and she'd been thrilled to get the chance to visit it with Brad's crew. Appearing on the television show was an added bonus. Like icing on a delicious cake.

The visit to the prison had been an eventful one, to say the least. She'd been paired with Brad, and one of the show's cameramen, who was named Jack, while they checked out one section of the large prison facility. Brad's cohorts were filming and investigating in another part of the prison; while she, Brad, and Jack filmed at the opposite end of the facility. The location she and Brad were investigating was one where the most sightings, and the clearest audio evidence had been reported. As they were standing in the center of a large, pitch black chamber, Brad began speaking to the spirits, asking them to make themselves known.

Suddenly, there arose a strong gust of cold wind, blowing her hair backward. A booming voice growling *"Get Out!"* accompanied the gale. Melissa literally jumped onto Brad, her heart racing, nearly skipping a beat. At the same time, she heard Jack crying out, and the clatter of him dropping his camera on the ground. Brad freed himself from Melissa's grip, fishing his high-intensity flashlight out of the bag he carried.

Brad panned the flashlight around the room as Melissa clung to his free hand for comfort. The bright flashlight beam revealed Jack, lying on the ground, dazed and bleeding. He had suffered a three inch gash across his right cheek. The cut was very deep, gushing blood that flowed freely across his face, and trickled down his neck. Brad handed her the flashlight, bringing a small first aid kit out of his duffle bag. As he sorted through the contents of the kit, he called on his walkie for Jason, who was back at the group's van, which served as a remote monitoring station, to summon an ambulance. He called for the rest of his group to immediately wrap up what they were doing, and to meet them out in front of the prison.

While they waited for the ambulance to arrive, Jack told them that when the gust of wind and the loud gravelly voice swept by him, he felt an icy claw rake across his face, accompanied by a hard impact, like a thrown rock, hitting him square in the chest. A second later, he was on the ground, stunned and bleeding from his torn open cheek, gasping in pain, from both the cut on his cheek, and from the impact to his chest. A week later, his cut became infected, and Jack developed a huge purple bruise in the middle of his chest. His sternum had been cracked. He spent a few weeks in the hospital recovering. The episode featuring the incident had been the highest rated episode of the whole television series.

That incident had cured Melissa of her ghost "addiction". It had also thrown her and Brad together for life. She hadn't even realized it at the time, but as the ambulance had come to take Jack away, she and Brad were still holding hands. It just seemed so natural at the time. Eighteen years later, they still held hands wherever they went…and it still felt natural.

Not even the harrowing Eastern State Penitentiary incident had shaken Brad's resolve to pursue the paranormal. The only sign that he was slightly rattled by the events of that night had been the sweat in his palm; something she'd noticed as she held his hand. He wanted to go back to filming there the very next week, but most of his crew felt differently. He couldn't get anyone to go back with him. Melissa was actually thankful for that.

This is what bothered her the most about these sudden, frequent nightmares that Brad had experienced for the last few days. Something in these dreams had scared him enough each night that he woke up screaming, covered in sweat, breathing rapidly, and even trembling. That wasn't like Brad. Another thing that bothered her was his silence about the content of these nightmares. He wouldn't discuss them with her...at all. He'd always been an open book with her; he was willing to discuss any topic no matter how uncomfortable.

When it came to these dreams however, he wouldn't talk about them. When she asked, he would always say that he couldn't remember what they were about. The steadfast claim that he didn't remember the content of these nightmares also gave her pause. She knew that he was lying, or at best deflecting. She'd never known him to lie to her before. Not ever. She could tell that he wasn't being truthful about the nightmares, because he always averted his eyes when he said he didn't remember what they were about. She knew that "tell" for what it was: a sign of willful, intentional deception.

What could be so bad about the dreams that he wouldn't share them with me? He's shared some harrowing, and sensitive, things about his traumatic childhood with me, but he won't tell me about his dreams?

She decided to just hold him and comfort him this time; not asking him about the dreams. If she didn't pry, maybe he would open up to her at breakfast in the morning. At least, that's what she hoped would happen, if she gave him a little space.

She also couldn't help but wonder if something about this town had caused Brad to start having nightmares. They'd initially come to Summer's Cove on the heels of the national news coverage regarding the weird events surrounding Halloween, 2015. While the murders, death, and destruction that occurred not far from here had been attributed to chemical poisons; poisons that had infected the town's water supply, they'd heard the whispered rumors of a mysterious ghoul the locals called The Pumpkin Man. Brad had wanted to check things out for himself. After spending a year coming back and forth to Summer's Cove investigating the case, the couple had found themselves quickly falling in love with the quaint, picturesque small town. Real estate in Summer's Cove was plentiful and cheap at the time. They'd gotten a great deal on a very nice home and moved here, fourteen years prior.

Brad was determined to write a non-fiction book, not only his own memoirs, but a book about the legend and mystery surrounding The Pumpkin Man as well. He'd tabled the project for the last several years, having landed a television show of his own, but since the show had been cancelled just last year, his interest in The Pumpkin Man, and the mysteries shrouding him, had become a near obsession once again. Could this obsession be the cause of the nightmares? Dreams that were so frightening and vivid that he couldn't talk about, or share with her?

What Melissa couldn't know was that Brad wasn't the only one starting to experience troubling nightmares in Summer's Cove. She had no way of knowing the deep significance of what these types of nightmares meant. Nor could she have known that the source of Brad's problems had begun with a fateful visit to Hunter's Glen...

JACK BEAUMONT

CHAPTER 11
OCTOBER 5ᵀᴴ, 2032

A week passed since Samuel's last visit to Hunter's Glen. He'd been going back to the Glen, without his mother's knowledge; careful to cover his tracks. Ever since his "Daddy" showed him the horrifically disturbing vision, he'd felt that he must go back to see if he could find out more information. He wanted to find out who the girl in the vision was, and if he could stop this terrible thing that was going to happen to her.

He'd never been scared of the voice prior to this. At least, not until it had shown him that graphic vision. The voice had always been cordial; comforting, like a trusted family member. Since the day of the nightmare vision, the voice had taken a much darker, much more sinister turn. He said things to Samuel that he didn't like hearing. He made nasty comments about people that Samuel knew from school; accusations that were disturbing. The voice told him that it wanted to do the same thing to Heather as it'd done to the girl in the vision; confirming that the disembodied voice belonged to the perpetrator. It told him that he, Samuel, wanted to do those same vile things to Heather too.

Samuel knew that he should probably tell his mother about what was happening, or going to happen, but he didn't want to disappoint her. She'd seemed so happy when he'd told her that the voice no longer came to him. He would hate to have to confess to her that he'd been keeping a dark secret from her for the last several years. He loved his mother so much that he couldn't stand to see the heartbreak in her eyes whenever he disappointed her. That's part of the reason that he'd told her that the voice was gone for good in the first place. He had wanted to make her happy. He couldn't tell her. Not yet.

But…he knew he had to do something…so he was on his way to Hunter's Glen, again. He had to see if he could find out why. Why was this happening to him? And, what did all of this mean?

Why did the voice show me that vision? he thought for possibly the one-millionth time. *What does it possibly want from me? What was the point in showing me this terrible event?*

It caused him more than a little angst that the voice was now able to reach him wherever he happened to be. Always in the past, the voice would recede in his head when he left Hunter's Glen; he'd not hear the voice again until the next time he and his mother visited. Now, he was hearing the voice all the time, everywhere he went; it was seemingly inescapable. In fact, he was having a hard time concentrating in school, when he was with Heather, and when he was at home, because the voice never seemed to be quiet. It always had something to say. It was like the obnoxious, opinionated friend that you just can't get to shut up.

He was on his way to the Glen this time to seek answers directly from the voice. He wanted to know why it would not leave him alone. He wanted to know why the voice had suddenly turned so dark; and why was it showing him these visions of horror?

Why the change?

Why now?

At first, he'd thought that maybe the voice had shown him the vision as a means of encouraging him to help stop the tragic events from happening. That's what he'd managed to talk himself into believing, at least for a few days. That is, until he realized that the dark and demented laughter that he'd heard in the vision was unmistakably the laughter of the owner of the voice itself. Anyone who could laugh at such horror couldn't be a force for good.

So, why the masquerade for so long as the kind and loving "Daddy" in my head?

He was so confused.

During a brief period of introspection, he began to wonder if he weren't going crazy to begin with. Maybe there was no voice. Maybe there never had been. Maybe the voice was just a figment of his imagination. A budding psychosis. But upon further analysis, he ruled that out. The voice had always been there; but it had always been limited to Hunter's Glen until just recently. Something had changed. He'd never heard it outside of the Glen, and it had never been violent. It had never shown him any violent and disturbing premonitions like this before. He wasn't imagining this voice; or experiencing a mental break. It was real. And, he had to do something about it.

Always in the past, he allowed the voice to take control of the conversations. Although spoken words were not used, the voice always led the "conversation" in his head. This time, he intended to take control of the dialogue. He was going to steer the conversation…and he was going to get some much-needed answers.

Starting with, why did he show me that vision in the first place? Samuel thought.

As he pulled his mother's car down the familiar path that led into Hunter's Glen, and that majestic, towering, huge oak tree on the hill came into view, Samuel had no way of knowing that his actions today would lead to widespread death and destruction in Summer's Cove yet again. He was leading the lambs to the slaughter…and he didn't even know it.

CHAPTER 12
OCTOBER 5ᵀᴴ, 2032

Brad Riviera had a lot of trouble concentrating as he sat at his desk trying to write. He just couldn't make his fingers put his fleeting thoughts down on paper. He'd have a moment of clarity, and a profound narrative would take form, only to have it dissipate before it could be recorded in written format. It seemed like he was always having trouble concentrating these days. Ever since starting to have those nightmares, each and every night, it seemed as if an impenetrable fog surrounded his brain, making it feel as if his limbs were moving through water. It was hard just getting through each day, much less trying to be productive. Sleep deprivation took a heavy toll on his cognitive abilities, and his motor skills, not to mention his efforts at writing and researching.

The guilt of keeping certain details from Melissa weighed down upon him; like a too-large anchor on a too-small boat. He never kept secrets from his wife. Not ever. He believed in maintaining an open and honest relationship, sharing all, leaving nothing hidden. The nightmares, however, were something that he just couldn't seem to find the strength to share. They were so bad. So violent. So terrible. So frightening. He couldn't share them. Not even with Melissa.

It was irrational to feel this way, he knew, but he almost felt if he shared the nightmares with Melissa, the very act of speaking about them would cause the things depicted within them to come true. He'd never known this sort of fear, or deep anxiety, before. At least, not since long ago, when he was a small child. And, it had all started just a few weeks ago when he'd visited Hunter's Glen, the supposed forsaken resting place of The Pumpkin Man...

▪▪▪

SEPTEMBER 20ᵀᴴ, 2032

Brad carefully navigated his car between the two thick oak trees lining either side of the small, narrow, dirt road that led into Hunter's Glen. It was clear that at some point the heavy iron chain that lay on the ground across the roadway was meant to keep people from entering, at least by means of the road. The rusted iron poles set in concrete on either side of the well-worn, narrow dirt road were leaning inwardly, leading him to believe that someone had either intentionally, or accidentally, run into the chain with their vehicle, causing the stout poles to bend inward, towards the road. In any case, the chain now sagged, lying flat across the dirt drive.

As he slowly drove further into the Glen, he was immediately struck by the stark beauty of the scenic wilderness setting. His eyes were instinctively drawn to the focal point of the clearing: a thick, towering oak tree standing at the center. Perched atop a rolling hill, the tree was a sturdy, silent, brooding sentinel overlooking a wilderness kingdom. It was this tree, or rather the prospect of what was supposed to rest underneath the tree, that he came here to see. He felt the familiar rush of excitement that came with the exploration of "haunted" places tingling through his body like an electric current.

■■■

He'd first visited Summer's Cove many years ago, to investigate the accounts of The Pumpkin Man. Rumors had leaked out, despite the media's willingness to accept the "cover story" provided by the locals. In fact, it was the secrecy surrounding these whispers, and the quickness with which those rumors of The Pumpkin Man were squashed by the locals, that made Brad believe that something *really* was going on here in the first place. In his experience with investigating supposed hauntings and paranormal activity, most of the time when locals or authorities were quick to state that there was "No there, there", there was usually something worth investigating. Some of the most famous and talked about "paranormal" or "haunted" places in the world were nothing more than a lot of hype; very little substance other than that a tragedy had once occurred there. It was in these lesser known places, like Summer's Cove, where a real story was often to be found.

He discovered a surprising reticence among the citizens of Summer's Cove to even talk about the events that had transpired here. He'd heard from a close friend of his that The Pumpkin Man was a local legend; one going back well over a hundred years. Supposedly something equally as tragic as the events of Halloween 2015 had happened in Summer's Cove previously. Way back in 1914, some event that the locals had attributed to The Pumpkin Man, had claimed the lives of many citizens of Summer's Cove. Several of the people arrested for crimes that occurred on, or around October 31st, 2015, also blamed this same Pumpkin Man character for causing them to go crazy. When he'd attempted to research the archives of the local Summer's Cove newspaper, he was told that an explosion had destroyed all records and historical town documents. Nothing existed up until to the last few years.

When he went to the local library, hoping to find more information about the legend of The Pumpkin Man, and the events of 1914, he was again met with resistance. He was told that the records he was searching for weren't there. It seems that the library had been leveled by an explosion, and had been rebuilt, but the records that he was looking for were missing. He could find no existing written records of the events of 1914 that had been attributed to The Pumpkin Man.

Brad refused to believe that, in this day and age of digital technology, even the most backwater town didn't have digital archives of their collective history. He'd been able to find information on the founding of the town, and the rich history of the community up until 1914. Then the records get scarce and sketchy until well after 1916. He couldn't figure out a logical explanation for why there would be such a huge, gaping hole in the records...unless the missing history had been purposefully omitted by someone. Such an omission of information only served to make Brad even more curious as to what had happened way back then.

The people of Summer's Cove seemed to be hiding something sinister from the outside world. On several occasions, as he attempted to gather more information surrounding the mysterious Pumpkin Man, he sensed that the person he was speaking to wanted to say more, but they seemed almost afraid to share what they knew with him. Some of these people cast furtive glances over their shoulders, or warily looked around themselves, as if afraid that someone else would hear their words. Some would quickly tell him that The Pumpkin Man didn't exist, that he was just a legend, but Brad noticed that usually this was stated with downcast or averted eyes, a sure sign of deception. Paranoia ran deep in this town. So did underlying fear.

Brad wasn't sure of what he believed about The Pumpkin Man himself, but he *did* believe that the citizens of Summer's Cove believed in the mysterious figure. In his twenty years of paranormal investigations, he'd seen enough to know that there *were* very real forces of evil that roamed the earth. While over ninety-five percent of supposed "hauntings", "demonic possessions", and "evil spirits" were nothing more than hysteria; or the product of overactive imaginations, that other five percent was made up of some truly scary, and sometimes very malignant stuff.

Could The Pumpkin Man be one of those "five percenters"? Why was he such a taboo subject among the residents of Summer's Cove, if there was nothing to his story? Why are people so scared? Too frightened to even talk about him?

It was these questions that gave him the motivation to dig deeper, search farther. He wanted to know the answers to these burning questions. He *had* to know the answers to these questions. The desire to know more, almost morphing into a burgeoning obsession; a need to get to the bottom of this mystery. It was the primary motivating factor in his and Melissa's relocation to Summer's Cove. He'd hoped that over time being a transplanted "local" would ease people's fears about speaking openly with him. Then, not long after moving here, he'd gotten a syndicated television show. His investigation into The Pumpkin Man got tabled; thrown to a back burner. An ever present, but distant thought.

After a run of nearly eleven years, his show was cancelled suddenly; with little warning. After taking an additional year off, traveling the world with Melissa, just enjoying the good life, Brad was finally getting back into investigating The Pumpkin Man in earnest. He was currently writing a book about him. That's why he was out here now. Research. Can't write a good book, or solve a tough mystery, without copious amounts of backbreaking, monotonous research.

It was only last week that he'd received an anonymous tip about Hunter's Glen. This much needed, and much appreciated, information came to him from the unlikeliest of sources: an anonymous note. A stranger had slipped a handwritten note under the front door of his house. He'd heard a car pulling out of his driveway, and when he went to the door to see who it might've been, he looked down, and saw the note. It was written on a blank sheet of plain white printer paper. The handwriting was neat, but lacking the flowing script that would have identified it as a woman's handwriting. He was pretty sure that the unsigned note had been written by a man. The message was short, to the point, although cryptic, taking up very little of the folded sheet of paper.

"The Pumpkin Man is buried under the Great Oak at Hunter's Glen. Seek answers there, but beware, evil lurks in search of those who it can inhabit. Do not lose your soul in your search for knowledge. Silence warns that evil is near."

He wished he knew who the mysterious messenger was. He didn't get a good look at the car, because he was distracted by, and too busy puzzling over, the cryptic message. It was obvious that the person who wrote this note thought that there was some knowledge that would help him in his investigation to be found in this place called Hunter's Glen. He just wondered who his mysterious benefactor was, and what their motivation could be, in providing him this clue. He wished he could've asked the mysterious note-writer some hard questions.

Later that same morning, he went to the supermarket to get some groceries. He casually asked the cashier where Hunter's Glen was located. The girl behind the register was probably somewhere between eighteen and twenty years old; pretty in a classic beauty sort of way, and friendly, with a smile to make all the boys adore her. She answered his question quickly. A little too quickly for her answer to be anything but a falsehood. Her face changed, the smile evaporated, and her previously warm green eyes seemed to quickly grow cold.

"I don't know," she said without glancing at him. While she'd been friendly, smiling warmly at him, asking him how he was doing when he entered her checkout line, she even wouldn't meet his eyes for the remainder of the transaction. Coldness emanated from her like it did from an open freezer.

He took his groceries home and put them away, pondering the oddness of the cashier's reaction to the mere mention of Hunter's Glen. After getting the groceries situated, he went to his office, sitting down behind his desk. He opened his laptop, beginning a Google search. He typed in "Hunter's Glen", expecting to find its whereabouts with relative ease. No immediate hits were forthcoming. He entered combinations of "Hunter's Glen" with "Summer's Cove", and various other reiterations. He gave up after about thirty frustrating, mind-numbing minutes of finding no available information. Not a single hit. He decided he'd have to ask around town, when he got home from New York, the following week. He was leaving that night.

■■■

The entire time that he he'd spent in New York pitching a concept for a new paranormal television show, he'd thought about Hunter's Glen, and The Pumpkin Man. He was going to solve this mystery for good when he got home. He vowed to find out what was at the root of the secrecy, and the crippling fear surrounding this legend.

Brad had gotten back to Summer's Cove just last night, and after a fitful, restless sleep, he got up to take a trip to the local Post Office. He had ventured out to mail the first chapter of his newest book to his literary agent, so that Gary could shop it around to a few publishers on his behalf. He tried once again to discover the location of Hunter's Glen by inquiring with the postal employee who assisted him at the mail counter. Resistance at the very mention of the place again met him head on.

"Why would you want to go there?" the female postal clerk asked him incredulously. Distaste for the notion noticeably apparent in her demeanor.

"I was just wondering. I've heard a lot about the place," he replied.

"I don't know where it is, but bad things have happened there. Stay away," she stated flatly, without meeting his gaze.

An aura of dark foreboding once again accompanied his inquiries into Hunter's Glen. It just wasn't normal for a place to engender such reactions. Not to mention that this time, he'd received a direct warning against venturing there. He quickly decided he'd get no further information from the postal clerk. He'd have to try to obtain directions to Hunter's Glen from someone else...if he could find someone willing to even talk about the seemingly accursed place.

As he exited the Post Office, a young man of about twenty, well dressed and well groomed, approached him. The man caught up to him just as he was about to enter his car. Brad turned, facing the man, wondering what the guy might have wanted with him.

"Excuse me," the man said in a casual tone. "I was in line behind you," he said, gesturing toward the Post Office doors. "I heard you asking about Hunter's Glen. I can tell you where it is," he offered.

"That's great!" Brad replied in excited disbelief. He couldn't believe that after several failed attempts the information he sought was going to be this easy to obtain.

"It'll cost you though," the young man continued quickly. "Information isn't free, and I don't think anyone else will help you, or tell you where it is."

I should have known, Brad thought, suppressing a groan.

He considered telling the guy to pound sand, but he didn't know where else to turn in order to find Hunter's Glen. So far, no one was willing to tell him anything. The man standing before him stood silently, waiting while Brad considered his options. The guy looked honest enough, so Brad figured it would be worth a few bucks to find out what he wanted to know.

"Okay, twenty bucks," Brad said reaching behind his back, pulling his wallet free.

"Fifty bucks," offered the other man, a slightly crooked grin on his face.

"Twenty-five, and that's my final offer," said Brad, hoping his pitiful attempt at a poker face didn't betray his bluff. He didn't want to telegraph his eagerness; lest the man increase his asking price.

"Okay," the young man said with a wider smile. "Twenty-five bucks for the location of Hunter's Glen."

Brad shook his head, pulling twenty-five dollars from his wallet. He would've been willing to pay fifty dollars, if he'd had no other choice.

As he handed the man a twenty accompanied by a five-dollar bill, he asked, "One more thing…why does everyone in this town avoid any questions about Hunter's Glen?"

The man took the money that Brad held in his outstretched hand, pocketed it, and smiled. "That'll be another twenty-five dollars for that kind of information," he said, another sly grin radiating on his features.

Brad shook his head, grinning back as he reached into his wallet again. "You better not be hustling me, kid," he said, forking over another twenty with another five-dollar bill.

"Never," the young man said, eagerly pocketing the additional cash.

He proceeded to give Brad detailed instructions on how to get to Hunter's Glen, which was located on the far reaches of Summer's Cove. It was technically outside the city limits. After he finished giving Brad the directions, he turned, starting to walk away.

"Wait a minute," Brad said. "I think you're forgetting something. You still owe me some more information. Why does everyone in this town shy away from the subject of Hunter's Glen?"

The young man pivoted, walking back toward Brad, leaning in close, and lowering his voice, after looking around to make sure that no one else was listening. "It's because that's where The Pumpkin Man's body is buried," he whispered.

Brad was a little surprised. At first, he wondered if this young man could be the same person who'd slipped the cryptic note under his front door. He quickly dismissed the notion though. *There's no way this kid could know where I live. Or, that I would be here, at the Post Office, today.*

"So, do you believe that The Pumpkin Man is real?" Brad inquired. He was shocked with the frankness, and directness, of the young man's answer. There was an undeniable note of genuine earnestness when he replied.

"I know he's real," he said, without hesitation. "I've seen him myself. So have most of the rest of the original people who still live in this town," he added, still speaking in a low whisper.

At first Brad was taken aback by this stunning admission. He wasn't used to anyone in Summer's Cove speaking so frankly about what was so obviously a taboo subject. Then, he was quickly inspired to ask another question, while he still had the chance.

"Why's everyone so secretive about The Pumpkin Man?" he asked. "What really happened here?"

"I've said enough," the man said abruptly, turning to walk away again. His entire demeanor seeming to change...quickly. He appeared scared.

"Wait! What's your name?" Brad asked him.

The man paused before replying, "Mitchell. Henry Mitchell."

"Listen Henry, would you like to make some more money?" he asked quickly. "Some *real* money?"

Henry looked torn between the chance to make some more easy cash, and the desire to escape this conversation. For a moment he stood there silently, studying Brad, weighing his options.

"Well, what about it?" Brad asked.

"How much?"

"Much more than the fifty dollars I paid you today," Brad said. "It would be a paid interview. Depending upon the amount of information you can provide, it could be as much as a five-hundred to a thousand-dollar payday for you."

Again, Henry looked torn between leaving and accepting the generous offer. Brad could see the conflict written on the young man's features. Henry ran a hand through his short, spiked hair, finally sighing.

"I'll think about it."

"You'll think about it?" Brad asked incredulously. "You just shook me down for fifty dollars for some lousy directions to a vacant field. It's obvious that you need the money."

Suddenly Henry looked past Brad's shoulder, back toward the closing Post Office doors. Brad noticed that he visibly paled, beginning to look nervous and agitated. He looked back to Brad, "We'll have to talk later."

As soon as he was finished speaking, he turned, walking briskly toward a red Ford Explorer, opening the door, and hopping inside quickly. As Brad shook his head, turned around, about to enter his own car, he glanced toward the front doors of the Post Office. Standing just to the side of the automatic double doors was a man in his late fifties to early sixties. He was staring fixedly, directly at Brad. The intensity of the man's gaze convinced him that he was the reason that Henry had taken off so abruptly.

Brad was not one to be easily intimidated; and standing at six-foot five and weighing in at nearly three hundred pounds, not too many people would even try. Still, something about the way the mysterious man was staring at him was slightly unnerving. He thought for a minute about getting into his car and quickly driving away. Instead, he returned the man's unblinking, unwavering gaze with one of his own. After an intense moment of staring each other down, the man turned abruptly, walking inside the building.

Brad couldn't help but feel a small measure of triumph, because he'd won the staring match. He smiled inwardly at the almost juvenile sense of satisfaction that such a small thing could bring.

Even the small victories count, he thought with a slight grin.

He'd always been competitive, even as a small child. He always hated for someone else to win. He was a typical "Type A" personality, a person who didn't like to lose, and who made even small matters a competition. It wasn't until he pulled out of the parking lot, and onto the main road, that he was struck by a startling thought.

What if the man who had stared him down was the author of the mysterious note that had pointed him toward Hunter's Glen?

He made a hasty U-turn, heading back toward the Post Office. He quickly parked in the first available spot, threw his door open, exited his car, walking rapidly toward the double doors. As he entered the Post Office, he scanned the three lines of customers for the man who'd stared him down. He wasn't there. Brad turned, walking to the other side of the building, where the walls were lined with PO boxes. He walked the length of the walls that featured hundreds of the small gray metal boxes and turned the corner. The man wasn't there either.

Brad turned around, walking out the front door, shaking his head and cursing himself under his breath for not considering the possibility of who the man might be sooner. He usually was a little quicker on the uptake than this. He got in his car feeling frustrated and beaten, but then began to feel better when he realized that at least he'd gotten what he'd been after all along: the directions to Hunter's Glen.

■■■

As he parked his car near the base of the upward sloping hill that led up to the large, grand oak tree near the center of the clearing, he took in his breathtaking surroundings. He marveled that such a serene setting had remained so undisturbed by time, and the endless residential development that had consumed much of the deep south. There weren't many areas like it left anymore.

Of course, given the reticence of the locals to even talk about this place, he was sure that there were some legends and rumors about Hunter's Glen that made the place unattractive to developers and investors alike. As with houses, a place that was considered "cursed or "haunted" would be hard to sell.

Still, he could envision a large, stately manor here, perched on the hill behind the large oak. This would make a perfect homestead for someone who enjoyed the raw beauty of nature. Maybe he should look into who owns this land. He wasn't scared of "haunted" places, and he'd always wanted to live on a large parcel of land. Especially one with a stream running through it. As far as he could tell, this place was as near perfect as one could ask for.

He walked over to the gurgling stream, watching and listening as the water rushed over the stones for a few minutes. The water made comforting, soothing babbling noises as it continued its task of wearing down the surface of the river stones, making them nearly as smooth as glass. As he stood there observing, a large fish quickly struck at an insect on the water's surface. He was taken back to a time when his father used to take him trout fishing, in streams much like this, in his native state of North Carolina. Brad stood there lost in thought for several minutes content to watch as the stream rushed by on its long journey to the ocean.

After a while, he turned away from the rushing stream, looking back toward the hill with the grand oak tree. *Might as well get to what I came here for,* he thought as he started toward the hill. Wading through the tall grass toward the tree, he wondered exactly what it was he was looking for. He pulled the note from his jeans pocket and read the words again.

> *"The Pumpkin Man is buried under the Great Oak at Hunter's Glen. Seek answers there, but beware, evil lurks in search of those who it can inhabit. Do not lose your soul in the search for knowledge. Silence warns that evil is near."*

Very poetic, he thought. *The author must read classic, gothic fiction.*

So, The Pumpkin Man was supposedly buried under this oak tree. *I wonder whether there's a marker, or something else to distinguish the grave?* He surely wasn't about to start digging for bodies with his bare hands.

As he neared the massive oak, he found one thing about Hunter's Glen that was deeply odd. Silence. Eerie, unnatural silence. It was the still and profound silence of a funeral home after closing time. As he stood on the banks of the Pumpkin Vine River a few minutes before, he'd silently wondered what bothered, nagged at him, about this place. Now, it suddenly hit him. It was the utter silence that seemed out of place. A place like this should be teeming with a multitude of the noises of nature. Bees and insects buzzing, squirrels barking in the trees, unseen animals rustling through the foliage, birds singing; all of that was missing on this side of the river.

He came to a stop about twenty feet from the base of the tree, turning to look back the way he came. Concentrating hard, he listened for the noises that should accompany any typical late summer day. No crickets chirping, no birds signing, no sounds of squirrels in the trees, no bees or insects buzzing, nothing. Not even the usual gnats; pests that would normally be swarming a person this near a body of water on a warm summer, or early fall day. The silence was near deafening in this open wilderness setting.

Something about this place is wrong, he thought. He didn't know any other way to classify it, other than "wrong". Looking down at the note that he still held clutched in his right hand, he reread the last, ominous line.

Silence warns that evil is near.

It was definitely silent, and growing even more so, as he neared the huge oak at the top of the hill. The sounds he'd heard coming from the other side of the river faded into quietness as he got further from the stream.

While he was not one to be easily frightened, Brad did have a keen sense for when something was amiss. This "six sense" was what helped guide him in his relentless pursuit of all things paranormal. In fact, he could usually tell if a place truly held a paranormal, or otherworldly, connection within minutes of arriving on scene. If he felt nothing upon entering a supposedly haunted venue, that's usually exactly what he and his team found: absolutely nothing. That was the case with most of the places that he and his team investigated.

There's definitely something here, he thought as the hairs on the back of his neck tingled, and he felt a current of unseen electricity traveling down his spine. The air suddenly became heavy, almost thick, making it harder to breathe. He began to wish that he'd brought some of his team members, along with their equipment, with him out here today. In his rush to find this place, he hadn't even considered doing so.

I should go back and get them now, he thought.

For just a moment, he was torn between going home and rounding up his equipment, and waiting for his crew to arrive, or exploring on his own. In the end his curiosity got the better of him, and he trudged the rest of the way up, to top of the hill, and the base of the ancient tree.

CHAPTER 13

SEPTEMBER 20TH, 2032

As he reached the base of the oak that stood at the top of the steep hill in the center of Hunter's Glen, Brad looked around the tree in mild confusion. He walked around the circumference of the massive tree's trunk twice. The oak was majestic, towering, and obviously hundreds of years old. The diameter of the trunk was nearly fifteen feet around. He wasn't quite sure what he was looking for, but he'd thought that maybe there would be something obvious. Something that would point to The Pumpkin Man's final resting place...if indeed this truly was his final resting place.

While he hadn't really been expecting anything as blatant as a headstone with the inscription *"Here lies The Pumpkin Man"*, he *had* expected something that would point him toward the grave that supposedly existed here. A small wooden cross, evidence of disturbed ground, a notch on the base of the tree, a makeshift rock monument; he expected something to mark the purported grave.

After walking around the tree several more times, in ever widening circles, carefully studying both the ground, and the trunk of the tree, for any indication of a grave marker, he decided to widen the search further out from the base of tree. *After all,* Brad thought, *Both the note, and Henry Mitchell, said that The Pumpkin Man was buried under the tree, but that doesn't necessarily mean at the "base" of the tree.* Looking upward, he estimated that the span of the branches and limbs of the oak tree must extended at least thirty feet in every direction from the trunk. "Under the tree" encompassed a pretty wide search area.

Brad decided on a methodical approach to searching the area around the tree. In the area immediately near the trunk of the tree, and extending out to about ten to twelve feet from the trunk, the ground was bare earth. Further out, the grass grew to at least thigh high. It would take longer to search this area, but he was determined to do so. As he started walking slowly in a wide circle through the long grass, he once again felt a tingling sensation vibrate down his spine. He felt as if he was being watched, although he was quite certain that there was no one else around…for miles. He ignored the sensation as he continued his search.

After about an hour of searching, Brad went back to the cool shade underneath the tree, sitting down, feeling defeated. He was sure that he'd left no area unsearched in his quest to find The Pumpkin Man's grave. As he sat under the tree, sweat rolled down his face, his shirt nearly soaked through. He still had the unshakeable feeling of someone hidden, watching him.

Ignoring the unnerving feeling, Brad considered his options. He was convinced that if he brought his crew, and their hi-tech equipment, out here that they might find something. The raw spectral energy permeating the air was nearly palpable in this location. While he began formulating a plan to officially "investigate" this area, Brad absentmindedly stroked the fingers of his right hand through the soft loam beside the spot where he sat under the tree. Stretching his fingers forward, then raking them toward his palm, he made little trenches in the soft earth.

After several minutes of distractedly raking the earth with his fingers, while lost in thought, his index finger caught on something hard. With each pass, his finger would catch on what he assumed was a tree root. As he finished his thoughts, resolving to get his crew out here tomorrow, he looked down to see that what his finger was encountering. It wasn't a root, as he'd first assumed, but instead looked like a small metal chain of some kind.

Curious as to what it was, he gave a small tug on the chain. Pulling harder, more dirt was displaced, revealing more of the chain, however it seemed to be caught on something. With more of the chain exposed, he was able to get a better grip on it. He slid four fingers under the chain, and with the exposed part of it resting on his palm, he gave it a firm pull. This time even more of the chain come free of the earth, but part of the chain must've been wrapped around a root or something underground, because it was stuck fast.

As determined as always, Brad gripped the chain even tighter, giving it a mighty tug. There was a moment of slight hesitation before he heard a small snap, and the chain came fully free from the dirt. Brad held it in his hand for a moment, turning it over, inspecting it, before realizing that what he held was a very tarnished, and dirt-stained, silver crucifix affixed on a thick silver chain. A shiver ran down his spine, as he realized what it was that he held in his hands.

Being well versed in the occult and supernatural, Brad was acutely aware that silver crucifixes were often used to "restrain" or "repel" an evil force or presence. Pure silver was said to be able to bind evil, keeping it at bay. Had he, by blind luck, stumbled across the very site where The Pumpkin Man was supposedly interred?

Have I been sitting on top of his grave the entire time?

Excitedly, Brad shoved the crucifix into his front left, jeans pocket, hurriedly making his way back down the hill to his car. He would have to get the entire crew out here tomorrow. They would have to conduct a full investigation around this entire area. He was positive that with their sophisticated equipment they would pick up paranormal activity. Activity that wasn't apparent to the unaided human senses. If such a thing as a "sixth sense" existed, Brad's was telling him that there was much more here than meets the eye!

As he opened his car door, jumping behind the wheel, he felt an involuntary shiver travel down his spine. As the hair on the nape of his neck vibrated with an electric tingling sensation, he glanced back toward the massive tree, where it stood as a silent sentinel over an unmarked grave. He again felt as if someone was watching him, a pair of malevolent eyes, searching his soul, although there was no one in sight. Shaking off the disturbing feeling, he started the car, reversed, and headed down the dirt road toward the entrance of Hunter's Glen.

Yes! Brad thought. *This might be the biggest hunt of my life! If I can get proof of this Pumpkin Man on record, this will put my career back into overdrive.*

Driving back toward his home, visions of several book deals, movie adaptations, media interviews, and more swirled through his head. While he'd enjoyed a pretty nice career already, his star was slowly fading.

Breaking open this case could catapult him to international stardom.

So caught up in his own plans was he, that he didn't feel the tendril of evil that had already gotten its talons hooked into his mind. He wasn't paying enough attention to hear the evil laughter that echoed far off, in a distant chamber of his brain...

JACK BEAUMONT

CHAPTER 14
OCTOBER 5TH, 2032

Jesse watched her husband, as he lay next to her in their bed, eyes closed in deep slumber. He was such a good man. A humble, honest, earnest man. An awesome father; a great and caring, gentle lover, a best friend, and an all-around stand-up guy. Any woman would be happy to have him in her bed, much more so to be married to him; helping him to raise their kids. She was one pretty lucky woman.

She was so thankful to have him in her life. She didn't know what she'd ever done to deserve him, and this blissful happiness that they shared together. They enjoyed what was, by all accounts, the perfect life. A traditional Rockwell painting type of life. A nice house on multiple acres of land, two newer model cars, three great, well-adjusted kids, and mutually loving spouses. What more could a woman ask for?

She rose from the bed, strolling over to the walk-in closet. She knew that he'd be really surprised by the unique anniversary gift she was about to give him. So would their kids. In fact, she bet the entire town would be abuzz, blown away by the sheer magnitude of her monumental gift. She smiled, grabbing the unwrapped gift from the closet, ready to surprise the love of her life in a way that he'd never been surprised before. She calmly and silently walked back toward the bed, stopping at the footboard, speaking softly to the love of her life.

She called out to David in a sweet, sing-song voice, "Oh, Daaaavviid! Wake up, honey. I have a surpriiizze for youuuu!"

David groaned, rolling over from his back to his stomach, still half asleep. "David. Come on now. Don't make me wait," she crooned. "I have something special I want to give you!"

David sat up in bed, blinking while wiping the sleep from his eyes.

"What is it, baby?" he asked sleepily.

"It's your anniversary gift!" Jesse said enthusiastically, at the same time swinging the gift up and over the footboard so he could see it. "I hope you like it!" she said breathless with joy, pulling the dual triggers, firing both barrels at once. The force of the sharp, twin recoil knocked her off her feet. She giggled with glee as she fell. She hit the floor, landing hard on her butt, but not before she caught the look of surprised horror on David's face… a mere instant before it disintegrated into a bloody, pulpy mess. The twin blasts of the double-barrel shotgun erasing all of his facial features instantly.

She picked herself up from the floor, yelling "Happy Anniversary!" to her dead husband, as she calmly grabbed more shells from their closet, reloading both barrels of the gun.

Now it's time to give the kids their presents too, she thought, making her way down the hallway, toward the kids bedrooms, suppressing the urge to giggle manically again.

■ ■

The Pumpkin Man smiled with deep satisfaction watching the carnage that he'd caused, playing out through the eyes of Jesse Parker. While he had no plans to give himself away early, as he'd done last time by making new disciples too soon, who could blame him for having just a little bit of fun? Now that the shackles holding him back had been loosened by the Ghost Hunter, and his act of removing one of the accursed silver chains that bound him, he needed a refreshing buffet of terror and pain to further restore his greatly diminished powers.

He enjoyed the show so much!

The sheer confusion and horror on the face of David, as he realized his doting wife was about to blow him away, was utterly pricelessness. The fear of the children as they realized their beloved Mama was about to murder them was, for him, like giving a steak dinner to a starving man. For dessert, he backed out of Jesse's mind, just long enough for her to realize what she'd done at his behest. He soaked up her heart-wrenching despair, as she viewed the results of her actions. He savored her anguish, as she recalled every terrible moment of killing her own family. Her confusion at having done so only adding to his delight.

To top it off, she'd hanged herself rather than face the reality and consequences of what she'd done. He couldn't take the blame for that one. While he had always planned on having her kill herself, she'd done it before he'd had the chance to make her. Still, her death served his purposes well. No one would know that he'd been involved. It would be viewed as a simple multiple murder-suicide. The bodies probably wouldn't even been found for several weeks since David was on leave from work. Jesse was a stay-at-home mother, and the kids were homeschooled. There was no one to miss them, which is why he'd chosen this family for some recreational fun in the first place.

Now, to see what else he could do to have a little fun, while recharging his powers…

CHAPTER 15
OCTOBER 5ᵀᴴ, 2032

Kory Millhouse went about making dinner for himself and his roommate, singing cheerfully along with the jaunty tunes issuing from his iPhone. He was glad to have a friend to share this big house with. After his mother and his father died years ago, at the hands of a crazy neighbor; he'd lived here alone for the last eight years. He'd been ten at the time his parents had tragically died; viciously murdered in cold blood. The events of that year had shaken his trust in people, forever changing his view of those around him. Even people he once thought he knew very well became distant strangers to him.

Of course, what transpired at the hands of his foster parents only deepened his already strong distrust of those around him. His foster father was nearly as much of a monster as the neighbor who'd killed his parents was. It wasn't until he could escape his foster home, at the age of eighteen, that he returned to this, his childhood home. Although this was where his parents had been murdered, this home had always been a place of safety and security; warmth and love for him, before that fateful Halloween ruined life as he knew it. He returned here despite the past, because this was the only home he'd ever loved. The only place he felt safe.

He'd become sort of a recluse after returning to Summer's Cove. He couldn't stand to be around most people, not for more than a few minutes at a time, at least. He found himself perpetually wondering what those around him might be thinking; what secrets they were harboring behind their smiles, beyond their friendly outward appearances. He came to the unfortunate conclusion that most people were hiding behind masks. It was only behind closed doors that one would see the real person behind the façade; penetrating the mask they presented to the outside world.

What made the loss of his parents even harder on him was that the man who'd killed them had previously been like a kind and beloved grandfather to him. Mr. Rush was known around the neighborhood as a kind, gentle old man. He'd lived next door to Kory and his family for years. In fact, he already lived there when Kory's parents first moved in, some fifteen years earlier. Kory knew the old man since he was old enough to walk.

They had taken walks together, and the man allowed Kory to help him with his garden and other tasks. In the late summer and fall, they would harvest the ripe apples from his bountiful apple trees. Then, they would cut the apples into chunks; using Mr. Rush's antique cider press to make fresh, refreshing apple cider. They'd shared a lot of wonderful things together; the old man always eager, and willing, to share his knowledge with his young neighbor.

On the Halloween that had changed his life forever, the day started off like any other. Mr. Rush said "Hi" to him in the morning, as he fetched his morning

94

newspaper from his long gravel driveway. Later that evening, Mr. Rush came to dinner at his house. Kory's family was having an early dinner; then Mr. Rush was going to drive him to the fair at Hunter's Glen when their meal was finished.

Instead, they had dinner as planned, and all seemed right with the world. Mr. Rush seemed to be his usual chipper self. Everyone who was present that evening shared good food, and friendly, light conversation throughout the meal. The old man brought over a homemade pumpkin pie for dessert. Kory wasn't a fan of pumpkin pie, so he'd passed on it. A few minutes after they'd finished eating their pieces of pie, both his mother and his father became violently ill. His father lurched forward in his chair, spewing vomit across the dining room table before collapsing into a limp heap on the floor. His mother vomited a second later, before falling out of her chair, collapsing right on top of his stricken father. Kory was so shocked at what happened, that he didn't know how to react. He was immobilized with fear and uncertainty. For what seemed an eternity, his brain tried to process what was happening. Shock making him incapable of action.

Even more disturbing was Mr. Rush's reaction to his parent's demise. Instead of rushing to help his parents, as Kory would have expected, the old man sat back and laughed; not just a chuckle, but an extended, raucous, mocking laugh. Kory would never forget that terrible, haunting, laughter. It was the sick, demented laughter of a person gone entirely, completely, utterly insane.

While Kory looked on frozen in horror, Mr. Rush stood up, walking calmly over to their kitchen counter, retrieving his dad's razor-sharp carving knife; the one his dad used to carve the Thanksgiving turkey. As his parents began convulsing helplessly on the dining room floor, his beloved neighbor began hacking at them relentlessly, again and again, with the huge knife. As blood began to fly about the room, Kory's trance was finally broken. He ran screaming from the house, into the woods out back. There, he climbed the wooden ladder up to the treehouse that his father had built him, and he waited, hiding until dawn. It was shortly after the sun arose when help finally came. When the police finally arrived, Mr. Rush was still inside their house, sitting in the living room, calmly watching television. Covered from head to toe in the blood of his neighbors, when the police confronted him, all he would say was: "The Pumpkin Man is coming."

Mr. Rush was sentenced to confinement in a mental institution, where he'd passed away just last year. Once, nearly five years ago, Kory had gone to see him. He needed to ask his former friend why; he needed to try to make sense of the situation. He had to know why Mr. Rush had betrayed his parents, and himself. He had to know what had driven that sweet old man to commit such heinous acts, seemingly without any provocation. He'd gone to the facility fully expecting to find a man devoid of his senses, a man who'd lost it completely.

What he found there instead broke his heart even more. The Mr. Rush he found was older, much feebler than Kory had ever seen him; a man who seemed broken in spirit. What Kory didn't see before him was the raving lunatic that he'd expected to find.

When Kory asked him why he'd done it, Mr. Rush's answered that he'd been possessed by a demon. He broke down in tears, asking Kory for forgiveness. He claimed that his actions were not his own; that he'd loved

Kory, and his parents too. Kory forgave him, but he never went back to see him again. It was as if in the space of a few hours, Kory had lost both parents, *and* a beloved grandfather figure. It was nearly too much for him to bear.

Kory had no family now. Mark, his roommate, was the closest thing to family that he had. The only reason Kory felt a strong kinship with Mark was because Mark was himself an outcast, an introvert, a societal reject. Someone who'd also suffered the loss of his family for no good reason, through no fault of his own. Someone who also rejected society, preferring to be at home, rather than out in the big, scary outside world.

We are two of a kind.

Mark had been disowned by his family for being gay. What was even worse about this betrayal, betrayed by the very people who claimed to love him most, was the fact that he wasn't gay at all. Mark simply wasn't interested in sex...with anyone...at all. Because he still lived at home by the age of thirty, and had never dated, people in town began to assume that Mark was gay. Once the folks in his hometown of Silver Springs began to gossip and whisper, his parents coldly threw him out of their house. His father was a Methodist minister. They just couldn't abide having a gay son living under their roof.

Damn idiots, Kory groused.

Kory found Mark sitting, with a small suitcase of personal belongings, outside of the grocery store in town, about two years prior. He'd asked Mark what was wrong when he saw him sitting there, desperation and sadness marking his shell-shocked countenance. He'd quickly realized that he and Mark shared the commonality, and kinship, of lacking a family...his was dead, while Mark's had chosen to abandon him without cause. They became fast friends, seeing in one another the hope of at least a type of kinship; a type of family. When Kory took Mark to his parent's house a few days later, hoping to gather the rest of his things, it had only solidified his parent's false assumptions that Mark was gay. Tragically, they asked Mark to leave their home, and never to return. That had been two years ago. Sadly, he hadn't seen, or heard, from his family since.

Now, he and Mark were almost like brothers. They ate together, they watched television together, and they spent most of their free time together when Mark wasn't working. Both preferred to remain at home rather than go out into the wider, wilder world where you never knew what others were thinking...or what they were plotting against you.

As he finished preparing their meal, setting the table, Mark entered the dining room by way of the living room. He'd been out tending to their flower garden earlier. He came in and showered, while Kory went about fixing their dinner. He pulled out a chair, sat down at the table, eyed the food enthusiastically and said, "This looks great! You've really outdone yourself this time, Kory!"

"Yes," Kory said, "We're eating well tonight! I even whipped up a homemade pumpkin pie for dessert. It's a recipe a dear neighbor shared with my family years ago."

∎∎

As he watched Mark twitching on the floor, gasping for breath, experiencing the same type of convulsions that his parents had suffered years ago, he pulled a heavy, serrated carving knife out of the drawer next to the sink.

Now it's time to see what's behind that mask of yours, Mark, he thought, malevolent laughter pealing through the dark recesses of his brain...

JACK BEAUMONT

CHAPTER 16
OCTOBER 5TH, 2032

Elton wondered for the hundredth time if he'd done the right thing in getting Brad Riviera involved with The Pumpkin Man. No one else knew what he'd done. Elton himself questioned his plans more than a few times an hour. He hadn't told his wife what he'd done yet. He really felt like he didn't have much choice in the matter.

My hands are tied.

Elton felt like a great evil was on the rise again. Something was brewing. Seething. He knew it couldn't be good. He knew it the moment that the dreams started up again. Sixteen years ago, Elton shared a psychic connection, however brief, with The Pumpkin Man; he had taunted Elton with the horrible acts that he'd caused Elton's kids to get involved in. Elton knew that somehow this psychic connection must have remained partially open, at least the smallest of cracks.

For the last sixteen years, Elton felt a tenuous, fragile peace. He'd been assured that The Pumpkin Man was destroyed, laid to rest forever. He'd actually bought into that theory for many years. He started growing complacent. It was his newfound faith, and his growing knowledge in that faith, that had shown him the errors of that way of thinking. Elton now recognized The Pumpkin Man for what he truly was: an eternal creature who inhabited the bodies of men in order to wreak chaos and havoc on mankind.

A demon. An actual emissary of the living devil.

His studies in his faith had led him to the knowledge that just like with mortal man, while the physical body can be destroyed, the immortal spirit that is the demon itself cannot. It was the same as the soul of man, once that man died. The man's physical body might die, but the soul that *was* the man lived forever. The body is temporary; the soul is eternal. Where he once thought that they'd destroyed The Pumpkin Man, Elton now knew that at best, all they had done was bought themselves some more time. And now, if his growing nightmares were an indication, it seemed that time was now running short.

They needed a more permanent solution to getting rid of, or containing forever, The Pumpkin Man...and they needed one quickly. When Elton started experiencing the nightmares, he knew that it could only mean one thing: The Pumpkin Man was becoming more active, getting ready to rise once more. As this unsettling realization set in, Elton came to the logical conclusion that decisive action needed to be taken now, before The Pumpkin Man solidified his evil grip on the town the way he had at least twice in the past.

That's where Brad Riviera came into the picture. Elton had seen his television show, researched the man himself. Instead of being one of those quacks on television, the kind who saw a ghost hiding behind every corner and a demon lurking behind every sound in a darkened room, Brad seemed to take the position of skepticism over gullible, blind belief. It seemed that while many in his field sought to prove all "haunting" claims true, that Brad was more likely to try to disprove the claims. Especially in those cases where he could definitively prove them to be false. It seemed like he possessed a lot more personal integrity than most in his field. It also seemed to Elton that he just might be the "real deal" when it came to dealing with true paranormal encounters and entities.

Elton didn't think the town could survive another encounter with The Pumpkin Man; nor did he have any desire to see if *he* would survive another face to face confrontation. The last engagement had been bad enough. Luckily, his children had come through the ordeal with little more than a few emotional, and mental, scars. Both his son and his daughter now lived a safe distance from Summer's Cove. They wouldn't be in any danger should The Pumpkin Man come back. Nor could they be used as unwilling pawns against him, as they'd once been so heartlessly used by the demon before.

Elton took the nightmares as a prophetic warning from above. He had not mentioned the nightmares, nor his intentions to seek help from Brad Riviera, with anyone else, not even his beloved wife, Juanita. While he trusted her implicitly, he was afraid that she'd try to stop him. He knew that saving the town would have to be on his broad shoulders. He considered it his penance, his cross to bear, for his failures of the past.

He wondered absently if this is what Elmira Camp felt like sixteen years ago, when she embarked on the arduous task of defeating The Pumpkin Man. She'd known what her mission was, and she had readily accepted it, knowing full well that she might die in the process. She hadn't shared her plans with anyone, including her most trusted confidant and friend; Juanita Tanner; Elton's current wife who'd been Elmira's live-in caretaker at the time.

That's how I feel now.

The Lone Ranger without a Tonto to rely on.

He knew in his heart why Elmira hadn't shared her plans with anyone else. She knew that The Pumpkin Man could read thoughts and minds. That he possessed some degree of telepathy, which could ruin any plans to defeat him. She feared if too many people were aware of her intentions, The Pumpkin Man might stumble across them too. He might have gained a chance to foil her designs; designs that led to his utter defeat. Elton felt the same need for caution and secrecy, as much as it pained him to have to hide things from his beloved wife. Sometimes, you had to do, what you had to do.

He kept his secret from her to keep her safe. A dark storm was coming. Elton could feel it. He knew it. Evil was going to rise again. He'd do whatever it took to keep The Pumpkin Man from returning. He'd give his very life, if that's what it took. He felt responsible in part for what had happened all those years ago, even now. He couldn't bear to see it happen again.

Perhaps if he'd not gotten involved, things would have been different…

CHAPTER 17
OCTOBER 5TH, 2032

Brad sat behind his executive desk, in his comfy oversized leather office chair, surrounded by floor-to-ceiling bookcases in his office, laptop open, Word pulled up, trying to write. For the third consecutive day, he managed to get a few words down, then his mind started wandering. He started contemplating the vivid, dark nightmares that plagued him. It was so unlike him to have *any* dreams that he could remember upon waking, much less nightmares of the sort that were haunting him nightly.

He thought he knew where these dreams came from. He'd interviewed a couple of the "insane" former residents of Summer's Cove. He knew about the haunting, relentless nightmares they experienced. He knew how all those who committed crimes in the name of The Pumpkin Man had professed to experiencing days, sometimes even weeks, of vivid nightmares before The Pumpkin Man made his presence known to all.

The problem was this: what was he going to *do* about it? He'd been trying to get his old crew back together. They needed to go with him to investigate Hunter's Glen. He needed at least two techs, and someone to monitor the readings on the equipment, while they ran their tests. He wanted someone else who could run the ground-penetrating radar, able to read the data output. That was far beyond his skill level. While Mark, one of his techs, was immediately available, he couldn't get the rest of the crew together.

He had hoped to get the entire team together within a day or so of discovering the silver chain, but here it was nearly two weeks later, and he hadn't been back to Hunter's Glen yet. While he told himself that he was waiting on his crew, he knew deep inside the real reason that he hadn't been back yet…the nightmares scared the crap out of him. He knew that something was there, in that serene meadow, and he knew it for what it was…pure evil. He also knew that no matter how much he kidded himself about the need to wait for more sophisticated equipment, that without the nightmares, he normally would have been back out there the following day with a shovel. Crew or no crew, he would have been digging by hand if necessary. As it was, he decided to wait until he had his team assembled before trying to tackle something this big by himself.

He sought out the foremost demonologist of the modern world, Jonathan Silver, in this matter. He knew that what they were likely to uncover would be something he couldn't handle alone. From what little information he had gathered about The Pumpkin Man, he thought what they were dealing with was a classic case of a strong demonic entity. If that was the case, he knew that it was well out of his league to deal with on his own. While he held no particular faith in God, or a savior, he had witnessed the power of the faith of those who *did,* when it came to demonic entities. He'd witnessed such firsthand.

In addition to being a celebrated demonologist, Jonathan was also a Minister who'd served as a Baptist pastor for over twenty years. When most people thought of casting out demons, they thought of a Catholic Priest; dressed in the full garb of that office. Brother Jonathan, as he preferred to be called, definitely didn't fit the preconceived notion of an exorcist. Not only was he not Catholic, but he also most often reported for duty wearing a faded flannel, button-up shirt and washed-out blue jeans. He readily accepted when Brad had asked him to come down to Summer's Cove to help with the investigation.

Brad was looking forward to finally getting some needed answers. The entire team finally had a break in their individual schedules, one that would allow them to all be here at the same time. Tomorrow at ten in the morning, they were going to begin investigating Hunter's Glen in earnest.

JACK BEAUMONT

CHAPTER 18
OCTOBER 5TH, 2032

The Pumpkin Man smiled a lascivious, invisible grin, where he lay, still interred in Hunter's Glen, underneath the big oak. He'd just enjoyed hitching a ride in Brad Riviera's head, while he and his wife made passionate love. *Melissa's quite the catch Brad,* The Pumpkin Man thought. *I'm looking forward to having some fun with her myself…once I'm free of this cursed grave.*

Although he was being very cautious about his psychic tendrils roaming outside of Hunter's Glen, The Pumpkin Man did need to know a little bit of what was going on in the outside world. He hitched a ride in Brad's mind, and when Brad slept, The Pumpkin Man enjoyed using Brad's mind as his psychotic playground.

I can't help myself.

When Brad tore the silver crucifix out of the ground, it caused his powers to grow stronger. As long as the other, larger silver crucifix remained firmly in place, wrapped around his skeletal neck, he wasn't at his full strength. However, that problem would be taken care of very soon. He knew what Brad did for a living, and he was having fun with him. He wasn't scared of a ghost hunter. He knew for sure that there was no such thing as "ghosts".

But demons?

Now that was something else entirely. And he was depending on Brad to help him rise from the earth.

When Brad was sleeping, he was vulnerable to the mental intrusion by The Pumpkin Man. His secrets were laid bare, betrayed by his sleeping mind. Oh, The Pumpkin Man saw it all. His hopes. His dreams. His worst nightmares. His weaknesses. The secrets that Brad had never shared with anyone but Melissa. He knew it all. And he would *use* it all too.

When you knew your enemy as well as your enemy knows himself, you have the upper hand.

So, The Pumpkin Man had been toying with Brad for several nights while he slept. He caused Brad to relieve those painful years, the things that happened when he was just a young boy. He replayed the scenes of Brad, forced to watch as his neighbor raped his sister over and over. He savored reliving Brad's sense of helplessness at being able to stop it from happening. He enjoyed the deep and enduring shame Brad felt. The guilt. The horror. The disgust. It was all like flavorful psychic candy to the sick, demented creature now known as The Pumpkin Man.

For days he made Brad remember things that he had long ago locked away in a dark and isolated corner of his mind. Locked away, but not totally forgotten. Like a burglar inside of his brain, The Pumpkin Man broke the lock on the door of forgetfulness, dragging those tortured memories out into the daylight…

CHAPTER 19

OCTOBER 5ᵀᴴ, 2032

A few days after the horrific nightmares first began, the troubling dreams began morphing. At first, they'd been true to what had transpired so long ago; now they took on a new, alternate life of their own. The facts became twisted. Things that *hadn't* actually happened in real life played out in his dreams…in full color, and vibrant detail. He was almost afraid to go to sleep at night; knowing the terrors that awaited him upon closing his eyes.

To make matters worse, last night, the dreams had taken another, even darker and sinister, turn. This time, it was Melissa featured in the dream, in the place of his sister. Instead of Lance Putnam, it was The Pumpkin Man who was her attacker. Brad was forced to watch as The Pumpkin Man brutally assaulted his wife, all while he hunkered down in the corner beside the bed, quivering in fear and guilt. The nightmarish assault seemed to go on forever.

Then the dream once again turned even more violent, and more terrifying. After The Pumpkin Man finished with Melissa, suddenly disappearing from the room, Brad turned toward Melissa where she lay on top of the sheets, cowering in pain and fear. Inexplicably, Brad projected disgust at himself, for his own weakness and helplessness during the assault, toward Melissa, where she still shook and shivered on the bed.

As his own fear subsided, he felt inexplicable anger toward Melissa starting to grow. Questions that defied logic began dancing through his thoughts. *How could Melissa allow this to happen? Was this something that she wanted? How dare she do this to him!* Anger and blame seethed in his mind.

As he stalked toward the bed where Melissa lay curled in a ball, he felt a white-hot anger, unlike anything he'd ever known. His face contorted in rage; his teeth were gritted. The sight of her just lying there, sobbing quietly, made him want to hit her.

"Get up," He growled.

Melissa laid there as if she hadn't heard him. She didn't even look up from where her face was buried deep in her pillow. The only movement she made was the slight rise and fall of her back as she breathed, and the occasional jerk, as she hitched with a sob.

Brad stood over her, watching her for a few more seconds. She continued to sob face-down in the pillow. *She hasn't even attempted to cover herself,* he thought, looking upon her nude, defiled form with disgust. He spoke to her again, barely concealing the rage that boiled beneath his words.

"I said, get up."

Still, Melissa made no move to comply with his order. For a split second, he wondered what he was doing. In a recess of his mind, he knew he should be lying there beside her. Holding her. Comforting her as best he could. He knew that *she* was the victim here, not him. He shouldn't be angry at her; he should be angry at himself for making no move to stop what happened to her. As soon as these sane thoughts flashed across his mind, they were shut down by the all-powerful rage that overtook him.

"I SAID GET UP!" Brad exploded into a fury of motion. He snatched a handful of Melissa's hair, jerking her toward him. She cried out in pain and surprise; he rained the first of many blows down upon her terrified, yet submissive face...

■■■

The nightmare had been almost the same nightly, ever since the first night when it morphed. It went from a factual retelling of horrific childhood events, to a fictional, but equally terrible account of the abuse of Melissa, first by The Pumpkin Man, then by Brad himself. Brad knew what was going on. These nightmares were the work of The Pumpkin Man. They had to be. He was trying to influence Brad to do something.

But, what? Stay away from Hunter's Glen?

Or did the demonic entity, for he was now sure that that was exactly what he was dealing with here, want him to come *back* to Hunter's Glen? That thought frightened Brad; and it was the primary reason why Brad had not ventured back to Hunter's Glen alone.

From what Brad pieced together, through painstaking, exhaustive research, The Pumpkin Man had attacked Summer's Cove not once, but at least twice before. Those attacks had happened in a space of slightly over one hundred years. This information told Brad something both important and interesting...The

Pumpkin Man was infinitely patient, willing to wait a long time between attacks. The second, and most important information he'd discovered, was that the demon needed a physical, human body with which to commit his worst deeds. The scant reports he'd read regarding The Pumpkin Man convinced Brad that he'd been a flesh and blood entity when he made his appearances in Summer's Cove. That could only mean that either he had the power of regeneration, wherein something could cause his physical body to put on flesh over raw, naked bone again; or that The Pumpkin Man was somehow able to possess a victim, thereby taking on a new physical body. The latter was what kept Brad out of Hunter's Glen until he could get his crew out there with him. Brad wasn't eager to try out his theory of bodily possession, at least not without someone there to witness, and provide help should it be needed.

Tomorrow.

Tomorrow, Brad hoped to get some firm answers…and he also hoped to get this monster out of his head. His full crew would be here tomorrow, and he would be glad to see them. One of the premiere demonologists in the country was coming with Brad's usual crew. He hoped to be able to, at a minimum, contain the entity; the best-case scenario being the team banishing him back to hell, where he belonged. It would be great if they could ensure that the Pumpkin Man would never rise again.

CHAPTER 20
OCTOBER 5TH, 2032

As Samuel awoke from the dream, he made came to a firm decision. He was ditching school today. This was something he'd never done before, but he knew he had to do it. As the fall season deepened, he knew that whatever was about to happen with the girl would be happening sooner, rather than later. If he was going to find a way to prevent these events, it would need to be in the next few days, because he knew that the clock was running out. Time was growing short.

He'd secretly gone back to Hunter's Glen several times in the past few weeks. The last couple of visits, he couldn't get the voice to acknowledge his presence. He would go there again today, trying to persuade the voice to speak to him again.

Why would the voice show me the vision, if it didn't want me to do something about it? Did it want me to prevent it from happening? Was it shown to me just to cause me nightmares? What possible reason could the voice have to show me the terrible vision, and then just go silent?

Questions that he couldn't answer kept arising like persistent weeds in a vegetable garden. He had begun believing that he would never get the answers he so desperately sought.

No. I will get answers today! I must get answers today.

He packed his lunch for school as he usually did. He noticed at breakfast that his mother was watching him very closely, studying him with keen interest. He put on his best false smile, trying to pretend that this was a day like all others. To put her mind at ease, he engaged her in light small talk. To his surprise, it seemed that she had more on her mind today than he did. She seemed preoccupied. Disturbed even.

I wonder if she knows something's up? If she's suspicious?

Samuel had already arranged for his friend Josh to give him a ride out to Hunter's Glen this morning. The great thing about having a friend like Josh was that he never asked questions. If Samuel had asked him to drive him to a bridge, so he could jump off, Josh probably would have just shrugged his shoulders and said "Okay". He and Samuel had been friends since the first grade. Josh had always been mostly a loner. Samuel was probably his only real friend. While Josh never said much about his home life, he knew that Josh had it rough at home. His father had run off when he was just a baby. His mother was an alcoholic, one who had a reputation around town for getting around. Josh never talked about his family, or anything else personal for that matter. Still, he and Samuel formed an early bond, and that bond had lasted over the years.

Samuel hadn't really thought about how he'd get home after his visit to Hunter's Glen. He could probably get Josh to come back at a certain time and pick him up by the road. He would ask him about it on the ride out there. He hoped that Josh didn't ask to accompany him to Hunter's Glen. He didn't know if he'd be able to get the answers he was looking for if someone else was present. Although Josh was what others often described as "weird", Samuel didn't want to have to explain why he was speaking to a voice in his head. That might be too weird, a road too far, even for Josh.

■■

Betty sat at the kitchen table watching him, as he methodically packed his lunch. *He's getting so big, so independent,* she thought. She knew she couldn't be his protector for much longer. *He's growing up.* Soon, he'd be leaving the nest, bound for college, starting his own life in earnest. She wasn't sure what she'd do then. He'd been her life; her reason for living for the last sixteen years. Still, she knew that one day soon, she'd have to let go, giving him room to live his own life.

She'd been keeping a close eye on him lately. She had been so worried about him since he'd begun acting so differently. Now on top of that, she began having nightly nightmares herself. Nightmares in which very, very bad things happening to him. She'd had an extremely rough nightmare last night. One with him getting attacked, and killed, in Hunter's Glen. The dream seemed so real, so vivid, that she awakened; visibly shaken, and sick to her stomach.

She wasn't sure why exactly, but she felt that this dream wasn't so much a dream as it was a foreboding premonition. It just had that sensation of "realness" about it. Watching Samuel pack his lunch for the day, she was quickly becoming more convinced of that now. A chilling sense of déjà vu swept over her, as he repeated the exact same words from her nightmare, while he went about getting ready for school; performing precisely the same motions and actions from the dream.

She'd never felt like Samuel would hide something from her in the past, yet if he was truly venturing to Hunter's Glen this morning, he was keeping that fact hidden from her. She decided early this morning that she was going to wait a little bit, then she would follow him to Hunter's Glen, just to make sure that things were okay. She didn't know what was going on, but she was determined to find out. She was determined that no harm was going to come to Samuel. She must prevent what the vision had shown her at all costs.

"Are you okay, Mom?" Samuel asked, as he finished preparing his lunch. She'd never really thought about it before, but her emotions must be just as easily readable as his own. She thought, prior to now, she was doing a decent job of hiding her fears. She was wrong.

"I'm okay," she lied. "Just have a bit of a headache."

"Okay," he said, grabbing his book bag, then gently kissing her on top of the head. "I love you. I hope you feel better soon."

"I love you too," she replied fighting back her fears and the urge to cry…

CHAPTER 21
OCTOBER 5ND, 2032

Samuel walked up the long, hard-packed dirt and gravel road that led into the Glen. Josh had dropped him at the entrance, promising to return around 3'oclock to pick him up. To his relief, Josh hadn't shown the slightest interest in accompanying Samuel on his quest. With a little luck, he'd find out what he'd come here to learn, and his mother would never find out that he'd ditched school to do so. He just hoped that the voice would be cooperative with him today.

As he made the long walk down the narrow pathway, toward the hill with the massive tree at its crest, he was struck by the sounds of abundant wildlife activity. Squirrels were running through the bushes, up and down the trees, in their busy attempts at the final harvest before cold temperatures arrived in earnest. Insects were thick in the air, several mosquitos already sampling his warm blood. He knew that within minutes, as the base of the hill where the great tree towered upon the rolling hillside came into sight, that these sounds would soon disappear, as if an invisible force-field kept all but human and plant life outside of the circle of the ominous tree.

By the time he reached the top of the hill, standing at the base of the tree some fifteen minutes later, he was winded, sweaty, and tired. It was an exhausting walk from the main road, and the hill the tree was perched on was steep. He sat down under the old tree, searching for the words with which to begin this conversation.

He finally decided on a direct approach; an attempt to reach the "voice" through familiarity. "Dad, are you there?" he asked out loud, to the open air.

"I'm here," came the immediate reply of the disembodied voice in his head. His hopes were buoyed by the fact that the voice seemed warmer, less petulant, than on the last several occasions on which they spoke.

He decided, since he was alone, he'd keep his part of the conversation verbal. There was no one else around to hear him, or think he was crazy. He found it easier to say what he wanted to convey out loud.

"Can you tell me why you showed me that disturbing vision? What does it mean?"

"I wanted you to help me save the girl," the voice said, much to Samuel's shock. This was not at all the response he'd expected. In fact, he'd already pretty much decided that the person behind the voice, whoever that may be, must also be the person behind the violent attack.

This revelation wasn't what he'd expected…and it threw him off.

"Why didn't you just ask me for help then? Why wouldn't you answer me the last few times I came out here?" he inquired.

"My power ebbs and flows. I cannot always speak; although I'm always here," the voice lied.

"Who is she?"

"I don't know her name. I only know what is going to happen to her," the voice lied again. "I know that together, we can stop it from happening."

"When is this going to happen? How can we stop it?" Samuel's mind was reeling because he had not fully expected the answers to these questions. Or, for them to be so easily obtained. He hadn't expected the voice to be cooperative. It did make an odd sort of sense that the voice had shown him these things for a specific reason. Now, he knew that reason.

"Why didn't you just tell me?"

"Would you have believed it?" the voice casually queried. "If I simply *told* you what was to happen, and your possible role in stopping it, you wouldn't have believed me. I had to make it real. Show you vivid images of what is to transpire, so you'd agree to help me stop it." The voice paused, allowing his words to be absorbed and carefully considered by Samuel. "So you'd feel compelled, by righteous outrage, to help me stop it."

"Okay, what can we do then? How do we stop this from happening?" Samuel eagerly asked. He was satisfied with the progress he was making. It would be great to stop the terrible attack on this innocent girl before it began. "Should I go back to town? Get the police involved?"

"No!" came the immediate reply, a little too forcibly in Samuel's mind. Then gentler, "No. The police would never make it back here in time. The killer would already be here, and long gone, before you returned with the police. I need you to help me stop this evil now."

"So, what do I do? How can I help? I don't even have a weapon!"

Samuel scanned the surrounding area for anything, a weapon of any sort, that could be used to fend off the girl's attacker. Now that the time had almost come to save the girl, he wasn't entirely sure that he was up to the arduous task.

How big is this guy? he wondered. Samuel had never been in a real fight in his life, so he was a little anxious about the prospect of fighting off an unknown attacker. *Is he armed? Does he have a gun, or a knife? I'm unarmed.* He felt woefully inadequate for the grave task at hand.

"Don't worry. I can help you. There's something here that can be used to ward off the evil that's coming this way, rapidly approaching as we speak," the voice said, as if reading Samuel's mind—and he was. "We have the element of surprise on our side. Together we can defeat any enemy. You'll end this day as a hero! You'll make history. That's guaranteed."

That thought had never really occurred to Samuel, but he couldn't say the idea of being a hero didn't appeal to him. More than that though, he wanted to save the girl; keep her from being so brutally harmed...simply because it was the right thing to do. He remained haunted by the graphic, bloody images of the horror the girl would suffer at the hands of her unknown, would-be assailant. Being hailed as a hero for saving her would just be sweet icing on the cake for doing the right thing.

"Okay," Samuel asked. "What do I need to do?"

"There's something here that will help you. Buried under this tree is a pure silver cross, on a thick silver chain. I need you to find that cross and chain for me. Dig it up...quickly."

Samuel looked downward at the surrounding ground. The area under the base of the tree comprised a large portion of land. Trying to find a buried silver cross over such a huge area would be like looking for a proverbial needle in a haystack.

I don't have a clue where to begin looking.

"Don't worry," the voice told him. "I know exactly where it lies. Look for a large, exposed tree root. Follow it from the trunk of the tree, toward your righthand side. When you see a recently disturbed area, where some of the dirt has been removed, you'll be in the right place. Just dig deeper, until you hit the chain."

Samuel quickly spotted the large, gnarled and twisted tree root, which rose two inches above the ground, traveling outward from the tree's massive trunk for about thirty feet, before disappearing under the earth again. Samuel walked beside the massive root until he came to an area where he saw the small hole, and accompanying tiny dirt mound, previously left behind by Brad, as he'd dug through the soft dirt, removing the smaller silver crucifix.

"Is this the place?" Samuel asked the voice.

"That's it," the voice responded eagerly. "You can dig with your hands. The earth is soft enough; you shouldn't need anything else. The chain shouldn't be far below the surface."

Samuel dutifully sat down, raking his fingers through the loosened dirt that had been left behind in the hole. The soil was cool, soft, and easy to move. He continued to rake his fingers through the hole; his fingers sinking deeper with each pass. He removed handfuls of dark, moist earth. After he'd deepened the hole to nearly eight inches, he felt something new; a hard and cold item under his middle finger. He explored, feeling the slight hump of something solid and continuous, wedged in the moist ground. Bending forward, peering closer into the hole, brushing aside loose soil, he saw what appeared to be a link in a thick chain.

"That's it!" the voice exclaimed in eager excitement in Samuel's head. "You need to uncover more of it, so you can pull it out."

With his target in sight, Samuel renewed his efforts. He continued raking his hands through the soft, dark earth, removing dirt by the fistfuls. After a few minutes more, he could feel the chain where it ran across the ground, at least four inches exposed now. Using both hands, he scooped more and more dirt out of the area around the chain, forming a larger, rectangular hole as he traced the outline of his target. He used his fingers as small spades, trying to dig dirt away from both sides of the chain, which ran perpendicular to the direction he was originally digging. He worked like a rabid archeologist uncovering a historic treasure in an ancient city. He could see the chain more clearly, as it slowly emerged from the dirt. It was quite thick. The chain was heavy, made from solid interlocking links. It took nearly a quarter-hour more until he could get one of his fingers underneath the chain. He hooked the index finger on his right hand under the chain, pulling hard.

The chain hardly moved at all.

Samuel spent the next ten minutes excavating desperately, methodically exposing more of the chain, until he finally could slip all the fingers on his right hand underneath it. Pulling forward, as if he were doing a bicep curl, he attempted to pull the chain free of the earth. It pulled taut in his grasp, but again barely budged from its resting place. The weight of the earth covering the bulk of the chain was still too much for him to be able to pull it free.

Sweat dripping down his face, his anxiety growing with each passing moment; fear that the girl, and her attacker, would show up before he was finished unearthing the chain making his heart race. He didn't even know what purpose this chain would serve. Wasn't sure how it could help. While it was heavy, it certainly didn't seem like the best choice of weapons to stop a violent, possibly crazed, violent assailant.

"Don't worry," the voice said, once again reading his thoughts; seeking to reassure him. "This chain has special powers."

"Okay, if you say so." Samuel wasn't sure he bought into that claim.

He continued to work diligently at freeing the chain. He didn't question the voice about the purported powers this chain possessed, much in the same way he didn't question the fact that he was speaking with a telepathic, disembodied voice in his head. The unusual had been "usual" to him for so long that it just seemed natural, a part of everyday life.

After another ten minutes of excavating by hand, he decided to try pulling the chain free again. He once again slid his fingers underneath the heavy chain. This time, leaning over the hole, he braced his left hand on the ground, pulling straight upward, with the chain closed in his right fist. After a moment of hesitation, the chain pulled free of the ground, showering him with dirt, and nearly causing him to fall over. He examined his find, as he knocked large dirt clods away from the links of now freed, heavy chain.

What he held in his hands appeared to be a thick, heavily tarnished, silver crucifix affixed to an equally thick silver chain. It was much larger than the type of jewelry that people typically wore around their necks, as a sign of their faith. This chain would be far too heavy for that. Neither Samuel, nor his mother, were overtly religious types. In fact, they'd never even gone to church, or held a conversation about God, that he could remember. He supposed that some people might be comforted at finding such an item, one that held deep religious meaning for them, but he couldn't really see how a silver crucifix was going to help him rescue the girl. Even if it was pretty heavy.

"Don't dismiss such things too quickly, Samuel," the voice said with a hint of urgency. "You'd be surprised how much superstition is based in fact."

As Samuel continued studying the crucifix, he was suddenly overcome with a deep, pervasive sense of exhaustion. It was as if the long walk, combined with the effort expended to uncover the chain, had used up all his reserves. He supposed that his building fear, and anxiety over what was to come, also contributed to his sudden lack of energy.

He yawned, contemplating his next move.

"You should lie down. Rest your head for a minute," the voice told him.

"But, if I do that, I might not wake up in time," Samuel replied.

"I'll make sure you are awake in plenty of time," the voice soothed. "You still have a couple of hours before you need to be ready. I already know what needs to be done to thwart your adversary. I can show you in your sleep. Let me guide you."

Samuel began protesting further, but he really *was* extremely tired, and a short nap couldn't hurt. He lay down beside the hole he'd dug, turning on his side, facing the river.

I'll only rest for a few minutes. Then I'll be ready to face whatever comes next. In fact, just my very presence here might be enough to keep the events of the nightmare from happening.

His eyes grew heavy, sleep coming on quickly. As he drifted off, he didn't notice something odd; barely visible in the hole he'd dug. A small, off-white fragment of bone peaked up from the rich, damp earth. Next to it, was a small, dark green pumpkin vine, already starting to grow with supernatural speed. By the time he'd been out for just a few minutes, the vine had already crept out of the hole.

After a few minutes more, it had grown halfway up the leg of his pants...

JACK BEAUMONT

CHAPTER 22
OCTOBER 5™, 2032

The Pumpkin Man arose in his new body.

Just as he imagined, his powers seemed to be magnified a thousandfold upon taking over the physical form of the child; one he had fathered over sixteen years prior. He shut Samuel's confused mind behind a thickly walled partition, but he could still hear the boy's angry and outraged protests. His indignation at being tricked. His anger at having his body hijacked.

Now...to wait on mother to arrive, The Pumpkin Man thought with glee. *It'll be so nice to see her again.*

He'd been toying with Betty's mind for several days now. It was a masterful plan...to not only use her son to help him rise in the flesh, but to also use Betty's concern for her son...to cause her to fall into his hands yet again. He wondered what Samuel would think when he discovered that not only was the girl in the vision his own mother, but that history was cruelly about to repeat itself, in part thanks to him. He was sure that the events to come, over the next few hours, would break the boy's mind...permanently.

His son.

As he tested the bounds of his new powers, he could "hear" the jumbled cacophony of the rambling thoughts of many, many others. His psychic range reached far greater distances than ever before. Flexing his fingers, he glanced down, pleased to see that he could once again create hellfire with a simple thought. It was a power he had sorely missed when he last awakened. Focusing, he could feel the raw, surging power within, just waiting to be unleashed. Stretching forth his mind, he tested his ability to control others.

He came across the thoughts the loving caretaker of an old man; a man who lived on the furthest outskirts of town. A "Visiting Angel", these caretakers called themselves. *Well, we'll see about that*, he chuckled. Seems this "angel" was visiting her last patient before she departed for a month-long trip to Europe.

Perfect, he thought gleefully.

As the nurse helped the old man down the front steps of his house, heading to his mailbox, The Pumpkin Man forced her to roughly shove the man in the back. The unexpected blow causing him to fly down the wooden steps like a rag doll thrown by an enraged child. His nose made a crunching sound when he face-planted into the concrete walkway. The nurse then dragged the unconscious man back up the steps by his ankles, his already ruined face smacking against each wooden step, leaving a crimson trail of blood, snot and broken teeth. She violently dragged him back inside the house, picking him up, taking him to the bathtub…where she proceeded to viscously drown him against his feeble protests. Then The Pumpkin Man had her go back outside, using the garden hose to spray the crimson blood and gore off the porch, the steps, and the concrete walkway.

Wouldn't want anyone finding their bodies too soon, now would we? he thought, chuckling inwardly.

As soon as the woman finished with her clean-up tasks, he had her go back inside, and mount the stairs to the laundry room. There, he caused her to grab a large bottle of bleach on the shelf above the washer. He watched as she helplessly screwed the top off the bottle, tipping her head back. Then he forced her to open her mouth wide, as she guzzled a mouthful of toxic bleach, followed by another, and another. In a final act of cruelty, he released his hold on her mind the second the last of the bleach first spilled down her throat.

As her mind became her own again, roaring back into full consciousness, her eyes widened in fear and pain; she immediately tried spitting the bleach up. Tears began streaming down her cheeks as she gasped, clutching her burning throat. She ran to the bathroom, attempting to cause herself to vomit. Along the way, she grabbed her phone, desperately trying to call poison control in hopes they could help her faster than 911 could. Her guts felt like they were on fire, as the bleach burned its way through her digestive system. As the operator on the other line picked up, she tried speaking, her ruined vocal cords wouldn't cooperate. All she could manage was a gurgling, wailing moan.

She rammed her index finger into the back of her throat, forcing her gag reflex to kick in. As the bleach made its way back up her throat, she realized she'd just made a big mistake. She doubled, over spewing blood, bleach, and stomach tissue, along with the remains of her lunch into the toilet. As the beach came back up, it wrought new damage to her esophagus, her stomach, and her bleeding mouth. She was suddenly wracked with gut-wrenching spasms, as the caustic bleach finished eating its way through the lining of her stomach. Stomach acid, digestive juices, and bleach leaked into her abdominal cavity. She fell to the floor in agonizing pain. Her ruined esophageal lining, making it hard to breath; the bleach and stomach acid beginning to eat through the soft tissue of her vital organs.

It took her more than ten minutes to die; an immensely painful, protracted death. All the while, The Pumpkin Man reveled in her pain, supping on her fear and despair. The sweet ambrosia of a person's raw, unadulterated emotions as they realized that they were about to die, mixed with the pain of the process of dying, was like the finest of fine wines to him.

He felt positively joyous, soaking up the psychic manna of fear, pain, and glorious death. He couldn't wait for what was yet to come!

CHAPTER 23
OCTOBER 5ᵀᴴ, 2032

Betty couldn't wait around any longer, she had to do something; anxiety her constant companion. She almost felt like she was being pushed out the door by some unseen, outside force. She had to go to Hunter's Glen…just to make sure. She had to be sure that her dreams weren't true; that Samuel was safe, at school where he belonged. That this was just a normal day, like any other. She'd thought about just calling the school to verify he was there, but then she'd quickly discarded the notion. They would have to find him to verify that he was on campus, and she didn't know what excuse she'd give them for calling. Then, if he really wasn't there, she'd be getting him in trouble for cutting class.

No, it made the most sense to put her fears to rest by going to Hunter's Glen herself. That way, if there was trouble there, she'd be able to stop it; to do something. She'd save her son, and she'd go through hell or high water to do so. No harm would come to Samuel this day. Not while she still lived.

She grabbed her purse and car keys, starting for the door. She paused momentarily before running out the door, looking into her purse, verifying once again that she'd put the handgun from her nightstand inside. She wasn't taking any chances with her son's life. She wouldn't allow him to be harmed…

CHAPTER 24

The Pumpkin Man smiled as he watched the nurse writhing on the floor, in her final throes of an agonizing death. *Not bad.* So far, he'd already racked up a considerable body count...and he'd only been back in action for a very short while. He was determined that nothing would stop him from destroying this town; this godforsaken community that had been the bane of his existence for far too long. Then, he'd move on to the next town, and then the next, until he had this entire nation quivering under his iron-fisted control.

As he waited for the boy's mother to arrive, he felt outward with his mental tentacles, seeing what other fruit he could find that would be low-hanging and ripe for the picking. He could sense Betty was coming this way, just as he'd planned.

Great, he thought, *I have time for one more little party before I get started on mother...*

■ ■

As Betty pulled into Hunter's Glen, she felt different about the scenic meadow than on previous visits. She had always loved coming to this place before. Today it seemed different; darker, more sinister somehow. The moment she pulled up to the base of the hill that led upward to the towering oak tree, she felt an oppressive weight upon her wary soul. She exited the car, her purse tucked securely under her arm, beginning the climb up the steep hill. Halfway there, she saw something that stopped her dead in her tracks, causing her soul to freeze.

There was Samuel, laying on his side, curled in fetal position, on the bare ground under the tree. Upon seeing him lying there, she ran the rest of the way up the hill. She feared that he was hurt, or even worse, dead. To her relief, as she got within a few feet of him, he sat up, looking around with a dazed, slightly confused expression. She was so relieved to see him moving that she nearly collapsed. She could feel her heart beating wildly in her chest, her body humming with adrenaline.

"Samuel, are you okay?"

Samuel stood, turning to face her, a weird, almost smug grin plastered on his face. He looked her over with a sneer, replying, "I'm just fine, Betty."

Betty?

His voice troubled her almost as much as the fact that he'd just called her by her first name. Samuel had never used her first name in addressing her. Not ever. *And his voice?* The voice that issued from his mouth was not the familiar voice of her beloved son. It was far too deep; too gravelly. It held an otherworldly quality, almost an echoing timber not naturally found in a man's voice. One thing for sure: this voice did *not* belong to her Samuel.

Something else about her son's voice troubled her as well; she knew without a doubt that she'd heard that same cringeworthy voice before. Icy fingers traveled up and down her spine, before gripping her heart in a tight fist. Her lungs seemed incapable of drawing enough breath, and it felt as if she was breathing under water. The color washed from her face, her brain desperately trying to alert her there was something that she urgently needed to remember.

"What's wrong, Betty?" he chuckled. "You look like you've seen a ghost."

Snap!

The lock on a hidden door, within a dark recess of her mind broke in half, falling to the floor. As the doors of forgetfulness slammed wide open, the memories that had previously been held within came flooding back with a whoosh, like water from a crimped garden hose, finally released.

"Oh my God, oh my God, oh my G--," she began stammering.

"I'd prefer you *not* use that name in my presence," the being impersonating Samuel said, stepping closer to her.

"W-W-William?"

"Well, that's a little better...but no. Still wrong."

Frozen in place, her heart nearly beating out of her chest, she silently relived the horrific memories of that day, so many years ago. The fateful day that Samuel had been conceived. The day she had been raped, and left for dead, by Samuel's father, William. The dark, terrible memories she'd locked away for so very long, now coming back to her like a raging torrent. Terror impaled her heart like a jagged, wooden stake.

"Who ar-are you?" she asked, taking a step backward for every step he advanced toward her. "Let my son go."

"Who am I? More like 'what' am I, don't you think?" he chuckled, savoring her growing discomfort and stress. "Your son? Oh, but he's my son too, isn't he?"

Horror mounting by the second, Betty weighed whether to turn heel and run, or stay to help her son, if she could. Fight or flight warred within her. Her brain, geared for self-preservation, wanting nothing more than to run, to escape, to live to fight another day. Meanwhile her heart, her love for her son, telling her to stand and fight, against this monster controlling her beloved child like a marionette.

"Let my son go!" she screamed. Striding forward with courage that could only be borne of a mother's love, she struck him an openhanded blow across the right cheek. "Samuel, if you can hear me, you have to fight him. Fight back"

"M-m-mo-mom?" Samuel's voice, weak and confused. "H-help me." His face contorted with intense inner conflict as he spoke.

"Samuel?" Betty gasped embracing him before holding him at arm's length, looking deep into his eyes. Searching. Holding both of his arms, she shook him gently. "I need you to fight him, Samuel. You can't let him have control!"

Samuel's eyes momentarily flashed, lighting up an impossibly bright orange before a deep, rumbling laugh escaped his lips.

"I really had you going there, didn't I? 'Samuel, fight him for mommy'…Oh, ha-ha," his laugh echoed through the quiet glen. "I hate to tell you this, but Samuel no longer exists. He's as dead as you'll be in a few minutes!" As he spoke, his voice rising with each word, Betty saw that there was no hope for her son at all. Again, her mind warred within her. One part of her wanted to collapse in grief at the loss of her son, the other wanted nothing more than to live. In the end, flight won over fight. She suddenly turned on her heels, running back toward the safety of her waiting car. As she began running away, déjà vu screamed a desperate, unheeded warning in the back of her brain.

The Pumpkin Man reached down, finding himself a sizeable rock. *History always repeats itself,* he thought as he lobbed the heavy rock toward his fleeing victim. *Whap!* His aim was just as sure and true as it'd been over sixteen years ago. Once again, the girl went sprawling, this time, into the dirt right next to the car, instead of across the hood.

Well, nobody's perfect, he thought, advancing on his victim.

As he approached, he saw that she was out cold. The rock had once again hit her right at the base of the skull, hard enough to cause some serious damage, and to cause her to lose consciousness, but not hard enough to kill her, or sever her spine.

Too bad, he thought. *This would be much more enjoyable if she were awake.*

This time, he'd make sure to finish her *before* he proceeded to town. He wasn't going to leave any loose ends for anyone else to discover. He had to admit though, there was a certain sense of pride, as well as convenience, in having created his own vehicle for resurrection. How fitting that the father begat the son; and now the son also begat the father. A little Biblical irony there.

Reaching down, he snatched a handful of Betty's long blond hair, using it to pull her up from the ground, roughly tossing her onto the hood of the car. Once he'd slaked his physical lusts, he'd move on to the town, where he'd attempt to satisfy that which could never be truly quenched: his lust for blood.

∎∎

As the assault on her body began, Betty retreated into the farthest depths of her own consciousness. She found the door of forgetfulness, where she'd stored the painful memories of the past, and she hid within, shutting out what was happening now, to her physical body. Somehow, she was able to read the intentions of the demon who was using her son's body to violate her. She could hear his demented thoughts as if they were her own.

She realized that he'd lied to her about Samuel. He wasn't dead. He was simply locked away, held deep within the recesses of his own brain, much like she was voluntarily doing with her own consciousness. She could hear the faintest echoes of his cries to be released. She heard the fear, confusion, and the desperation in his small, far away voice. She knew she had to live for him. She had to find a way to save her only son. If that meant she had to endure this pain, this utter humiliation, this dehumanizing torture, she'd gladly bear that cross for her son, in hopes she could still save him.

Closing the door to the saferoom within her mind, she shut out her consciousness, shutting down her thoughts. She held the door closed with both hands, willing herself to appear dead...

∎∎

As he neared finishing, he felt a cold, blankness slam down that could only mean one thing. Death. His play toy must've been more damaged from the rock's impact than he'd initially thought. He could no longer detect any of her thoughts, her body seeming to grow colder by the second.

"Oh well, it was fun while it lasted, Mom."

He finished, tossing Betty's body off the hood of the car. He sat behind the wheel. Thankfully for him, the keys had been left in the ignition by his victim in her haste to "save" her son. He started the engine, slamming the gearshift into reverse, and turning the car around.

"I'm coming home once more!" He laughed out loud. "One, two, three, four...ready or not, here I come!"...

JACK BEAUMONT

CHAPTER 25
OCTOBER 5ND, 2032

Time was on his side. He constantly reminded himself of that nugget of fact. Perhaps the only thing he bore in common with these maggots, called humans, was that his kind was also known to pursue instant gratification. A design flaw common to all creation, it would seem. Close analysis of his other attempts at bringing these worms to heel, revealed that his lack of patience, and impetuosity, had led to fatal mistakes. He wouldn't allow those same weaknesses to hamstring him again.

He was eternal. He existed before the human stain appeared on the face of creation. He would continue to exist even after they were gone. He would help lead them into oblivion. To do so, he would have to be more careful than he'd been in the past. The humans had made many technological and weaponry advances in the last couple hundred years. These advances made them far more dangerous to him, and his carefully laid plans.

He drove to the outskirts of town. He'd already scouted a perfect place for his base of operations. An old widower lived out here, on thirty-five acres of farmland, alone and with no family. He also had no frequent visitors. So long as The Pumpkin Man avoided the local mail carrier, he should be able to use this base of operations until he was ready to reveal himself to the town. Too bad for the old geezer living here, because he wasn't looking for a roommate. The old man's appointment with his maker just got moved up several notches. With no neighbors on either side of the property for a couple of miles, there'd be no one to hear his desperate screams...

∎∎

"Noooooo!" Elton slammed upright, a scream dying on his lips, sweat dripping from his brow. Visions of what happened to that girl in Hunter's Glen years ago still fresh in his head. *No, no, that's not quite right. Not an exact vision. Something was different. Off somehow.* He racked his brain, trying to grasp what the dream was trying to show him. Sleep still holding on to part of his consciousness, like a lion refusing to let go of its helpless prey. He forced himself out of bed, swinging his arms back and forth and stretching, hoping to snap out of his deep mental fog. He tried to recall the dream before it was snatched away, as dreams so often are upon waking. Something about the dream was off.

That's it! That's the problem. This wasn't a dream based on what happened before. The details were off. First, the girl. It was the same one from before, but she was older; different. The car. It wasn't the red muscle car from the distant past. It was a late model car. It was new. A current model.

A sick, sinking feeling gripped Elton's stomach.

It can't be. This can't be real. It can't be happening again.

Frantically, Elton started pulling on his clothes. Juanita was out of town, visiting her mother for a few days. He wouldn't have to explain to her where he was running off to. She'd probably have tried to stop him were she here. He almost wished she *was* here, so she could do just that. As he finished pulling on his polo shirt, he was already halfway down the stairs. He snatched his car keys off the little table by the door, rushing out.

Please God, let this have been nothing more than a bad dream...

JACK BEAUMONT

CHAPTER 26

Elton felt it the moment he entered Hunter's Glen. Something was different. Something nagging, yipping at the back of his mind like a small dog, begging for his attention. He pulled into the meadow, proceeding slowly, not quite sure what he would find, or what he was looking for. He stopped well short of hill that featured the large oak at its pinnacle. He parked his car and got out.

A stark change in Hunter's Glen struck him immediately, as a flying insect buzzed by his face. Something that would be expected elsewhere, but stood out as extraordinary here, were the birds. A large flock of coal-black crows perched in the branches of the massive oak tree. Having been here before, and having known the history of this place, he knew that usually no wildlife ever ventured over to this side of the river.

The fact that birds now cawed, perched in the giant oak tree, underneath which The Pumpkin Man had been interred, made his blood run cold. He was afraid of what that might, and probably did, mean. Without thinking, he ran through the long grass, up the steep hill toward the tree. The birds in the tree scattered with an indigent chorus of raucous cawing as he approached.

Scouring the ground around the base of the tree, he didn't see anything out of place…at first.

Then he saw it.

A small, disturbed patch of dirt. It looked like someone had dug it out with their bare hands. He supposed it *could* have been the work of a small animal, burrowing for a hidden treasure. However, that idea was quickly discarded. Small animals didn't venture into Hunter's Glen.

*Not since **he** was buried here.*

It had to be a human who dug this hole.

Continuing to examine the disturbed area, he saw something that caused his breath to catch in his chest. Realization of the truth hitting him like a vicious, invisible punch to the solar plexus. After the gravity of what his discovery meant truly hit home, and he recovered from his shock, he spoke aloud.

"He's not here. God help us all. He's not here!"

Elton bent down, picking up a single, broken link from a heavy silver chain. The silver chain which he himself had placed over the charred, blackened skull, and around the neck of The Pumpkin Man, nearly seventeen years ago. The same talisman that had held evil at bay previously, for over a hundred years.

That the silver chains, both the small crucifix and this heavy, linked chain of silver, were gone could only mean one thing. One very, very horrible, disastrous, nearly unthinkable thing. The Pumpkin Man was loose upon the town again.

I have to warn the town. I have to stop him. We can't let this happen again. Last time, it was my fault. If I'd only just listened, so many lives wouldn't have been lost.

Elton's inner dialogue was running nearly too fast for him to keep up. An old familiar friend suddenly came back home; uninvited, and definitely unwanted. Guilt. For nearly a year after the previous encounter with The Pumpkin Man, Elton had suffered from soul-crushing, heart-wrenching guilt at having ignored, even ridiculed, those who'd tried to warn him of the dangers. In the end, Elton had become a believer, even helping to destroy the monster; but that victory came at a heavy, heavy price in both human blood, and lives lost. Not to mention the physical destruction of property, and the lasting impact upon the survivors.

His turn to play Paul Revere had come. Only instead of warning the town that hostile British forces, forces that were entirely human were approaching, he was tasked with a much more difficult task. He had to convince the town that something much eviler, and much more inherently dangerous, was headed their way. Pocketing the link from the silver chain, he ran back down the hill.

So immersed was he in his inner thoughts, that he didn't notice the pile of clothing on the ground, until he stumbled over it, sprawling to the ground, face first. Elton lay still for a moment before pushing himself up off the ground. Thankfully nothing seemed broken. He'd have to bear some bruises in the coming days, but other than his pride, nothing else was damaged too badly. He spat out a little dirt from where he'd faceplanted, turning toward the pile of clothing that he stumbled over as he did so.

His already racing heart kicked into an even higher gear when he realized that what he'd first taken for a pile of discarded clothing wasn't what it appeared to be at first glance. Curled into a ball was his very reason for coming here: the girl from the vision.

She lay on her side, naked once again, with her clothes lying loosely on and around her; just as she'd been found when he'd discovered her so long ago, near this very same spot. Like last time, she appeared to have been savagely attacked, blood matting her lustrous blond hair, lips split and severely swollen. Elton felt her wrist, searching for a pulse, relieved to find a weak, but steady throb. Watching her chest, he could see that she was drawing in very shallow breaths.

Working gingerly, but urgently, he quickly used the discarded clothing to dress her the best he could. Then leaning over, he scooped her up, struggling briefly with her dead weight, and headed toward his car. Although she couldn't weigh more than ninety-five pounds, he soon regretted not having the foresight to pull the car closer to her, before attempting to move her.

Panting for breath, he gently laid her on the ground beside the back door of the car. He opened the door, scooped her up again, then gently placed her across the back seat. He then popped open the trunk, grabbing two of the blankets he kept inside with some emergency supplies. One of these he spread under her head to act as a pillow, and to keep her blood from seeping into his car seat. The other he used to cover her from chin to feet, tucking her in. He knew that keeping a victim who'd entered shock warm was vital to their recovery.

As he sat down behind the wheel, another problem presented itself. He couldn't just show up at the hospital with a woman who had been physically and, most assuredly, sexually assaulted. The hospital would be required to call the police if he took her there. In the best-case scenario, he'd be stuck for hours on end explaining how he found the woman, what he was doing in Hunter's Glen in the first place, and why he hadn't called 911 for help. In the worst-case scenario, he'd likely be arrested and charged with rape, assault, and attempted murder; at least until the DNA test results that proved his innocence came back from the lab and were reviewed. That process could take weeks, even a month or more. He knew from the past that the people of Summer's Cove didn't have that long. Not if he were correct, and The Pumpkin Man had indeed risen again.

I'll take her home. I'll call Juanita and explain that I need her to come home as soon as possible. She's a nurse. She'll be able to help her.

In considering again whether to take Betty to the hospital, another, more disturbing thought came to mind...

He'll know. He can invade minds, read thoughts. He'll know that she's alive, that she's in the hospital. He'll come after her. He'll come after us. Elton fingered the crucifix around his neck. *Lord, protect me, shield my mind from this predator,* he prayed.

As he drove out of Hunter's Glen, and back toward his house, he said a lot of prayers along the way. He wished that he had a spare crucifix for the girl. He knew they had one at home. He found himself hoping that it was harder for The Pumpkin Man to read the minds of the unconscious.

Otherwise, I could be leading him right back home to me.

"Oh my God, Elton. This can't be happening again. Please tell me it's not happening again," Juanita implored her husband.

"I'm sorry dear. I think we must face reality. The Pumpkin Man has risen again. This proves it." He held up the broken link from the silver chain. "As does she," he added, gesturing to the bed, where the girl lay unconscious and unmoving, but resting comfortably. She represented a living testament to their dire circumstances.

Juanita came home as soon as he called her. Within a short time, she had the girl bathed, her wounds stitched and dressed. A three-inch gash in her scalp, and a concussion, and a battered face seemed to be the extent of her visible injuries, although Juanita believed she was in some sort of self-induced coma. Probably shock at what she'd endured, and at whose hands she'd endured it, causing her to retreat far within the depths of her own mind.

Juanita checked her patient's vital signs again, hooking up a new saline bag to her IV tree. *I'd be happier if she were at a hospital*, she thought, as she went about her work. *She needs to be checked for bleeding in the brain.* Medical concerns aside, she knew that Elton was right. A trip to the hospital would lead to questions they couldn't answer; and even if they could, it was doubtful that anyone would believe the only answers they could truthfully give.

Beyond that, since The Pumpkin Man could read minds, the possibility that he'd find out that the girl yet lived was very high. That would make her a prime target, and he was sure to come back to finish his work. No, this arrangement might not be ideal, but it was probably for the best, until Elton could figure out how to go on from here.

She pulled at the crucifix around her own neck; a nervous habit she'd developed over the last several years. As she did so, she said a silent prayer for divine deliverance from evil once again. An identical silver necklace rested upon the chest of the injured woman. As a precaution, Juanita had outfitted her with one. She hoped it would be enough to shield the woman from The Pumpkin Man's prying mental tentacles.

For all our sakes. If he discovers she's here, we'll all be doomed...

JACK BEAUMONT

CHAPTER 27
OCTOBER 6ᵀᴴ, 2032

Brad tingled with nervous excitement, ready to begin what promised to be an exciting venture. Assembled and waiting in his driveway, were eight of the best of the best in the field of paranormal investigations. Jonathan Silver had yet to arrive, but Brad didn't want to wait for him any longer. Maybe he could catch up to them later. They could give him GPS coordinates to Hunter's Glen.

No one in his crew would ever be confused for one of those "something went bump in the night; it must've been a ghost" types. Nothing burned his hide more than the "ghost hunters" who treated every single speck of dust flying in front of their camera lens as a mystical "spirit" orb, or who considered every wayward shadow a "ghost".

In his career, he'd debunked more cases of the paranormal than he'd proven...by far. Most of the time, people were relieved to find that they weren't being haunted. However, in other cases, he had faced wide-ranging array emotions, ranging from disappointment to anger, and even all out hatred, for informing someone who'd seen the possible dollar signs in being a "haunted" attraction, that the only thing haunting them was their own imaginations. One thing that he felt sure about was that something malevolent did indeed still linger, infecting Hunter's Glen. He intended on finding out what that malevolent force truly was.

The crew he'd assembled fed off his excitement about this outing. They'd never seen him this fired up, this eager, this gung-ho about an investigation prior to this. Several members of his team, those who'd known him for decades, were stunned that they'd heard him openly stating that Hunter's Glen was infested with a paranormal entity. Never, in their experience, had he proclaimed a place "haunted" before the official investigation had even gotten underway. Usually he kept his proclamation, the final findings of an investigation, to himself until it was time to reveal their results to the client.

He called a brief team meeting before they departed. There were some important ground rules that he wanted to go over before the team arrived on the scene. They could not afford to screw this up. If he was right about what lay interred in that beautiful, yet forsaken meadow, this could also end up being one of the most dangerous assignments they'd ever tackled.

"Okay guys, listen up."

The team formed a semi-circle facing Brad, their undivided attention on him.

"Today, we're going into an investigation that's different. We're not going out there today to determine whether something paranormal exists there. This time we are going into the field because we *know* something paranormal exists there. This isn't our usual type of assignment in other words."

"Excuse me boss," said his field electronics technician, Kevin O'Malley. "What do you mean, we know there's something there? How can we *know*, if we haven't done any work out there yet?"

A couple of murmurs of agreement rose through the group. Brad had expected this and was prepared for it.

"I've been to the site already. I've seen enough in my time to know when a place is the real deal, and when it's not. Most of you have that same gut level intuition. It just comes naturally, after years of experience," he began.

Nods of agreement met this assessment.

"I can tell you that this place is different."

"Different how?" James, the team cameraman asked.

"Well, for one, there's the wildlife. Or really lack thereof. Where we're going, there's no wildlife." He held up a hand, warding off the coming questions before they came. "Let me explain. We're going into the woods. A serene, secluded meadow, far away from any homes or businesses. A beautiful woodland, far enough from the road that you can't hear passing traffic. A place one would expect to find teaming with animal and insect activity. A river flows through the meadow. On the opposite side of this river, you can hear all sorts of wildlife. Squirrels, birds, small animals, even buzzing insects. However, on the side of the river where our target lies, there's nothing, nada, zilch. Not even a fly or gnat buzzing around your head. It's almost as if an invisible barrier blocks any living creatures, other than man, from entering the area."

He could see the looks of skepticism on his team member's faces. This was not a group that was easily swayed, not even by him. That was one of the reasons that he valued the people on his team so much. Their objectivity, and their reasoning skills, would not allow for them to be swayed. Not without positive proof and concrete findings. They were hardcore skeptics, down to the very last team member.

"Bear with me for a minute, please. Before I go into more details, I'm going to lay down some solid ground rules. Number one: We will be using a strict buddy system on this assignment. No one goes anywhere once we're at the target site without their assigned partners. I don't want anyone straying, not even five feet away from their partner. Got it?" He paused for a moment, for emphasis, before continuing. "Number two: I'm imposing a strict gag order on this assignment. No one talks to anyone, outside of this team, about this case. No one shares any information about this investigation, unless specifically authorized by me to do so."

"Don't you think that's a little excessive?" This came from Jill, his data analyst. "It's broad daylight. What's going to happen to someone, in an open field, in broad daylight?"

"Those are the rules. You'll hopefully understand the rationale behind them by the time I'm done. Anyone who doesn't wish to abide by the rules can feel free to stay behind."

He gave her a pointed look, and after meeting his eyes for a moment, she nodded, looking away. He wasn't used to having to lay down such strict rules. It wasn't his usual style. His team wasn't used to this sort of rigid structuring either. "I have something to show you." Pulling the silver chain from his jacket pocket, he held it up for all to see.

"This item came from our target location."

"What's the significance?" Billy, the team medium asked.

"It's a silver crucifix. It was buried at our target location, and it fits in with ancient superstitions that claim that silver can hold evil entities at bay. It also fits in with the local lore of what lies buried in that preternaturally silent meadow."

He then went on to explain everything he'd been able to dig up on the history of the town, and purported legend of The Pumpkin Man...

■■■

As their matching black vans pulled into Hunter's Glen, his heart began racing, his adrenaline beginning to surge. This could be *the* case that catapulted him to international stardom. He and Melissa would be set for life, if his findings could be documented, and proven to the world. Book deals, movie deals, and television shows would be offered for years to come. A few years of hard work would mean a lifetime of luxury, as well as the option of never having to work again.

But beyond that, there would be the deep personal satisfaction, derived from knowing that he'd solved the riddle of the evil that had plagued Summer's Cove for well over a hundred years. He could prove to the masses that demons actually *do* exist. That the paranormal wasn't just wayward dust particles floating in front of cameras, distorted audio tapes manipulated into menacing words, or shadows shaped by the mind into mysterious ghostly figures. He could prove that his life's work wasn't just entertainment for the gullible, as so many people viewed the paranormal field.

It's funny how so many people willingly embrace the possibility of ghosts, and yet scoff at the idea of demons. In my experience, I've never seen a ghost, but I've come across more than a few demonic entities, or cases of possessions.

Brad knew that within hours, his life would be changing forever. He couldn't wait to hop out of the van, getting this party started...

■■■

As the vans parked at the base of the hill, leading to the massive oak tree, under which their target lay, he sensed it. Something was off. Different. Something had drastically changed. A palpable transformation was in the atmosphere. He jumped out of the van, immediately making his way up the hill, forgetting about his team for a moment.

Something's wrong. Something's changed about this place.

Sweat started beading on his forehead as he made it to what he suspected was the grave of The Pumpkin Man. It wasn't until a fly landed on his face that it hit him...like a ton of bricks.

A fly? On this side of the river?

Then he heard something that he hadn't taken note of earlier. The birds. There were birds roosting in the branches of the oak, high above him. Confusion marred his features, as he considered what these substantial changes to this area might mean.

Even the very atmosphere feels different, he thought. *It no longer feels like something, or someone, is watching me.*

With feelings of dejection and deflation mounting, he went back to the vans, helping the team prepare their equipment. Intuition nagging him that this would be a wasted venture, he decided to soldier on with the investigation, not sharing his reservations with his peers. It was too late to turn back now. He had to see this investigation through to completion.

■■■

"Well, boss," Marty patted him on the back an hour later, "I think that about wraps it up."

Brad couldn't contain his dejection and deep disappointment. His head hung low; his reputation having suffered a great hit. "Okay guys, let's wrap it up."

They had found nothing to speak of. This investigation was, by all accounts, a complete bust. A colossal waste of time and resources. What was the most frustrating of all for Brad was that he *knew* that he hadn't imagined what he'd seen, felt, heard, and experienced here before. He knew that *something* malevolent *had* been here. He knew that someone had pointed him here for a reason, and that reason was to find whatever was hidden here, waiting to be discovered. Someone had wanted him to know about The Pumpkin Man. To discover the evil hiding here for himself.

As he watched the team packing their equipment away, he was still reluctant to give up. He couldn't begin to explain what had happened, but he knew there was more to this mystery than meets the eye. He was missing something. Something vital. Usually, if his team could find no trace of paranormal activity, they'd close the investigation, just as they were in the process of doing now, without further digging.

Brad, however, wasn't ready to give up just yet.

"Marty, do we still have the GPR unit on one of the vans?"

"Yes, but why?" Marty seemed puzzled by the question.

"Would you be willing to stay behind with me, and help me lug it up that hill?"

"Sure boss, but I don't know what you hope to accomplish. I'm as sure as I've ever been that there's nothing here."

"There *was* something here. The question is whether it's still here; and if not, where did it go?"

They bid the rest of the team goodbye, Brad asking them to reconvene tomorrow morning at his house, where they'd go over the collected information and review any findings that they might have overlooked. This was standard operating procedure, but Brad already knew they wouldn't find anything new upon further review.

Brad and Marty lifted the Ground Penetrating Radar unit out of the rear of the remaining van. The GPR unit closely resembled a manual lawnmower. It consisted of a similar frame, with a view screen located on the handlebars. Instead of a body consisting of a motor and blade assembly, the GPR unit featured a rectangular block, suspended above four wheels. This radar unit sent out powerful radar waves that penetrated the earth as far as thirty feet down before bouncing back. The unit was operated by slowly rolling it across the ground, forward and then a second pass back. The result was an image, or virtual map, of what was under the ground.

If the area they were going to search truly was a grave, they'd get an image that would indicate as much. The GPR model that they used in their investigations was one of the most powerful on today's market. It had the ability to show what was hidden beneath tons of soil, with remarkable detail. If bones lie beneath the ground under the massive tree, they'd find them.

I know the best place to start from, the most likely spot to find remains, is where I pulled the chain from, but I want to remain objective. I'll have Marty sweep the entire area, coming to his own conclusions.

Brad sat under the oak, watching as Marty began the slow process of scanning the ground. The GPR unit made long, sweeping patterns back and forth across the ground, starting close to the base of the tree and moving outward with each pass. Each pass around the tree took about five minutes. Lost in thought, Brad was nearly pulled into a hypnotic state as he watched the slowly swinging GPR unit hovering, gliding over the uneven ground. His thoughts were interrupted by something splatting on his right shoulder. He looked over to see a small spot of bright white mixed with gray, as bird poop started dripping down the front of his shirt, leaving a trail from his shoulder.

Insult to injury, he thought, wiping the mess off his shoulder with a handkerchief that he took from his front pants pocket. *As if I needed a reminder that things have changed in this meadow.*

"Come look at this!" Marty suddenly called out excitedly.

Brad rushed over, peering at the small screen. On the righthand side of the display near the bottom of the screen, there was a clear indication of a human skull. "That's awesome! At least this venture won't be a complete bust. Keep going. We'll see if we can find anything else. My research says that there should be at least two bodies buried here."

"So, what're we going to do with this information?" Marty asked.

"You'll see," Brad replied cryptically, as he started back toward the van. "Mark the location of that skull on GPS, so we don't lose it."

"Where're you going?" Marty called behind him.

"To get the shovels!" Brad replied.

■■■

Three hours later, they'd finished the arduous task of digging. They had unearthed the jumbled skeletal remains of not two, but *three* bodies. That wasn't all they'd uncovered either. Elton found additional links of the same silver chain that he already possessed, as well as several links of a different silver chain. One that was much thicker, almost as heavy as an iron towing chain.

This is consistent with what my research said I'd find here.

Even more compelling evidence that the story of The Pumpkin Man was at least partially true existed in the form of the skulls themselves, or rather the condition of the skulls. All three were charred; deeply burned as if they'd been through an intense fire.

Blackened would be a better word, Brad thought.

According to legend, The Pumpkin Man had met his demise under this very tree in the early nineteen-hundreds. Accounts claimed that as he perished, hell-fire issued from his mouth, instantly killed the preacher who confronted and defeated him, broiling his entire head down to a charred, smoking skull instantly. Reports said only a blackened skull remained from the neck up, and that the preacher was dead before his body ever hit the ground. That same hell-fire was said to have had the same effect upon The Pumpkin Man himself. Both men were purportedly interred here, with The Pumpkin Man having had the heavier silver chain placed around his neck, as a barrier to restrain him, preventing his return. The third skeleton, also with a blackened skull, must have come from the last supposed battle with The Pumpkin Man; which took place sixteen years prior.

This skull must belong to the unfortunate soul who The Pumpkin Man used for his resurrection.

Reportedly, both the minister who'd died fighting him, and The Pumpkin Man himself, were buried here over one hundred and seventeen years ago, as was the new body of The Pumpkin Man, after being defeated in 2015. The second silver chain had been added to the first, when The Pumpkin Man was laid to rest once more. Brad shared the significance of the skeletons, and the charred skulls, with Marty.

After listening closely, Marty looked at one of the scorched skulls he held in his hands, asking exactly what Brad was thinking.

"So, if he was buried here, imprisoned so to speak, why didn't we find anything with any of our equipment, Brad?"

Brad sighed, telling him about the first time he'd set foot in this place. He relayed how oppressive and thick the atmosphere had been. How no signs of life existed on this side of the river; and the malevolence he could feel just sitting under this very tree. Then he pulled the silver chain out of his pocket again.

"I know why we didn't find him here," Brad said realizing the grave truth of the words as he spoke them. "God help us. I think I might've set him free."…

JACK BEAUMONT

CHAPTER 28
OCTOBER 7TH, 2032

Brad and his team assembled in the "war room", a modified room in the basement of his home, that he used to go over their findings, and where he did most of his intensive research. There were three bulletin boards, where Brad could keep track of their findings, mapping their investigation, computers sitting at three workstations, a radio, and various other technical equipment adorning the walls.

All three blackened skulls from Hunter's Glen sat in the middle of the large, rectangular table in the center of the room, hidden by a white sheet, as he relayed his findings to the team. Brad began telling the crew that their mission was far from over.

Before he could even finish speaking, Jill cut it.

"But we couldn't find anything. Nothing on film, nothing on audio, nada. Simply nothing at all. I've seen more indications of the paranormal inside of an empty Walmart. Even our best medium couldn't find anything interesting. Not even a trace."

Brad had expected this.

His team, the people who he'd personally trained on ethics in the field. The same people he'd taught to be skeptical of everything, and anything, were now being asked by him to believe that, even though they had found nothing they could quantify, there had indeed been an evil force occupying the picturesque meadow just a short time before their arrival.

"Wait, a minute," Brad pleaded. "You've all known me a very long time. You know how I feel about having real, solid, tangible proof in our hands before proceeding further with an investigation. You know me well enough to know that I don't engage in publicity stunts, or self-aggrandizing behavior. This isn't about me. It isn't about selling books, or a syndicated television show. Before you judge what I'm saying, let me share the full story of The Pumpkin Man with you...and all that I've uncovered in regard to this entity."

Brad looked around the table, seeing he had their attention, if not their belief. Yet.

"It started back in 1914 in this very town..."

CHAPTER 29

So, the famous ghost hunter and his team now know that I've escaped, huh? Well, that's something I'll have to deal with sooner, rather than later. Still, it'll take a while for them to find me, or to become a thorn in my side.

Letting out a small chuckle, he went back to work, laying the careful framework for his plans. He had begun the process of subtly influencing the minds of those he found vulnerable. He was cautiously laying the vital infrastructure for his triumphant return. Carefully, oh so carefully, he implemented his plans, with the care of a master artist slowly adding brushstrokes to a velvet canvas, in hopes of creating a great masterpiece. It was more difficult than he originally thought, this whole "patience" thing.

Definitely takes some getting used to, he thought.

He happened upon the stray thoughts of a police officer, sitting about twelve miles away, in his patrol car, off the side of a busy highway. Officer Wes Baxter.

Nice to meet you sir, The Pumpkin Man thought. *What's that? Feeling a little racist tonight, are we? No? Well, you will my friend, just give it a little time, and you will.*

The Pumpkin Man continued watching through Officer Baxter's eyes for about an hour. Seeking the perfect opportunity to cause a little chaos. Reading the man's mind was nauseating. A good little church fellow, he was. One who, just six months ago, had lost his beloved wife of twenty years to a bout with cancer. He'd then dedicated most of his free time to helping at-risk youth in the community. Most of the kids he mentored were minority kids. Many had tough home lives, broken families, or abusive parents. *How generous. How loving this selfless man was. Makes me sick*, The Pumpkin Man thought, literally trying to spit the bitter taste out of his mouth. *We'll have to tarnish that reputation. I know just the thing for that.*

He saw his chance when he witnessed, through the officer's eyes, a car, with a black family inside, passing by the cruiser that Baxter sat in. He caused Baxter to flip on his cruiser's lights, pulling out behind the car. Blue lights flashing, he watched as the car in front dutifully pulled over to the curb.

The driver rolled his window down, as Officer Wes Baxter approached, unexplainable hate seething in his heart, rage searing his brain. He approached the open window, his right hand resting on his firearm.

"Good evening, officer," DeAndre Freeman greeted him. "Oh hi, Wes! Didn't know that was you at first," Freeman said with a smile, upon noticing it was his friend Baxter who'd pulled him over. Freeman was the Pastor at Silver Springs Methodist Church. He and Wes worked together, helping several of the youth they ministered to. Sitting in the passenger side of the car was Keisha, his beautiful, sweet wife, and in the back of the car were the two children that they'd adopted, after having tried for years to have kids of their own. Baxter had known the family for several years. He thought the world of them. They were 'salt of the earth' type of people.

At this particular moment though, Wes Baxter couldn't explain it, but he'd love nothing more in this world than to see them all bleeding. Dying at his feet. Horrible thoughts, the likes of which he'd never experienced in his entire life, screamed through his brain. Terrible thoughts. Racist thoughts. And, rage. An all-powerful rage. It was like nothing he'd ever felt. He needed to quench this rage. It caused him great pain. As he stared down into Freeman's smiling face, he realized how much he suddenly hated this man. Hated his entire family. With a burning, white-hot hatred.

Noticing the change in his friend's features, Freeman started growing concerned. "What's wrong, Wes?"

In answer, Officer Wes Baxter pivoted his holster toward Freeman's face. Without removing the gun first, he pulled the trigger. The bullet smashed through Freeman's skull, leaving a blue-tinged, smoking hole in the center of his forehead. Blood and brain matter splashed across his lovely, confused wife's face, as the bullet tore out the back of his skull. Freeman pitched forward at the same moment the car broke out in a cacophony of confused, shocked, and frightened screams...

• •

It was over rather quickly.

Just one shot apiece was all it took to dispatch the entire family. Like shooting fish in a proverbial barrel.

The small space of just a few seconds, and four lives were snuffed out, confused expressions now painted permanently on their stunned faces for eternity. Wes Baxter remained seduced by The Pumpkin Man, a hostage within his own brain. Forced to watch horrendous events, in which he was an unwilling participant, play out before his shocked and horrified eyes.

Now, let's add some extra flair to this wonderful occasion, The Pumpkin Man thought gleefully.

He had Officer Baxter dip his index finger into the still warm blood running out of the wound in Pastor Freeman's forehead. With it, he watched in delight as Baxter, at his direction, used the blood to paint every noxious racist term The Pumpkin Man could think of across the exterior of the Freeman family's car. Once he was done, there'd be no question as to why Baxter had committed this heinous multiple homicide. Even if none of it was really his doing.

Just another case of a racist white cop losing it, and killing some black folks, is what the media will say. The Pumpkin Man let out a roaring, raucous laugh. *And, there'll be no investigation, no case, no trial, and no defendant. No one to know that I orchestrated this whole thing.*

He released his hold on Officer Baxter's mind, watching triumphantly, as the man realized what he'd just done to an innocent family. One who he dearly loved. The Pumpkin Man watched with demented joy as the broken officer sank to his knees, looking at his bloodstained hands, as if they belonged to someone else. He laughed as the man screamed, "Nooooo!" repeatedly in wailing despair. He smiled as the completely shattered man wept bitter tears of disbelief, grief, anguish, and desperation.

After he'd dined on Officer Baxter's despair long enough to sate himself, he seized control of the broken cop's mind again. *Can't leave any loose ends around to do any talking,* he thought to himself. *Time to say goodbye, Officer Baxter,* he thought with a childlike laugh. *Time for you to pay for your crimes.*

He had Officer Baxter unholster and raise his service weapon to the right side of his head. Releasing Baxter's mind again, for just a second, he sent a message loud and clear, directly to his brain.

Now, you're going to die!

He enjoyed the final few seconds of Baxter's life, as the man realized that he was about to be forced to blow his own brains out. He struggled within himself, desperately trying to lower the gun, to force it away from his head, but no matter how much he tried, his muscles wouldn't obey him. His eyes grew large with fear, his breathing becoming panicked, as he felt his finger beginning to involuntarily apply increasing pressure to the trigger.

Seconds later, it was over.

The Pumpkin Man sighed, smiling happily. He felt contented and full, like a man who'd just enjoyed a sumptuous Thanksgiving Day feast.

No time for resting now, he thought. *There's a lot more work to be done, and much more fun to be had.*

That night, the local news channels were all reporting on the wayward officer who'd harbored secret racial hatred, disguised as a caring nature. The evil man who'd slaughtered an innocent black family of four, covering their car with vicious racial slurs, before killing himself. No one even gave a second thought to any other possible motive for the killings, because all they needed to see was written in plain sight...

CHAPTER 30
OCTOBER 7TH, 2032

Nurse Janet Kramer went to the kitchen to prepare Mr. Knoblocher's dinner tray for him. She'd performed this same routine, day in and day out, for the better part of four years now. Her patient was nearly ninety years old, and he required round the clock assistance.

The old geezer's become like family after the last four years, she thought affectionately. *I can't imagine life without him at this point.*

While caring for someone twenty-four hours a day could be tiresome, she *did* love the special old man. He was patient and kind, and he reminded her a lot of her own grandfather, who'd passed away when she was still a teenager. He wasn't like some of the older people she'd served in the past, those who seemed to grow grumpier, and more impatient, with age.

While many people of advanced years suffered the cruel effects that age wrought on the mind, Mr. Knoblocher's mind was crystal clear, his speech concise, lacking confusion. He could recall events from a young age, and he often shared his life stories with her. At first these stories had been a minor annoyance. Over time, she'd seen them for what they were: the cherished memories of a man's long life. Memories that he cared enough to share with someone he considered a trusted friend.

I'm the only family that he really has now, she thought. *We have that in common, I guess. He's really my only family now, also.*

Mr. Knoblocher had outlasted all his immediate family. One of three children, he'd lost a sister to cancer when she was only fifty-nine, and both of his younger brothers had passed on before they'd seen their seventieth birthdays. "I'm still here because I was the orneriest one of the bunch," he'd often told Janet. His second wife had passed on four years prior, and that's when Janet had come into the picture as his primary caretaker. Although he often joked about it, it had to be tough having survived all of your siblings, two wives, and your only child.

Having never married, Janet no longer had any living immediate family either, which is what made her the perfect fit for this job. She'd lost her parents in a tragic car accident when she was just twenty-two years old. There'd been no time to say goodbyes. They were just here one minute, gone forever the next. Then, she'd lost her fiancée five years ago this summer. Oh, he hadn't died, although she often wondered if losing him to death would have been easier to take, had that been the case.

No, she lost Quinton to another woman. In many ways, that was also an anguish, like losing someone to death itself, that would never heal. She knew that he was still out there somewhere, living a happy life, while she languished with a completely broken heart; this was why the hurt would never fully heal. He'd never even given her an explanation for why he left. They'd shared an apartment, having pledged to share their lives together, forever a couple. Only five months before their upcoming wedding, she'd come home to find a cold, empty apartment. All traces of Quinton gone, as if he'd never existed. His cellphone had been shut-off, his friends wouldn't return her desperate calls. He'd been out of a job when he'd disappeared, and she didn't know how to reach his parents.

She'd lost him…just as surely as if he'd died on her.

One night, after Mr. Knoblocher shared the pain of his losses with her, she'd told him her story. The kind old man had listened patiently, nodding his head, but saying very little. When she was done, tears streaming down her face, he gently reached up, brushing a tear from her cheek. "Don't worry, dear," he said. "Love will find you again. This young man just realized that you were too good for him. He let you go, so that you could find your prince."

The old man was a good liar, but she loved him for it. It was that same night when she stopped viewing him as a patient, starting to view him as family instead. Just like she was his only family, he was also hers. She lived in his house, cooked his food, washed his clothes, helping him do all the things that he could no longer do for himself. He *was* her life. At least for now. No one else in the world cared for her, or really knew that she existed. It was this kinship, this isolation, that made the pair perfect targets for The Pumpkin Man.

This'll be a gas, he thought, watching events begin to unfold from Janet's point of view.

He observed as Janet first brought the old man's dinner tray, and then her own, into his bedroom. In the last few years, she'd taken to eating her meals with him, sitting in an overstuffed chair by his bedside. They shared light conversation while they ate together each night. Janet helped the old man sit upright, placing his tray, adorned with roast beef, mashed potatoes, corn, a dinner roll, and a homemade chocolate chip cookie across his lap. Smiling, she asked the blessing over the meal; something her old friend was adamant about.

The Pumpkin Man stifled a chuckle in his mind. *There'll be no blessings coming from this meal. You'll both be dead soon, one of you before your food has time to digest.*

He enjoyed his role as a spectator as the two shared the meal with some friendly banter. The loneliness of the pair was a sweet savor to his mind. After they finished eating, he abruptly seized control, right as Janet stood, walking over to the bed to retrieve the dinner tray, and its now empty dishes. As she bent over, picking up the tray, The Pumpkin Man struck.

Neither party saw it coming.

Gasping, fighting, and struggling. Desperately trying to break free of the powerful hands crushing the throat, making it impossible to breathe. Several moments of intense thrashing, a mind screaming out in confusion and panic, voice silenced prematurely by inability to draw a breath. Hands beating at the other hands that squeezed life away, so brutally. Another mind filled with inexplicable rage and raw hatred. More thrashing and struggling, as burning lungs frantically try drawing in air, despite a windpipe that's being crushed. More frantic, desperate thoughts; pleas to God for mercy. The brittle crunching of neck bones crushed and broken; a windpipe collapsing. Shock, pain, the realization that death has come to claim its prize. Hate, fear, pain, confusion, denial, rage, pity, and regret providing The Pumpkin man a veritable buffet of emotional delicacies.

A body collapsing heavily in death. Hands relaxing their deadly grip, only after death fully arrives. Rage dissipating, leaving only confusion and deep despair in its wake. Sudden realization of a crime committed; an unimaginable atrocity completed. Hot, bitter tears of heartbrokenness at a precious life cut short; a life taken without cause.

The life of a dear friend, taken before their time.

Ahhhh, he sighed taking it all in. *Such a savory dish.*

Mr. Knoblocher held his shaking, age-spotted hands before his face in horror. He stared at the pale, thin flesh covered with blue veins, and dark spots, as if they were dripping crimson blood instead. Disbelief marking his countenance; fear shaking his delicate heart. Grief at his unexplained actions threatened to overtake him. He didn't know what had just happened, or why it happened.

Janet's lifeless body lay sprawled heavily across his lap, her once beautiful, sparkling blue eyes bulging and bloodshot, tongue lolling from slightly parted, blue lips. Her accusing, bloody glare turned obscenely upward in his direction. In her struggles, she'd knocked over the serving tray, the dishes and remaining food spread across the bed. His unwilling efforts at snuffing her life out had exhausted him. He didn't have the strength to attempt push her body off his lap, which would have been a taxing, probably impossible chore, even on his best day. Shock began setting in. He drifted into a restless unconsciousness. As his mind shutdown, he heard a deep, ominous laughter rumbling in his head.

Oh, this is good! The Pumpkin Man thought. *This'll be more fun than I had envisioned. I'll watch for the next few days as the old coot starves to death or dies of exhaustion trying to get that body off his lap.* This dire situation had the capacity to keep him entertained for days to come…

CHAPTER 31
OCTOBER 7TH

A ringing doorbell sounded, punctuating Brad's finished tale of The Pumpkin Man for his team. He could tell by the looks written on their faces that many of them weren't buying the story. Even after he reiterated his own experiences in Hunter's Glen, several of his team looked at him with open skepticism.

Guess, I'm to blame, he thought. *I've taught them well. Maybe too well in the department of skepticism.*

As the doorbell sounded again, he discarded his initial notion to ignore it. *It might be good to give them a minute to process the information he'd provided them before continuing.*

"I'll be right back," Brad said turning, trudging up the wooden basement steps. Before he got to the top of the stairs, the doorbell rang a third time. "Geez, I'm coming!" he shouted.

He made it to the front door just as the unknown guest rang the doorbell yet again. *This had better be something urgent.* Brad flung the door open, surprised to see, standing before him, the same man he'd seen watching him at the Post Office, the day that he'd discovered the whereabouts of Hunter's Glen.

Was this the same person who'd left him the mysterious note? Guess I'm about to find out.

"Sorry to interrupt you," the man began. "I'm here about something vitally important."

"You're the one who left me the note, aren't you?" Brad asked.

"Yes," the man replied, looking frazzled and exhausted, running a hand through his graying hair. "We need to talk, and we don't have much time. He's free."

"What do you know about all of this?" Brad asked, warily. "Why did you leave me the note? Why didn't you come to see me face to face? Who's free?"

"I was afraid. I didn't think you'd believe me. I had sworn never to tell this story to anyone. But now I'm afraid. I'm of afraid of what's coming, and we have to do something to stop it."

"Come on in," Brad said stepping aside. "I have some people I think you need to meet."

"We don't have much time," Elton said warily.

Brad surveyed the man in front of him. He looked scared. He also looked tired; no, not just tired. He carried the look of someone who was flat-out weary. The kind of exhaustion borne of sleepless nights and extreme anxiety. The kind of tired that permeates a person's very bones.

"Can you tell me more about The Pumpkin Man?" Brad asked.

"That's why I'm here," Elton said.

"Okay, let's go meet my team then."

They descended the stairs to the war room, Brad hearing the team arguing amongst themselves as they approached. He couldn't believe the good fortune of the timing of his guest's arrival. Hopefully, this man would be able to answer any nagging questions that he couldn't.

Brad knew that he'd need some seriously convincing backup to persuade the team, *if* they were going to accomplish what Brad had in mind.

As the team realized Brad was no longer alone, the room abruptly fell as quiet as a funeral home at closing time. The once vigorous debate now temporarily forgotten. They were not used to having strangers within their circle. The team looked toward Brad expectantly, waiting for an explanation for this unusual intrusion. When the team was assembled, and an investigation was underway, outsiders were never allowed in the war room. Nor were they ever involved in a case, unless they had knowledge in a related field that happened to be pertinent to the investigation.

"Okay team, this is unexpected and unorthodox, but I think this gentleman can shed some light on this affair. Let me introduce you to..." He waited for Elton to fill in the blank. Realizing, after an awkward pause, that the floor had been yielded to him, Elton introduced himself.

"I-I'm Elton Crosby," he stammered. "Former Mayor of Summer's Cove. I was the Mayor the last time...when *he* came."

"Who's *he*?" Jill asked.

"The Pumpkin Man," Elton said. Cutting off questions, he continued, "I saw him with my own eyes. I saw him while he was attacking the town. I saw firsthand the death and chaos he brought to this community."

"You mean what Brad's been telling us is true?" Jason asked. "Is that what you want us to believe?"

"I don't know what he's told you, but I know the truth," Elton said. "I know the horrors that I narrowly lived through. I also know that I'm largely to blame for him being loosed back then."

Elton scanned the room as he spoke.

He saw the room was split, about half of Brad's team looked interested in hearing more, while the other half appeared to be waiting for the proverbial punchline. As he looked from face to face, his eyes landed on the white sheet in the center of the conference table. His face blanched completely white, his eyes bulged, and his heart threatened to hammer its way out of his chest as Brad, noticing his gaze, pulled the sheet away. Sitting on the table were three blackened skulls, and part of the silver chain that he'd help place around the neck of The Pumpkin Man, so long ago.

"Wh-wh-where did you g-g-get those?" he stuttered pointing to charred skulls and silver chain links. "Oh, dear God, what have I done?" he wailed, suddenly collapsing to the floor in a heap.

∎∎

Brad and a couple of members of his team tended to Elton. He was now seated in Brad's leather chair, at the head of the long conference table. A mug of hot coffee sent tendrils of steam upward where it sat on the table, cradled on either side by Elton's trembling hands. A thick blanket was wrapped around his shoulders; his color beginning to return slowly.

The team was still seated around the table, even the most skeptical of the bunch now ready to hear Elton's story with rapt attention. As he began speaking, his tale and his mannerisms very much resembled those of an accused man finally confessing his guilt, racked with feelings of relief, mixed with apprehension.

"For me, this story begins seventeen years ago. It was then that I came to Summer's Cove with hopes of using this small town as a stage to advance my budding political career. Little did I know at the time that I would be the catalyst for bringing so much death and destruction to this place..."

■ ■

It took nearly three hours for Elton to fully unburden his soul by telling the team his entire story, from the moment he stepped foot in Summer's Cove, up to this point. Throughout it all, the team listened with silent, captivated attention. A few took notes. Studiously, they held their questions until Elton finished speaking.

"And now, from the looks of things, my good intentions have once again helped to unleash this demon upon the people. God help us all."

As he finished his story, he cradled his head in his hands, beginning to sob. Brad placed a comforting hand on his shoulder, giving it a slight squeeze.

"I wouldn't blame myself, if I were you. You were trying to help. Also, if you're correct, and this entity needs a body to resurrect in, someone else had to come along, remove the second crucifix, unwittingly becoming his host."

Elton stopped sobbing and looked up at Brad.

"You didn't influence whoever that was. They acted on their own."

"What do you mean?" Elton asked.

"Even if I hadn't removed this chain, which seems to be one of the barriers that kept him at bay, the other person who removed the second crucifix still would have come along. The person whose body, presumably, The Pumpkin Man is now inhabiting."

"Oh..." Elton said, still not fully grasping his meaning.

"Even had I never found Hunter's Glen, this mystery person would've still removed the second chain, probably this one was well. Your involvement is what served as a catalyst to bring this group together." He gestured to the team. "Without your note garnering my interest, they wouldn't be here. If any one group in the world stands a chance of subduing this menace, you're looking at them."

Elton nodded his head. Some of the guilt he'd experienced since finding Betty in Hunter's Glen beginning to abate. He'd left out that one small detail from his story. He didn't think it wise to share the details regarding Betty. Not until he had to. The fewer people who knew about her, and where she was, the safer she'd be.

"Now, it's time to discuss what we do now. Where we go from here. How do we go about finding this demon, and send him to a place where he'll never be able to rise again?"

No one seemed to be forthcoming with an answer to that all-important question. Brad did note however that after meeting a credible, lucid, and convincing eyewitness to the events surrounding the legend of The Pumpkin Man, and seeing the charred skulls for themselves, not a single skeptic remained among the group...

CHAPTER 32

Making plans against me, huh, Ghost Hunter? Well, I'm not some little timid ghoul that rattles chains, moaning in the night, child. You'd best be prepared to face me, he thought with a sinister chuckle.

He did realize though, that Ghost Hunter and his crew did have the potential to cause trouble for him. They'd have to be dealt with, sooner rather than later. He needed to find a way to deal with all of them, preferably as a group. A one-and-done hit. In the meantime, he continued to seek those whom he could corrupt, or use for his cause. Instead of torturing these folks with nightmares for weeks ahead of time, he was planting subtle little thoughts in their heads, prodding them gently toward the direction that he wanted them to go.

He likewise continued to seek those with which he could have a little fun, psychically feeding off them at the same time. Anyone without close family, or deep personal connections, was fair game for him. He'd checked in a few moments before on old Mr. Knoblocher. The old man's despair and growing desperation made for great entertainment. Starving to death slowly, the decomposing body of the friend he'd murdered pinning him to his bed, he fell deeper into hopelessness with each passing hour.

With any luck, he'll live for several more days.

The Pumpkin Man continued with his plans, undeterred by the threat of the few gifted individuals who might stand in his way. He was confident that he would prevail in his plans this time. He couldn't see how he could fail. He'd learned from the past and was determined not to repeat the mistakes of yesterday again.

He would bring this town, and eventually this entire country, to its knees...

CHAPTER 33
OCTOBER 20ᵀᴴ 2032

A couple of weeks had gone by, and Brad was growing increasingly frustrated. His team had been unable to follow any leads that panned out for them. Each place they turned, they found nothing. Elton shared with him that bad nightmares were usually a precursor to The Pumpkin Man's attacks on the town. While he and Elton seemed to be suffering nightmares, no one else they spoke with were.

Elton said the tension that had steadily built among the townsfolk during the prior attacks didn't seem to be detectable. At least not currently. No one seemed to be missing, no one seemed to be acting oddly or openly hostile toward others. For all they could tell, life in Summer's Cove was no different than before The Pumpkin Man had risen.

As a safety precaution, Elton gave Brad, and his entire team, silver crucifixes to wear. The paranormal expert balked at this request at first, but Elton's persistent arguments eventually won him over. Brad had to admit that there seemed to be some truth to the fact that pure silver did seem to have the effect of holding evil at bay.

It'd definitely seemed to work in the case of keeping The Pumpkin Man confined to his resting place.

Elton and Brad had a harder time convincing Brad's crew of the benefits of wearing the chains. Most of the team were avowed atheists, while one was of Islamic faith, and one a devout Jew. It was hardest to convince those two to wear the sacred symbol of another religion...for obvious reasons. In the end, Brad won out. He basically commanded anyone who didn't follow his rules to sit the investigation out; and in this case, the rules included wearing the silver chains...at all times.

Elton believed that a recent police officer shooting of civilians, a multiple murder-suicide in fact, had been the work of The Pumpkin Man. The problem with his theory was that there were no witnesses, and the perpetrator killed himself before being caught. There was no one who could shed any light on the motivation for the crimes, other than the awful racial slurs written in the victim's blood at the scene.

Still, Elton had a point.

Why would a decorated officer, a man who'd dedicated his life to serving the public suddenly snap, killing an entire family? Especially a family he was known for working closely with, in the pursuit of helping others? Brad's understanding was that the officer had been deeply committed to mentoring minority, and at-risk youths of all backgrounds. Why would such a man suddenly kill four people, and then himself, in a streak of racist, murderous rage?

Of course, the media came up with all sorts of scenarios and conjecture. Possibly the man had gone off the deep end after the recent death of his beloved wife. Or perhaps he'd molested one of the kids, killing the entire family to keep them from telling, finally killing himself to protect the secret. Elton was convinced that The Pumpkin Man had conducted the murder-suicide through mind control, having the officer kill himself to avoid anyone detecting his involvement.

As the calendar worked ever closer toward Halloween, Elton grew ever more frantic, more paranoid. Since events in the past always spiked, coming to a head on Halloween, he was sure that they were in a race against time. If The Pumpkin Man was not found and neutralized before Halloween, they were doomed. Brad had to admit that his own sense of apprehension also grew with each passing day.

It was highly unlikely that the demon had risen from his grave, only to walk away without lashing out at the town. This was a community that he seemed to harbor an intense personal grudge against. That meant that he was likely hiding somewhere, plotting, setting things up for a triumphant return. They needed to find out where The Pumpkin Man was, and they needed to find out quickly. He was obviously operating with a different MO than previously known for. He'd adapted his style, making himself harder to detect. Which meant he'd be harder to stop. If Elton was right, he could have numerous eyes and ears among the townspeople, and was likely even aware of the team and their intentions.

The woman who Elton had saved at Hunter's Glen had yet to regain consciousness. After the team had accepted the silver crucifixes, vowing to wear them, he shared Betty's story with them. It was their hope that she'd regain consciousness, so that they could possibly glean some valuable information from her. It would be immensely helpful if they had a clue regarded who The

Pumpkin Man was inhabiting. This might help lead them to his location…before it was too late.

With each passing day, they moved closer and closer to Halloween and it looked less and less likely that they'd get any information from their comatose patient. Not to mention, if the woman died while at Elton's house, they'd have a lot of explaining to do. Brad had checked local police reports. No one had been reported missing in the last couple of weeks. The sands of time where flowing through the hourglass. Time was running out. They needed a break, and they needed it now.

■■■

I should've known, Elton thought. *God must have a keen sense of ironic humor.*

It was roughly seventeen years prior when others from town had come to his mayoral office, trying to convince him to take decisive action to prevent The Pumpkin Man from rising. Back then, he'd thought that those people were superstitious rubes, backwoods hicks, backward in their thinking. Today, he'd just received a very similar reception; his own dire warnings likewise falling upon deaf ears.

No help would be forthcoming from City Hall.

They wouldn't be receiving help from local law enforcement either. At least sixteen years prior, the sheriff and everyone else, had quickly become a believer. Most knew the legends from a prior generation. Old age, retirement, and death had claimed most of those who held positions of power back then. All the new people who had replaced them over the years, unfortunately had not lived through what happened in 2015. Equally unfortunate was the fact that the agreed upon silence of those who *did* know what transpired, had the effect of limiting the amount of people familiar with the story.

Which was the original intent. A purpose that now backfires on us when we need help the most.

He now knew what it felt like to know, without a doubt, that a threat was very real, and to have others fail to take you seriously when you try to warn them. It made you begin to question what you knew to be true. It made you feel like the world's biggest fool. Like everyone else knew the laugh was on you, but you just couldn't see it. More than that, it was a source of unbelievable frustration, having others openly mock you, while you knew that Halloween could see half of the town destroyed, and dozens, if not hundreds, of people dead. All within a few weeks' time.

He was feeling building apprehension and dread, ramping up with each coming day. They needed help if they were to have any hope of finding The Pumpkin Man before it was too late. He'd tried his best to convince the Sheriff to at least dedicate two men for door to door searches. The Sheriff was having none of it. He'd have better luck trying to fight a hungry lion away from a fresh kill than he'd had at convincing Sheriff Feldman to help with their quest.

He hated to think it, but someone, or many people, would probably have to die before the Sheriff would be of any help…

JACK BEAUMONT

CHAPTER 34

So, they're having no luck marshalling their forces to come against me, huh? Imagine that, he smirked with mirth.

They wouldn't be getting any help from the Sheriff's office, because he had control over the Sheriff's mind. Not that the Sheriff knew it, of course. He'd been careful not to cause the Sheriff to have even the slightest single unpleasant dream. He was completely oblivious to the fact he was being subtly controlled. True, it wasn't as much fun this way, but he carefully prodded the Sheriff in the direction he wanted him to go.

There was no way that he'd be dedicating any of his people to the search for me. Not this time around.

Same thing applied to the mayor. He'd influenced her in the same way. When the former mayor visited her, The Pumpkin Man had already made sure that she was firmly set against his story as well.

She wouldn't be offering any assistance. The best part of that encounter was when she called Elton Crosby "paranoid", to his face. I thought the man was going to have a stroke.

His plan was on schedule, things ticking into place like a finely tuned clock. He was beginning to see how patience could pay dividends in the long run. The lack of any credible evidence leading back to him, and his ability to influence the minds of others from a distance, ensuring his success in this endeavor. Come Halloween night, this town would be leveled; brought down to so much rubble. Most of its inhabitants either dead, or his willing disciples; warriors in the unstoppable army that would advance on the next town, followed by the next. He'd been working on a plan to take over the military base, sitting only two towns away, like a ripe apple, ready to pick.

Just imagine what I could do with the might of modern weaponry at my command!

The commandeering of one military base would allow him to take over nearby bases with relative ease. From there, anything was possible.

He felt an incessant, all too familiar need beginning to pull on him again. It wasn't bloodlust, which he could slake from far away, remotely. No, this was another need; a need that could only be fulfilled in person. He recently discovered just the person who could fulfill this need without arousing suspicion. With her parents gone to Paris for two weeks, they wouldn't even know she was dead until after his work here was done, and he had moved on.

He just needed to see if he could test something that would help him in this task. He couldn't very well show up over there with this oversized jack o' lantern sitting atop his shoulders. If he could cast a glamour, making his head appear to be that of his earthly son once again, he could pull this off with relative ease. He stood in front of the bathroom vanity, concentrating intensely on masking his true appearance. Not long after taking over this body, his head had undergone severe changes.

Where he'd once appeared as normal as any teenage boy, his head had become a very large, bright orange jack o' lantern, complete with triangular holes for his eyes and nose. His mouth was a sinister grinning maw. His facial features were illuminated from within, just as a jack o' lantern with a lit candle inside would be. He focused forcefully on changing his appearance. After roughly ten minutes, just he was about to give up, thinking he'd have to take the girl the old-fashioned way. Moments away from deciding that it wouldn't work, he did it. Working from the mental image he retained of the boy, he'd recreated his face in a strikingly convincing illusion.

He smiled. The boy's youthful, tanned face smiled back at him in the mirror.

Not perfect, but it would do.

He would have all the time in the world to enjoy the girl, and even better, if his plan worked, she'd be a willing participant in tonight's festivities...because she would think she was making love to her boyfriend...at least until he was ready to kill her...

JACK BEAUMONT

CHAPTER 35

Heather heard the doorbell ringing, wondering who it could be at the door. Her parents were away for the next fourteen days, and God only knew where Samuel and his mother had taken off to. She hadn't seen or heard from him in two long weeks. It was very odd that he'd take off without telling her. She assumed that maybe there'd been an emergency in their family. Something that made them need to leave town, quickly.

Still, he wasn't returning her calls, or her text messages. That was very much unlike him. At the very least he should have called her, letting her know where he was, and that he was okay.

It was obvious that wherever he was, he had to be there with his mother. She'd gone by his house several times in the last couple of weeks. He'd shown her once where the spare key was located, inside a faux rock located near the front door. She'd used the key about ten days ago, entering his house. Nothing seemed out of place; nothing seemed amiss within the house. His cellphone charger was still plugged into the outlet near his nightstand, although his phone was gone. While she supposed that this could explain why he wasn't calling her back, or getting her texts, she also knew that it was extremely easy to obtain an iPhone15 charger nearly anywhere.

Where the heck are they?

She'd asked the father of her best friend, Chloe, if there was any way they could search to see if there'd been an accident or something. He'd told her that it wasn't a crime for a mother to take her son out of town, and that since nothing seemed out of place at his home, they'd likely just had to leave in a hurry to deal with a family emergency. Police resources couldn't be used to search for someone who wasn't necessarily missing.

As the doorbell rang again, she looked through the peephole in the middle of the front door, expecting to see a schoolkid selling something, a security system salesman, or possibly the mail carrier holding a parcel that needed to be signed for. Instead, she nearly cried out in relief when she saw the last person she'd expected to see standing there. She jerked the door open, throwing her arms around him.

"Where the hell have you been?" she asked. "I've been worried sick about you."

Having read her mind ahead of time, The Pumpkin Man was prepared for this question. He fed her a line of bull. One that he knew she'd buy. He also knew that she'd be sympathetic, lending him compassion.

"It was my grandma. Mom's mother. She had a massive heart attack. We had to leave immediately to see her."

Still holding him, she pulled him tighter into her warm embrace. "I'm so sorry, Sam. Is she going to be okay?"

"I don't know. Mom had my aunt bring me back from Tennessee. She's staying with Grandma until she gets out of the hospital...or until she dies."

"I'm so, so sorry. I'm sure she'll make it. Is there anything I can do to help?" she asked again, hugging him tighter before releasing him from her embrace.

"Just spend some time with me, I guess. Can we talk for a little while?"

"Of course," she said as she led the way toward the leather couch in the living room. "Come sit with me," she said, before playfully punching him on the right arm. "Of course, next time, you could at least call."

"I'm sorry, I forgot my phone charger. And, Mom...well, she's a real wreck right now," he lied. "She's really taking things hard. I spent most of my time trying to keep her spirits up."

Being what he was, telling these lies were so easy for him; it came very naturally. Like breathing. Or water to a fish. Lying was part of his very existence. And, because he intended to use, and then kill this girl, it bothered him not at all to lie to her, stoking her sense of compassion and empathy. From what he could tell, his ruse was working very well.

"Your grandma's in Tennessee?"

"Yep. Nashville," he lied again. "She's at the Baptist hospital there."

"Do you think your Mom needs anything? Maybe we could drive up there tomorrow. Maybe I can help?"

"No," he said. "I think she wanted me to come home, so she didn't have to worry about me as much. She knew you'd help take care of me."

As he said this, he looked deep into her eyes, false tears starting to well up in his own. She reached down, taking his right hand in hers, giving it a firm squeeze. She leaned in, kissing him lightly on the lips.

"I'm going to fix us a quick dinner. Then, I'm going to make you forget all about your pain and heartache," she promised. She stood up, starting toward the kitchen. "Wait here and I'll be back shortly."

■■

Ah, patience. Must always have patience. Just a little longer, and then she'll be mine. She even practically promised me as much. Of course, she thinks I'm her precious boyfriend. I can almost taste her right now…and I will taste her later!

While he waited, he reached out with this mind, looking for, and easily locating, a new victim. He settled on Tina Raines, a lonely and much despised occupant of apartment 310 in the Summer's Place apartment complex. A bitter, mean person by nature, Tina didn't have any close friends, or living family members. Even her closest neighbors despised her, wishing the mean old crone would either die, or be moved to a nursing home. So hard to get along with was she, that she was alone on the top floor of her building. No one even wanted to live near her if they could help it. Drawing a Social Security Disability check monthly for mental and physical disabilities, she didn't work, and she rarely left her apartment for any reason beyond getting her mail or buying groceries. When the other renters saw her coming, they either turned their heads, or quickly ducked inside their own apartments to avoid having to speak with her. In her ten years of renting apartment 310, she'd shared harsh words with nearly everyone in her building. Most of these confrontations were unprovoked, unwarranted attacks on her part. Paranoia serving to further isolate her from her neighbors. She became known as "the crazy lady of 310".

As he watched through her eyes, she went about making her dinner, a cheap, store-bought pizza. She opened the oven door, sliding the cookie sheet holding the frozen pizza inside. The entire time, grumbling and grousing about her neighbors. *The idiot in apartment 205 let his mangy little mutt crap in the grass again. Someone should poison the wretched little beast.* She'd stepped in a fresh pile this morning, nearly going down as a result.

"I oughta slip some rat poison in the little mutt's food bowl. That'd fix him," she laughed out loud, talking to herself. "He wouldn't be leaving little poop bombs for people to break their necks on anymore, that's for sure."

The Pumpkin Man invaded her mind without her even knowing it. When she pulled the cooked pizza out of the oven, he had her turn on all four of the gas burners on the stovetop, without igniting the flames. She turned them all to the highest setting, without ever questioning why she did so. She took her pizza to the next room, turned on the television, slouching on the couch. She didn't notice that the room began to smell of the pungent odor of natural gas because The Pumpkin Man willed her not to take note.

After she'd finished eating four slices of the pizza, he caused her to fall fast asleep. Soon, night would fall. When she awakened from her nap, she'd turn on a light to see by. By the time she flicked a switch, the apartment would be filled with gas, and the whole thing would go up like the Hindenburg.

■ ■

Heather felt horrible about Samuel's grandmother falling ill. She remembered just few years ago, losing her own grandmother and how difficult that was. They'd been very close, and her passing had affected Heather greatly. She imagined that both Samuel and his mother were going through a wide range of raw emotions right now. Under the circumstances, she figured it was understandable that he'd disappeared on her without remaining in contact.

She remembered Samuel talking about his beloved grandmother in the past. Outside of his mother, she was the only close family he really had. Since he never knew his father, he didn't know who his paternal grandparents were. So, she knew that he must be talking about Granny Worosello. It'd be tough on him if he lost her. He often spoke about their relationship, so she knew that Samuel's grandmother was very dear to him. Seeing him beginning to tear up while talking about her nearly broke Heather's heart.

While she prepared their dinner, she decided that she wanted to do something extra. Something to help. She'd like to call Samuel's mother and ask her if she needed anything. Possibly send some flowers to his grandmother's room. She picked up the home phone and punched a few buttons. She had left her cellphone in the living room.

"Nashville, Tennessee," she spoke in response to the automated 411 voice. "Baptist Memorial Hospital." She waited while the number was provided, then she opted to auto-connect to the number. A few seconds later, the hospital operator picked up the phone. "Nashville Baptist Memorial Hospital, how may I direct your call?"

"Can I have the room number for a Mrs. Worosello?"

"One moment, let me check..." the operator replied. A few seconds ticked by before she responded. "We don't appear to have anyone by that last name. Is there another name you'd like for me to try?"

"Are you sure? An older lady brought in with a heart attack, about two weeks ago? She should be in the ICU? Her last name is spelled W O R O S E L L O."

"No Ma'am. There's no patient in the ICU, or this hospital, by that last name. Have you tried Erlanger General? She might be there instead."

"Okay, thanks. Maybe I have the wrong hospital." Hanging up the phone, Heather frowned in confusion. There was no other hospital that Samuel's grandmother could be in.

I wonder why he'd lie to me? Could he just be confused? Maybe he meant a hospital in Knoxville, and he misspoke when he said Nashville?

She decided that she'd gently prod him about it after dinner. She knew there had to be a reasonable explanation...

■■

Time for sleeping beauty to arise, he thought.

Thirty minutes had elapsed since Tina had begun her catnap. *Long enough. The apartment should be primed and ready to go by now.*

His anticipation for the coming fireworks grated against his impatience. Were he patient enough, he could have waiting until morning. That would have made things far more spectacular; a veritable Fourth of July show. Although the chances of his plans being foiled by another resident smelling the noxious odor of the permeating natural gas would increase as well.

Can't have that, now can we? Wake up, he roughly prodded Tina's mind. *Get up. It stinks in here. You need to light a candle.*

He spoke to her, in her own mind, without her realizing that her thoughts were not her own. She still couldn't smell the rotten-egg smell of natural gas, because he willed her not to. Instead, all she smelled was the overly full litter box that her multiple cats used. That's one of the reasons her small apartment was filled with scented candles. When the odor got too strong, she'd light the candles to mask the smell of cat feces and stale feline urine.

He couldn't help but smile as she reached for the butane lighter, the instrument of her death, that rested on the small coffee table in front of the couch where she sat. He watched with growing impatience, anticipation, and the eagerness of a small child awaiting their chance to tear into their abundance of wrapped Christmas gifts, as she slowly removed the glass top off the candle jar, setting it aside. His eagerness turned to near giddiness as she lowered the tip of the lighter to the candle wick, pulling the trigger, igniting the flame.

For a fleeting moment, Tina's searing pain flashed through his brain, as the woman's eyes relayed the blinding flash of orange that accompanied a massive concussive blast. Then he was no longer able to see through her eyes as they, along with the rest of her body, the apartment, nearly the entire top floor of the building, and much of the second floor below were obliterated; blown into non-existence.

206

Reaching out mentally, he felt their sharp pain and emotional distress as three others lay severely injured, possibly dying, in the rubble of the second and third floors. Their misery was like ambrosia of the gods to him. Sweet, savory, delicious. Pain, fear, distress, regrets, all flooded his mind, making him nearly drunk on psychic narcotics…

■■

Upon returning to the living room, Heather was taken aback by the inexplicable, terrible expression on Samuel's face. While he appeared to be staring directly at the wall, not focusing on anything in particular; his face looked different, twisted, and distorted. His mouth was contorted into the evilest, sneering, most vicious snarl she'd ever witnessed. Hate was written across his features, his eyes seemingly lit from within, burning with raw hatred. She nearly dropped the tray, upon which their plates of food rested, upon seeing his face.

"S-Samuel? Wha-what's wrong with you?"

With an abruptness borne of someone surprised in an embarrassing act, by another person entering the room with them, The Pumpkin Man whipped his head toward her, attempting to once again fix his mirage of the boy she loved into place. His efforts fell short. Distracted by the death, pain, and destruction he'd wrought, he'd let his guard down. As Heather startled him, his glamour flickered, momentarily showing his true features in all of their bright orange, jack o' lantern-from-hell glory.

"Wh-wh-who are you?" Heather screamed as she dropped the tray, attempting to run. Dropping the façade entirely, he answered with his own voice, rather than Samuel's, hellfire issuing from his sneering maw.

"Your worst nightmare, dear."

Heather attempted to make it to the back door. She nearly made it too, before The Pumpkin Man reached inside her brain, forcing her to stop.

"Guess we'll be doing this the hard way," he laughed. "Not that I mind that. In fact, I like it more when people resist me."

His demonic laughter echoed through the small house...

■■■

As he finished with the girl, he wondered what to do next. The girl was still alive, but he'd remedy that very soon. Before he did anything else, he checked back in on his previous endeavor, to see how things were going there. He found a spectator among the crowd of people who'd gathered outside the apartment building. He took a moment to see and hear things through this man's eyes and ears.

"They said at least five residents are dead," the woman standing next to him said. "Crazy old lady on the top floor must've left the gas on. That's what they're saying. Took out the whole darn top floor, and half the one below it."

"How many others were hurt?" he asked her.

"They said ten people were taken to the hospital, still alive. Some in critical condition. One guy had his arms blown off, is what I heard."

"Wow. That's bad. All cause some old broad made a big mistake."

It galled him to know that the credit for his work was going to others. That was one of the problems with this new way of doing things. No one knew that he was responsible. He didn't like this guy, whose eyes and ears he'd borrowed. He'd have to make sure to look in on him real soon. Maybe he could enlighten him as to who was actually responsible for these deaths.

I'll bet you piss your pants when we meet.

Letting his mental tentacles stretch out further, he checked in on some of his other unwitting thralls. None of them, as of yet, knew he was their master. None knew that the thoughts and feelings that they were experiencing were not their own. They were his. Mind, body, spirit, and eventually soul, they would bend to his will, doing his bidding on command. They were his pawns in a deadly game of chess between himself and the human contagion.

As his consciousness spread far and wide, a stray thought came to him. It was one of Ghost Hunter's team members. Since the former mayor handed out his pitiful religious talismans, The Pumpkin Man hadn't been able to invade the minds of these people. He'd known that he'd have to deal with them soon, but he'd nearly forgotten about them since they started wearing the silver crucifixes. It was as if they had winked out of existence. Now, he picked up the thoughts of a lone team member. Being Muslim, the man had not taken kindly to being made to wear the symbol of a competing, nay polar-opposite, religion. He wanted to obey his boss, yet at the same time, he also wanted to please his God. As a result, he'd taken to removing the chain whenever he thought he could get away with it. He didn't buy into the power of the crucifix anyway.

Just a stupid Christian superstition, Akkad thought.

That disobedience is going to cost you, The Pumpkin Man mused. He read the mind of this man, getting a complete update, and full picture of what the team was up to. Their plans regarding what they were going to do next were laid bare.

They're going to be a threat soon. I'll use Mr. Akkad against them. He implanted a suggestion that Akkad would not wear the crucifix again; convincing him that he had heard the voice of Allah, speaking in his head. Always wanting to please Allah, Abdullah Akkad was more than willing to do as asked. He would not wear the crucifix again.

It would be an affront to Allah. A symbol of shame and reproach.

With that handled, The Pumpkin Man continued to scan Abdullah's psyche for any other information that he could use. There was some development involving an unnamed girl that Ghost Hunter and the mayor considered important. She held some key information that they hoped to glean from her as soon as possible. On the surface, this information didn't seem to matter very much. Akkad didn't even know who the girl was, or where she was located, he'd only heard snippets of their conversations about her, and a frustration that his boss couldn't get the needed information.

He didn't place much emphasis on the girl...until...

Another consciousness suddenly slammed into his mind with tremendous force. He knew this person well...very, very well. The more familiar a person was to him, the easier a mental connection with that person was established. In some cases, their minds would seemingly seek him out. This was one such case.

How? How is she still alive? Where has she been?

When he attempted to probe her mind, he found only confusion there. She didn't seem to understand where she was, or what happened to her. Amnesia, possibly due to head trauma, had wiped the memories of what he'd done to her, and who she was, completely from her mind. At least for the moment.

She can't be allowed to live. She must die. If she recovers her memory, that could ruin everything.

Alive, there was a danger that she'll recover her memories, being able to warn the others of who he was and where me might be. He couldn't have that. He needed to eliminate the acute threat she posed, and he needed to do it soon.

First though, there was something pressing that he needed to finish here…

JACK BEAUMONT

CHAPTER 36

He gazed upon the body of the young girl where she lay, splayed out on top of the bloody mattress in a bold and shocking mockery of the crucifixion. He nodded his head smiling in approval of his own brutal handiwork. Satisfied his message would be well received by his intended audience, he remained content for now.

She looks good, he thought. *A true work of art.*

The completed work was a culmination of several hours of viciously torturing the girl, using her in every way possible; he was very satisfied with his finished production indeed. His driving, insistent physical lust had been slaked for the moment; his spiritual lust for blood never to be quenched, had at least been temporarily sated. Both cravings would return soon; the craving for bloodshed taking precedence over the lesser need for physical satisfaction. Already, he'd begun formulating plans for his next victim; dreaming of the blood he would spill next.

He was going to go about things much smarter this time, and he was confident in and well pleased with his superior planning. Sixteen years had passed since his last stunning defeat. He wasn't about to let an old woman, or a fallen preacher, or even a ghost hunter stop him. *Never again.* This most recent term of interment, spent trapped and buried in Hunter's Glen, had allowed him to think, to watch, to analyze his failures, to come up with a better plan of attack.

He was too powerful, too eternal, to be thwarted by these weak and pitiful creations of his former master. As he felt that familiar, ever present hate for these lowly, pitiful creatures flowing through him, he felt alive. He felt free! The fear and the pain this young girl had given voice to as she suffered, bled, and finally died, had invigorated him, making him strong again after his insufferable sixteen-year nap. He surveyed his handiwork a final time before turning to leave the room.

The girl was lying on the bed completely naked, arms stretched straight out to the sides, as if reaching for either edge of the mattress, her legs extending straight down from her body, ankles overlapping each other. Her lustrous mane of long, silky brown hair artfully arranged on the fluffy pillow upon which her head softly rested, framing each side of her unmarked and uncommonly beautiful face. Her light blue eyes remained open, staring at the ceiling; the glaze of death dulling their once brilliant shine.

The palm of each delicate hand turned upward, pinned to the mattress with a sharp steak knife. He hated that he'd had to improvise, but he was left without choice, because he couldn't find any nails in the garage that were long enough to do the trick. But such was life.

It would suffice.

The girl's ankles were crossed and pinned together with a razor-sharp, wooden-handled, carving knife that had been driven through them, deep into the mattress below. Atop her radiant head sat the green, rough-hewn crown of thorns he'd hastily woven together from the knockout rose bushes that graced the front of her house. Blood trailed down the sides of girl's pale face in thin trickles from where the sharp thorns had pricked the tender flesh of her scalp.

She became a nearly perfect mirror image of the crucifixion...with exception of the missing hole in her side. Instead, a ragged, bloody, gaping hole marred the girl's chest, right where her heart should have been. While not an *exact* recreation of the scene that he wished to mockingly portray, it was close enough.

It would have to do.

He only wished that his fun hadn't had to end so quickly, but alas, he had other pressing matters to attend to. He let out a long, ominous chuckle as he raised his right hand to his mouth, taking a large bite out of the girl's rapidly cooling heart.

Maybe I should go visit mother now, The Pumpkin Man thought with a sneer, as blood dripped from both sides of his sinister jack o' lantern grimace.

Checking in on Betty, he tried to ascertain her location by reading her scrambled mind. All he found there was disorientation and scattered thoughts. Pain, confusion, weakness, terror, and a deep prevailing sense of dread warred with each other in her head. He stayed in her head for a moment more, soaking up the tumultuous emotions, savoring them like a selection of fine wines. He tried to implant a suggestion within her mind, only to find he couldn't control her the way he could others. Something, whether it was the damage he'd done with the rock, or her deeply disoriented state, was blocking him as assuredly as a concrete barrier. He would have to find someone else who could lead him to her.

Then, he would enjoy her once again, a final time, before ensuring she was dead for sure…

CHAPTER 37

What's this?

She pulled the silver crucifix over her head, setting it down on the nightstand that stood next to the bed, in the strange house she'd awakened in. She wasn't religious at all; didn't even go to church. She'd never worn a crucifix in her life and didn't have a clue why she would be wearing one now.

At first, she'd assumed that she was in a hospital of some sort. An IV tree, with a vital signs monitor stood next to her bed. Upon awaking, she'd found herself hooked up to an IV drip. A catheter snaked from beneath the gown that she didn't own, terminating at a urine collection bag. She didn't know where she was, how she got here, or what had happened to her.

The back of her head throbbed fiercely.

She tried to stand, falling backwards on her butt, waiting several minutes before trying to stand again. It took three tries before she was successful at maintaining an upright position. On legs that were as wobbly as a newly birthed foal, she gingerly walked toward the bathroom, fighting nausea with each tenuous step, hanging the urine bag on the IV tree, pushing the IV pole in front of her, using it for support and balance. As she slowly made her way across the room, she realized that wherever she was, it was no hospital, even if she was hooked up to professional medical equipment. This was obviously someone's personal bedroom, inside of someone's private residence.

But whose?

And why was she here? Why was she hooked up to medical devices? What had happened to her?

She entered the bathroom, inspecting herself in the huge mirror hanging above the double vanity. She was surprised to realize she didn't know who the woman staring back at her was. Racking her brain, she couldn't remember her own name. She knew the year. She knew that she had a son, and she knew his name. She knew who she'd voted for in the last presidential election…She just simply couldn't remember anything personal thing about herself.

One thing she *could* see in the mirror was the reason why her head throbbed so rhythmically hard. Turning as far as she could, while still being able to see her reflection, she could see that a large patch of hair had been shaved across the back of her scalp. In the center of the shaved area was a large, wicked looking, jagged gash that'd been neatly and professionally stitched together. Something had sliced her head open, and the wound had required quite a lot of sutures to close. She couldn't remember anything happening to her to cause such a grisly wound.

She turned, slowly walking back toward the bed on wobbly, shaking legs. She needed to get back to the edge of the bed quickly, lest she fall. She again pushed the IV tree in front of her feet, holding on to it with both hands for stability. As she neared the bed, she noticed a framed picture of a handsome, middle-aged white man, smiling, with his arms around the waist of a pretty black woman of similar age. She too was smiling the wide, toothy grin of a person madly in love. She tried to conjure the couple's names. If she was in their house, being cared for by them, she must know them in some way.

Nothing.

A complete blank. Not even the slightest indication that she was familiar with these people came to mind. Sitting on the edge of the bed, she picked the photograph up, studying it further. She tried focusing on the people in the photograph, one at a time. There was nothing about the woman's face that rang a bell. As far as she could remember, she didn't know who this person was. She appeared kind, with a warm, loving smile; she just didn't seem like someone that was familiar to her. Then, she turned her focus to the man pictured with the woman.

He looked kind and good-natured too. Obviously, they were married, or at least lovers. Still, something about the man, upon closer inspection, set off alarm bells in her head. She knew him but didn't know how she knew him. There was something vaguely familiar about him; something she couldn't put her finger on. Echoes of panic sounded an alarm in her brain. For some reason, her mind was trying to warn her that something unpleasant occurred to her, and this man was close to, or the cause of, whatever that was. She wished she could recall what was troubling her so deeply. She racked her mind for anything that would connect herself to this man.

Her spine suddenly went rigid; a realization striking her with the force of a lightning bolt hitting a tall tree.

Why am I here, in this man's bedroom, instead of a hospital? Obviously, someone has treated my injuries, but if they needed treatment, if I need an IV, and sutures, why aren't I in a hospital?

Her injuries, along with the realization that it's very weird for a person with such considerable injuries to be treated at a private residence, beginning to cause her to panic. Combined with her amnesia, and the warning bells going off in her head about this man, and the fact that she was in a stranger's house made her very uneasy.

Something was off about this whole deal.

It's as if they don't want anyone to know where I am. Why, though? What if he's the one who hurt me in the first place?

Like the clap of thunder that closely follows a blinding lightning bolt, a dark memory assaulted her mind, unbidden: She was lying on the ground; cold, confused, naked, and in terrible pain. Consciousness coming and going in waves. Something terrible happened to her, pain and trauma causing her brain to block the excruciating details. Fighting hard to cling to consciousness, the will to live warring with her body telling her mind to give up. A presence near her, bending over her. A face coming close to her own...this man's face!

Oh no! I have to get out of here!

Heart racing, mind working in overdrive, she considered her options. Knowing that she couldn't stay put, she decided she needed to leave this place, and leave now, before *he* came back from wherever he currently was. She couldn't be here when he returned. She wouldn't be a sitting duck for anyone. But...where would she go? She didn't even know where she was. She wasted another several minutes in trying to come up with a plan.

First, she decided to remove the IV and catheter; she wouldn't get far pushing an IV tree in front of her. Next, while she was trying to figure out where she'd go upon making it out of the house, she decided to test her ability to walk again. She'd not make it far on weak and wobbly legs. It would do her no good to try to escape, only to end up prone on the floor, unable to walk or run away.

After removing the IV from her hand, she used the IV tree to support her weight as she walked back and forth across the room several times. She was encouraged to find her legs getting stronger with each pass she made across the room. After five minutes of practice, she had to rest for several more before trying again. Once again, she made several more passes across the room. Then she sat down on the bed again, deciding to take another moment to rest, while formulating a getaway plan. While she contemplated her next move, she tugged the catheter out, grimacing at a sharp pain when it came free.

She could remember where she lived, although her exact address was still a mystery. Would that be enough to guide her home? Would she recognize the street that this house was on? Was she even in Summer's Cove any longer? Should she just try to make it to a neighbor's house, banging on the door until they opened, begging them to call the police?

First things, first, she thought. *I must make it outside the house. Then worry about where to go from there.*

She had no idea what was on the other side of the closed bedroom door. *Was anyone home? How big is the house? Would she be able to make it outside before being caught?*

She knew that if she could at least make it to the street, she'd have a much greater chance of being saved. She could scream her head off if necessary, so that someone heard her. Surely a woman screaming in the streets, in broad daylight, would garner enough attention to ensure her safety? She looked toward the bedroom window. The curtains were drawn, allowing her to see outside from her vantage point, seated on the edge of the bed. She was heartened to see that this bedroom faced the road. That means the front door was likely somewhere close by. If there was no one waiting in the hall, or the front room, she should be able to make it out the front door without issue.

Screwing up the courage to make her escape, she stood, exhaling slowly. *Here goes nothing,* she thought. She almost ripped the door open, before thinking better of it. A sudden noise might alert someone in the house that she was attempting an escape. Instead, she carefully pulled the door open a couple of inches, listening for a moment, before cracking the door even wider, peering out. Listening and watching for a little longer, she couldn't see or hear anyone else in the house. She slowly crept out the bedroom door, keeping her back to the left-hand side of the wall. She could see the front door, not thirty feet from her, dead ahead. She made her way slowly toward the door, keeping her back pressed to the wall, creeping along, trying to remain as small as possible. Across the entryway, she could see into the formal dining room. No one was inside it.

Just a few more feet, she thought.

Her legs were already beginning to tire. She'd have to make it out of the house soon and find a place to rest for a moment before trying to figure out where to go next. She reached the door, after what seemed like an eternity slowly stalking down the empty hallway, pressed against the wall like wallpaper.

As she reached the door, beginning to turn the doorknob, she heard a toilet flush somewhere deeper in the house. Panic overcame her; she violently flung the front door open, running from the house. Her legs gave out when she hit the brick steps. She went sprawling across the concrete walk. Ignoring the stinging pain in her palms and her aching, skinned knees, she crawled like a wounded animal to the side of the walk. She couldn't let the person in the house catch her again. She had to find somewhere to hide, *now*. Glancing up, she saw the garage of the neighboring house just twenty feet away. The garage door was up, a car parked on the inside. If she could just get over there, she could perhaps hide behind the car. Scrambling to her feet, she half ran, half stumbled into the garage, falling to the cold concrete floor once she was safely inside. Thankfully, there was no one else inside the garage at the moment. She hid behind the car, contemplating where she'd go from here.

From her hiding place, she could see a street sign that said, "Pine Grove Place". She knew where she was! Her house was only a little more than two blocks from here. With a little luck, she could make it home without being caught. Then she'd call the police. She'd be safe from whatever these people intended to do to her. She just needed to get home.

Suddenly she *knew* that she *needed* to be home. Home was safety. Home would make everything okay. Home was where her son waited for her...

• •

Yes, come home! The Pumpkin Man thought. *Home is where I'll be waiting for you, mother.*

He directed her thoughts toward home, leading Betty to her doom. He wasn't sure why, but his access to her mind had been restored. He could now lead her to right where he wanted her.

This is almost too easy, he thought to himself with glee. *It's a wonder that the human race has survived this long. They're little more than slightly evolved cockroaches. Although cockroaches were a little harder to snuff out.*

Now that mother is on the way home, let's see what everyone else is up to...

• •

Juanita Crosby heard the front door slam open, as she washed her hands in the bathroom just outside of the kitchen. Immediately she assumed that *he* had come for the girl. She rushed into the bedroom, expecting to see the girl dead, or worse, or to find The Pumpkin Man standing there. What she found confused her instead. It looked like the girl must have awakened, taken out her IV and catheter, and then fled the house in confusion or panic. There were no signs of violence, and surely The Pumpkin Man would have dealt with her here; probably killing Elton and herself as well.

Juanita ran to the front door, looking out. The girl would be in grave danger if she's roaming the streets alone. Especially in a weakened state, with The Pumpkin Man hiding only God knows where.

Not only that, if she goes to the police, we're in deep trouble, she thought.

She walked out to the sidewalk, looking both ways, up and down the street. Pacing the driveway, she considered what she should do next. Running her hands through her hair in frustration, sighing, she made the decision to call Elton immediately; he'd know what to do. She went inside to retrieve her cellphone.

∙∙

Betty watched from her hiding place behind the car, as the woman searched up and down the street, pacing her driveway, obviously upset that her captive had escaped. She watched as the frantic woman ran back inside the house, probably alerting her husband that she'd gotten away. She needed to move, now, before the woman called in reinforcements.

She knew if she shot straight across the street to the backyard of the house on the other side of the road, she could travel through the backyards of the houses along this street, staying hidden, for the most part, from the main road. There would be plenty of hiding places along the way, if she needed to rest for a moment to catch a breath or rest her weary legs. With a little luck, she'd be able to reach the safety her own house within the next hour.

Safety was calling out to her. Home called out to her, playing a siren tune in her head. If she could just get home, she'd be safe. She'd be free.

I must get home…

■■■

Yes, come on home, Mama, The Pumpkin Man thought with glee. *Nothing will ever hurt you again, if you just make it home…well, at least after I'm done with you, nothing will ever hurt you again…because the dead feel no pain.*

He continued pushing her fragile mind with the subtle, imperative command to return home. He guided her toward his direction, relishing the moment when he helped her rediscover her lost memories. She'd know who she was again soon, then she'd realize who he was also, right before she died. He would make sure that she was dead, truly dead. No mistakes this time. He couldn't afford to have her around, a loose end waiting to be traced back to himself. No, he needed a little more time before he was ready to make his grand debut to Summer's Cove, and the world beyond.

While he waited for her to arrive, he checked in with his unwitting minion, Abdullah Akkad. He could sense the frustration of the man, and that expressed by the rest of the team, as they sat in yet another long strategy meeting. They'd had no luck in getting help from the local authorities, just as he knew they wouldn't. They were brainstorming for ideas regarding how they could locate him. As Halloween rapidly approached, they were quickly growing short on time. Even the supposed expert among demonologists couldn't seem to locate him.

The Pumpkin Man sat in on the meeting, using Akkad's eyes and ears as his own. Through their planning, he began to formulate a design of his own. One that would allow him to take out the entire group, as one. With one blow, he'd be able to crush the only feeble resistance that this small town had to offer.

He watched as the former mayor of Summer's Cove received an urgent phone call. He witnessed as the man spoke for a moment with the person on the other line, and then hung up. Moments before, the team had been discussing the possibility of the girl awakening and thus leading them to The Pumpkin Man. Elton Crosby let them know what he'd just learned.

"She's gone," he said dejectedly.

"What do you mean, she's gone?" Ghost Hunter asked.

"I mean, she woke up, must've panicked, and ran from the house. My wife heard a commotion while she was in the bathroom, and when she came out, the girl was gone."

"We have to find her! She's the best lead we have."

"Not to mention that if The Pumpkin Man finds her first, she's as good as dead."

"Okay team, we need to fan out, start closing in a perimeter from here, to the mayor's house. We need to find her before she gets to the police or before *he* finds her. She might be the key to breaking this case."

The Pumpkin Man chuckled inwardly as he pulled back from Akkad's mind.

Time to bring the lambs home to the slaughter…

JACK BEAUMONT

CHAPTER 38

I've got to get home, Betty thought desperately. *I've got to get back to Samuel, back to safety. Home is the only place where I'll be safe.*

Each time she heard a passing car, she nearly fell over as panic threatened to disable her. With each engine she heard, she wondered if her captors were closing in on her.

Halfway home. I'm nearly there. Hold on, son. I'm coming.

She watched from her resting place behind an oval, above ground swimming pool in a neighbor's backyard as another car drove slowly by. This one was obviously driven by someone looking for something, or someone. The car passed by deliberately, braked, turning around, and then coming back, making another slow pass. As soon as the car was out of sight, she bolted, running across the yard to the house next door. There she found cover behind an outdoor storage shed. Panting, breathing hard from exhaustion and exertion, she held her position as she continued watching for more signs of relentless pursuit.

I'm coming son!

She didn't know why, but it was almost as if she could hear her son calling out to her. Willing her to come home inside her head. Beckoning her. Pleading for her to return. The need to get back home, to get to him, nearly overcoming her need for caution...

■■■

Yes, come on home, Mama, The Pumpkin Man mentally sent. *I'm waiting for you.*

Contemplating his reflection in the mirror, he concentrated on changing his appearance again. It took several moments before he got it right and he could no longer see the sneering jack o' lantern face, instead seeing the features of the son who the woman loved so dearly. As the boy's facial features solidified, settling into place over his own true, ghastly features, he tried on a tentative smile.

These weak little bugs. Their sentimental notions of love always making them pitiful and weak. They would never be anything more than pathetic, scurrying little insects. Love. The word caused bile to rise up in his throat. Love was good for nothing. It made the powerful weak, making the weak even weaker. Hate. That was a truly powerful tool. Hate was power! Hate removed the constraints of love, allowing those who would embrace it and harness it, to thrive. All the world's greatest leaders, throughout history had embraced hate, making it their own.

He looked at his reflection in the mirror again. *Not perfect, but good enough*, he thought. Reaching out with his mind, he sent out another urgent thought.

Come home, Mama. Come home to safety.

■■■

I made it. I can't believe I made it.

A breathless Betty ran up the front steps of her home, heart hammering in a chest that was heaving for air. The sudden realization that she was without keys, causing her to have a brief moment of doubt. She held her breath, reaching hesitantly for the doorknob. Fully expecting to find the door securely locked, she breathed out a sigh of relief when the knob turned freely in her hand. Opening the door quickly, she barged inside, slamming the door shut behind her. With trembling fingers, she turned the cylinder lock, then put the chain lock on for good measure.

As the relief of the safety of home washed over her, she nearly collapsed on the sofa. Legs that had not supported her body weight for a couple of weeks finally giving out. She didn't think she could walk a step further if she had to. As she sprawled across the couch, legs beginning to cramp painfully, she heard a noise from another room.

"Samuel, is that you?" she called out. "I'm home."

"I'm glad you made it back, Mother," Samuel said from somewhere behind her. "I've been waiting for you."

Betty broke down, sobbing. Tears of relief cascading down her face. Realization that she was safe, and the love for her son, overwhelming her already fragile emotional state. She was home, safe at home. Free from her captors. Somewhere in the back of her mind, she realized that she had been inexplicably worried about Samuel too.

A shiver rolled down her spine suddenly, threatening to overshadow her relief, as something important urgently tugged at the back of her mind. Some knowledge was desperately clawing, trying to climb to the forefront of her brain. Like a foghorn screaming through a dense, foggy mist, alarm bells rang in her head. She couldn't grasp what it was that her brain was attempting, in vain, to warn her about.

Suddenly, for an unknown reason, home didn't seem so safe any longer.

Samuel came from one of the rooms near the back of the house as he spoke. Heart still gripped tightly by an icy-clawed talon; Betty's brain screamed at her in a seemingly indecipherable language. *What was the reason for this sudden sense of dread and unease?* She was on the verge of a panic attack; and didn't have a clue as to why.

That's when Samuel walked around the corner, and into her line of sight.

"What's wrong, Betty? You look like you've seen a ghost." The Pumpkin Man, sensing her distress, dropped all pretenses of being her son, Samuel, knowing he could never really fool her.

As she took in the monstrously large pumpkin sitting upon her former son's shoulders, nightmarish jack o' lantern face fixed in a cruel, sneering grimace, the dam holding back her traumatic memories cracked, bursting wide open.

Orange flames licking around the triangular holes of his eyes and nose, flames flicking inside his mouth, an odor of sulfur and brimstone punctuating his speech, he openly mocked her, the Pumpkin Man savoring her terror.

Betty recoiled, feet scrambling, trying to backpedal into the couch as he approached. She almost made it over the back of the couch before his command slammed into her mind like a fifty-car freight train. "Stop moving," the voice in her mind commanded. Like a marionette on a string, her body had no choice but to obey its puppeteer. She fell limp on the couch, her body no longer hers to control. She tried screaming but couldn't get her body to cooperate.

"Welcome home, Mama!" The Pumpkin Man exclaimed with insane glee. "It's so nice to see you again, Betty. Are you ready to have some more fun?" His echoing laughter reverberated off the walls as he advanced on his prey.

"P-p-please don, don't k-kill me" Betty managed to stutter in a defeated, desperate whisper.

"Oh, I'd never do that, mother," The Pumpkin Man said in a nearly perfect imitation of Samuel's voice. He laughed again, a raucous, deep-throated, and hearty laugh. "Oh no, you're going to do that all by yourself, my dear, Mama." ...

■■

"Great, thanks!"

Brad hung up the phone.

He was able to obtain an address for their missing victim from one of his friends back home. Ted was a master of Google "searchology". Give him the slightest bit of information, and he could turn up reams of knowledge on the most stubborn of subjects. Ted had been largely responsible for most of the information that Brad had discovered on the historical aspects and lore of The Pumpkin Man. He was one of Brad's most invaluable resources.

"I have the address," he said turning to Elton. "Who's driving?"

Elton looked at the address. "No need for that," he said, indicating Brad's phone, where he was already entering Betty's address into his GPS app. "I know exactly where this is, and it isn't far at all."

"Let's go!" Brad said, automatically breaking into a sprint for his own vehicle. Elton ran behind him, jumping inside the passenger seat. While he was putting the truck in motion, Brad used the conference feature on his phone, contacting all his team members at the same time. He gave them the address, asking for them to meet him there. No one was to enter until they all reached the house.

▪▪

He watched the boy's mother as she lay convulsing on the floor. He hadn't had time to enjoy her properly again, but he'd dined quite nicely upon her sumptuous fear and delicious pain. Now, it was time to leave this forsaken place. He'd picked up on the thoughts of Abdullah Akkad. He subsequently knew that Ghost Hunter, and his merry team of investigators, were headed this way. He wasn't prepared to face them in person. At least not just yet.

Halloween.

The day when he would be at his strongest. The day when the veil between the spirit world and the land of the living was the thinnest. The day when darkness spilled over into this world in greater volume than any other. The day when hell reached forth its dark claws, eagerly touching the hearts of man.

He wanted to be at his full power when he met them head on. He wanted them to see the destruction that he'd set in motion. He wanted them to know that their puny efforts were futile, all for naught, as their town collapsed into rubble around their ears. He wanted them to know that their God had abandoned them. That, he, The Pumpkin Man, was now the master of their world. He wanted to dine on their despair...before he killed them all.

No, he'd leave for now, avoiding a direct confrontation. He'd have to watch his "mother" breathe her last gasp through the eyes of someone else.

Such a shame, he thought. *We could've had so much more fun together, had we only had more time...*

■■

When they first arrived, Brad felt a familiar creeping sensation, a chill of dread traveling the length of his spine. *He's in there,* he thought. *I can feel his evil seeping out of the house like a thick fog.*

"I think he's in there," he told Elton. A look at Jonathan Silver told him that the preacher had noticed the same repugnant aura.

He watched as Elton subconsciously tugged at the shiny silver chain around his neck. Brad wasn't sure, but it looked like he might have been whispering the faintest of prayers, through slightly parted lips. His brow covered in sweat, his face showing his apprehension.

"Where the heck is Akkad?" He turned asking to Eric.

Pulling his phone from his pocket, he punched a number, waiting for Akkad to pick up. "Where are you?" he demanded impatiently. "I think he's in the house. We need you here before we can go in."

"I'm around the corner. I got caught behind an accident," Akkad lied. "I'll be there in thirty seconds."

Less than a minute later, Akkad pulled into the driveway. Brad huddled briefly with his team. "I think he's in there, guys. That means we stick to protocol, and let's take down this SOB. You got it?" Watching everyone give a quick nod, he broke the huddle. "Okay, let's go."

It took two men nearly a minute to kick the door hard enough, ripping the chain lock from its mooring in the doorframe. They door flew open so rapidly when the lock broke free, that one of the men went sprawling, face down across the decorative rug in the entryway. The team quickly filed inside the house.

"Check each room, top to bottom. Buddy system. No one left alone, even for a second. As soon as you see or hear anything, alert the rest of us," Brad gave the orders.

Something's off.

It hit him nearly immediately. The oppressive, pervasive presence he'd felt before they entered was no longer in the immediate vicinity. It was if the ambient air pressure had suddenly lessened.

How long? he thought. *How long has he been gone? It can't have been more than a few minutes, maybe less.*

In the excitement, and adrenaline rush, of the anticipation of confronting this demon, he hadn't been focused on the thick aura of evil that previously permeated the air. Rushing to the back door, he yanked it open, running outside. He scanned the backyard for any hiding places big enough to conceal a person. He didn't see anything large enough to hide someone. He scanned the tree line, watching the dense woods beyond for any signs of movement.

Nothing. He was gone. The lack of the presence of the thick, heavy air told him that much. He ran his fingers through his hair, stomping his foot in frustration, cursing loudly. Just then, a yell from inside the house caused him to rush back inside. As he entered the back door, he nearly collided with Jane, who was on her way out to find him.

"We found her."

"Is she alright?"

He knew the answer before he asked, but he held on to the slightest hope that their sudden appearance had scared The Pumpkin Man off, before he had the chance to kill or mortally wound the woman.

"I think you'd better see for yourself," she said, turning and leading the way. She led him upstairs to a small bathroom situated between two tidy bedrooms. As they approached, the rest of the team moved to the side so that Brad could see inside. The woman was lying on her side, convulsing as she vomited blood and viscous fluids. A discarded, empty bottle that previously contained a product used to unclog drains lay near her head. 911 had been called, and an ambulance was already in route, but Brad could tell that it'd never arrive in time to change this woman's fate. Her lips had nearly melted off her face, her nose was sloughing off as well; both the effects of the acidic gel having been vomited up violently, the thick, corrosive fluid exiting through her nose, as well as her mouth. He could only imagine the exponential damage that her esophagus and stomach had sustained. Judging by the vast amount of blood, pooling on the floor, it was substantial. As he watched, she launched into a fit of violent coughing before finally exhaling one last breath, and then lying still.

The Pumpkin Man has claimed yet another victim.

Something about the situation nagged at the back of his mind, but he couldn't quite place what it was. Something was off kilter just enough to bother him.

Where do we go from here?

From everything he knew, it seemed that The Pumpkin Man needed to inhabit the body of a living person. *The question is who? What victim was he residing inside of?* If they had that piece of information, they could possibly get some much-needed answers. Maybe a line on where The Pumpkin Man was hiding.

As they waited for police, and an ambulance to arrive, he walked through the house. The bedroom adjacent and to the right of the small bathroom obviously appeared to be that of a teenage boy. Portraits of a young man playing various sports hung on the walls. The room was tidy by teenage boy standards. Nothing much he could glean from this room, so he walked on. He assumed the police would have to break the news about his mom to this kid, when he returned home from school.

Brad didn't envy them that task.

His search turned up nothing that would point them to where The Pumpkin Man might have gone. He was going to try to speak once again to the Sheriff, and see if they could get some help with this case. He swore in frustration as they waited for the authorities to arrive…

■■■

The Pumpkin Man watched the gruesome death scene, and the ensuing investigation, playing out with glee. His "eyes" and "ears" on the scene enabled him to see and hear everything, as if he were there himself. Almost as satisfying as the death and confusion he'd wrought was the frustration of Ghost Hunter and his team.

By design, his attacks were working as planned. By making each death, thus far, appear entirely normal, he'd diverted suspicion that anything was out of the norm; a suicide, a murder-suicide, an accident...all unfortunate, but common occurrences in life. He hadn't even had to use his powers of persuasion to guide the Sheriff on this occasion.

"I'm telling you Mr. Riviera, there's no sign of foul play. This is a textbook suicide. Plain and simple."

"But, I'm telling you, the killer was here when we arrived," Brad protested.

"There was no 'killer'. The woman drank a half-gallon of drain cleaner."

"And, I'm telling you, this woman did not kill herself. Where's the suicide note? A woman with a teenage son would've left a suicide note."

"And, I'm telling you, again," the Sheriff said abruptly. "Get your people and get out of this house before I have you all arrested for tampering with a live crime scene, and obstruction of justice. I've just about had it with your Hardy Boys routine."

Brad started to protest further, but a glance at the Sheriff's face told him that the man was deadly serious. He knew that getting himself locked up wouldn't help anyone in this town.

Brad rounded up his team, deciding to regroup back in his basement...

JACK BEAUMONT

CHAPTER 39

"The local authorities are going to be no help at all," Brad told the group, who were assembled around the conference table in the war room. "I've spoken to the Sheriff and he's not giving me any information. He's also forbidding us from stepping foot in that house again, even going as far as to threaten me with breaking and entering charges."

A low murmur of whispers and side conversations arose. Brad held up a hand before speaking again.

"But, an unnamed source within the department gave me a piece of interesting information. The woman's son never came home last night."

The group began peppering him with questions, but before Brad could answer, Elton clapped his hands together loudly, interjecting himself into the suddenly lively conversation.

"Wait a minute. Just wait a minute. We've gone over some scenarios, and multiple possibilities that we wanted to present to the group before we go any further into the weeds on this."

The group gave him their full attention as he began speaking.

"We have two main ideas on this. First, we must ascertain, is he a victim; possibly being held, or maybe even already murdered, by The Pumpkin Man?"

"Or," Brad picked up the lead, "Is he our target? Is he being used as the human host for The Pumpkin Man?"

"For my money, I believe he may in fact be the target. It would make sense if he were the one being inhabited by The Pumpkin Man. I see a scenario wherein he was possessed by the demon, then turned, attacking his mother before leaving the scene," Elton said.

"However, just as easily, The Pumpkin Man could have been waiting in Hunter's Glen and might have killed the boy and attacked his mother, before leaving the scene," Brad said. "Of course, he could be someone else entirely, and could be holding the boy hostage for some reason as well."

"Based on his past actions, I think a hostage situation is the least likely scenario. We can't afford to be chasing down false leads, so we're going to have to split up," Elton said. "We need to either, find the boy, find his body, or find where he's being held."

"So, here's your assignments," Brad said as he began fleshing out the details of their search...

■■■

Two days later, the team met back in the war room at six pm to discuss their findings.

"So, from what I was able to gather through the school, no one has seen the victim's son, Samuel, since the same day that Elton found Betty in Hunter's Glen."

"So what does that mean? Were they both attacked, and the boy killed, or is the boy now The Pumpkin Man?" Martin asked.

"That we don't know. We also don't know whether the boy was even with her at the time."

"Anything further from the Sheriff's office?" Jane asked.

"Well, as you know," Elton said, "The Sheriff himself won't share any information with us. He's declined to comment further. However, a friend inside the force alerted me to the fact that the boy has *still* not returned home."

"Are they considering him a suspect?" Marty asked.

"Suspect?" Elton replied. "No, not at all. They don't feel there is a "suspect". The official line is that when the victim learned that her son ran away from home, she committed suicide in her distress. In their opinion, this is an open and shut case of a depressed mother taking her own life. Nothing more, nothing less."

Brad turned to the rest of the team. "What else did we discover from interviewing his fellow students?"

Kevin spoke up first. "He has a girlfriend named Heather. She also seems to be AWOL. Parents are supposed to be on an overseas trip, while she stayed at home alone."

"Is it possible that while her parents are away, Samuel is holed up with Heather somewhere? Skipped town? Went on an adventure of their own? Or are they maybe even cuddled-up at her place, playing house?"

"I think that's the next place we need to look," Brad stated.

"I agree," Elton added.

"Anyone have an objection? Or better idea?" Brad asked the room. Pausing for a second, he scanned the room. When no response came, he said, "Okay, let's load up. I have the address plugged into my phone."

CHAPTER 40

So, they're about to discover my little masterpiece, are they? I hope they enjoy her as much as I did...but I doubt they will. He let a raucous laugh echo, reverberating through the house.

"Still," he said to himself, "Can't have the Sheriff's department on my trail too soon."

Scanning through the many thoughts he was able to read from afar, he picked up on one that'd do just fine. Frank Cleary. The neighbor two doors down from Heather's house.

Poor boy. He just never really got over Heather breaking up with him a few years prior. Except, he was too much of a weakling to do anything about it.

"Well, Frankie-Boy," The Pumpkin Man said under his breath, "Today's the day you find your courage, and do something about it. You'll go down in history, sir." As he reached out to the boy's mind, he let another laugh peal through the house, echoing in the otherwise silent structure.

CHAPTER 41

The team arrived at the unassuming home of Heather Long, which was just a short drive from Brad's house. They gathered just outside the front door ten minutes later, most displaying signs of nervous energy in anticipation of entering the silent house. A possible confrontation with The Pumpkin Man was brewing.

Brad's adrenaline rushed as they prepared to knock at the front door, before attempting to forcibly enter the house if necessary. They were taking no chances. They couldn't afford to. Brad sent four members of his team around, to the back of the house. Should someone attempt to slip out the back, they wouldn't be successful in fleeing undetected or unchallenged.

Brad didn't feel the familiar oppressive weight to the air around this house, but his senses were still on edge. It was clear to him that something was amiss. He didn't know what they'd find inside this house, but he was convinced that it wouldn't be good. He spoke into the radio in his right hand, engaging Marty, who was leading the team out back.

"Marty, let me know when you're in position. Be prepared for anything." He let go of the "speak" button on the radio. A short burst of static came through the line before Marty's alarmed response came back.

"Boss, we're in position now," Marty said. "Proceed with extreme caution. Repeat. Proceed with extreme caution. Back door's been kicked in. From the terrible smell, there's something, or someone, dead inside."

Brad looked over at Elton and the rest of the crew with raised eyebrows. He didn't have to tell them that knocking was no longer a necessity…or that they needed to proceed with extreme caution.

He spoke into the radio again.

"Marty, on the count of five, I want you and your group entering the back. Leave two outside to guard the door. The rest should join us inside."

"Copy that," Marty responded.

Brad counted down from five to one, giving a curt nod to the group before trying the doorknob. Surprisingly, it turned easily in his hand. He slowly pushed the door open and went inside. The rest of his team fanned out as soon as they entered the doorway. Closing the door, he stationed two of the team by the front door, motioning for the rest to follow him further into the house. He let his nose lead him. Fighting back the urge to vomit, he had to breathe through his mouth. He heard someone behind him fighting back their gorge as well.

He found the stairwell and began climbing. Three doors opened off the left-hand side of the long hallway at the top of the stairs. One bathroom, three empty bedrooms. No sign of anything amiss. The smell came from further up the hallway. The door to what must be the master suite loomed before him, at the end of the hallway. Closed and foreboding. A horrendous odor, that of death and decay, seemed to ooze out from under the door, seeping through every crack and crevice where the door met the doorframe. Pulling his t-shirt up, covering his nose and mouth, Brad hesitated for a moment before opening the door. He wasn't sure he was prepared for what he'd see beyond it.

He wasn't.

When he turned the knob, entering the room, the full-scale assault of his senses began with the increased depth of the stench of death and decay. Through watering eyes, he beheld the spectacle on the bed. A young girl, presumably Heather, had been murdered, her heart ripped from her chest. Her desecrated body arranged in the fashion of a mock crucifixion, her hands and feet pinned in place with large knives. A crown of thorns had been fashioned and placed upon her head. This was obviously the work of someone with a grudge against God. The work of a very sick, twisted individual.

The work of a crazed demon.

The room seemed to spin before him, the smells and sights before him making him dizzy and nauseous at the same time. Behind him, he saw Jane ducking into the bathroom. He heard her vomiting a moment later. Kevin leaned over the railing in the hallway, proceeding to do the same. Brad slowly backed out of the room, closing the door.

He told Marty to call the Sheriff's office, as he ordered everyone else back downstairs and out of the house. He didn't think that the killer was here any longer. In fact, he knew for sure that The Pumpkin Man was not. The aura that followed the demon wasn't present in this house. Still, Brad couldn't shake the feeling that something else was out of place here.

He herded his team out the front door. Marty was the last to leave, following closely behind Brad. Out of nowhere, a thunderous boom split the air, and chunks of wood and splinted shrapnel flew from the open door that Brad held. Marty dove for cover out the doorway. Brad hit the deck, rolling to the right, in front of the couch. He heard the *snicket* sound of a pump shotgun chambering another round, and he snuck a peak over the top of the sofa. He jerked his head back just in time as the top cushion of the sofa exploded in a shower of fluffy white cushioning material and torn fabric.

Before ducking for cover, he saw a teenage boy, a sneer of pure hatred and rage fixed upon his face, a split second before he fired. Immediately after the shot rang out, Brad launched himself from the floor, hurling himself in the direction of the teen with the gun. He hit the gunman just as he heard the sharp *snicket!* again. Both he and the teen hit the floor hard. The impact drove the breath out of the boy with a loud *whoosh!* Acting quickly, he tore the shotgun from the teen's hands, tossing it to the side. Then with lightning quickness, he slammed his fist into the kid's temple. With a small grunt, the boy quit resisting, falling limp.

Brad stood up, looking the kid over.

He wondered if this was Samuel, their missing target. Just then, he heard the wail of incoming sirens as the Sheriff's deputies, and other emergency vehicles, approached. He decided to let the Sheriff try to sort things out from here. Hopefully, he'd get the chance to interview the kid later.

Brad had just made it back to the driveway when the first cruiser screeched to a halt at the edge of the road. He wasn't surprised to see the Sheriff himself getting out, striding directly toward him. He looked none too pleased to see Brad, and his team, at the scene of yet another tragedy.

"What's going on here?" he demanded tersely.

"A dead girl inside, a teen boy with a shotgun; unconscious and disarmed. He tried shooting me and one of my team members. I knocked him out."

"Where's the gun?" the Sheriff asked.

"Still inside," Brad replied, cursing himself for that oversight.

"You left the gun inside with the perp?" the Sheriff demanded, voicing rising with each word. "This is why you amateur detectives need to stay out of my way!"

He turned, storming toward the house. Before entering, he unholstered his firearm, cautiously peering inside. A moment after Brad saw him disappear through the door, another thunderous boom echoed through the night. The first blast, obviously from the shotgun, was followed in quick succession with six more blasts, one right after the other.

Brad started toward the house, before being yelled at by a deputy who'd just arrived on the scene, "Stay back! Everyone stay back, and get behind some cover!" The team watched from behind the van as more and more deputies arrived, along with an ambulance. The paramedics waited by the curb for an "all clear" to be given by the deputy charged with making sure that no one else entered the line of fire.

After several tense minutes, the Sheriff came back outside, being assisted by a deputy. Blood ran down his left shoulder and arm; his shirt was tattered from taking the blast from the shotgun. His Kevlar vest likely saving his life. The ambulance backed down the driveway to meet him, now that the "all clear" signal had been given. After putting the ambulance in park, the driver got out, opening the back, motioning for the Sheriff to sit inside. His wounds were not life threatening. He declined being taken to the hospital. As the paramedics began treating his injuries, he motioned for Brad to come forward. The several other deputies on scene were already busy interviewing his team.

"Now, why don't you tell me how the hell you junior detectives keep showing up at these crime scenes before we do? What is it with you guys?" the Sheriff asked, obviously in pain and more than a little perturbed.

"You wouldn't believe me if I told you," Brad replied.

"Well, you sure as hell better try to convince me," the Sheriff grunted. "Because I'm just about as close as a hair on a frog's ass from arresting you, and your whole darn outfit."

"We're investigating The Pumpkin Man..." Brad began.

"Not this nonsense again!" the Sheriff barked, cutting him off before he could even explain why they were here. "Get your people off this property as soon as they've had their statements taken. If I see your face, or even smell you, at another crime scene, I'll have you arrested on sight. Got it?"

Brad couldn't stand being talked to like a child, but he knew better than to press his luck. He nodded his understanding, turning away. A deputy approached, taking a brief statement from him. As he finished giving his statement, he saw a second set of paramedics carrying a gurney towards the house. This ambulance had arrived without fanfare. As Brad waited for the rest of his team to finish giving their own statements, he watched the paramedics wheel the gurney with the body of the teenage boy laying on it, covered by a white sheet, out of the house.

Suddenly, something that had bothered him since they'd found Betty, dying in pain from ingesting the drain cleaner, struck him like a sharp slap.

He's killing without leaving witnesses. No survivors. No loose ends. No one to point back to him.

Always in the past, The Pumpkin Man had used others to do most of his killing, often leaving them broken and confused, with the terrible knowledge that they'd been his unwitting pawns. This time, it seemed he was leaving no one behind. He'd had Betty kill herself before they could question her. He felt sure of that the night that they found her. Likely, he'd killed the girl inside this house himself, then used this boy to cover it up. No doubt the police will assume that the teen did it, and that he acted alone. The boy was now dead, basically the victim of "suicide by cop". No loose ends. All of the perpetrators were dead, leaving no one to suspect that an outside force might be pulling the strings.

I bet Elton was right. That cop over in Silver Springs was probably a victim of The Pumpkin Man too. He'd probably been made to kill that family, before being forced to kill himself.

It was all very neat and tidy.

Too neat and tidy by far to be coincidental. But how did that knowledge help them? They still had no knowledge of where he was hiding, or any clue where he'd strike next. For all Brad knew, anyone around him, including the Sheriff, or even the deputy who'd just wrapped up his interview, could be pawns of The Pumpkin Man. For once in his lifetime, an investigation truly had him entirely stumped. What made being stumped even worse was the fact that this wasn't just an owner of a hotel, business, or home who wanted to either prove or disprove they were haunted, this was the real deal. A high-stakes game of cat and mouse that he could ill afford to lose. Losing would mean that the lives of countless people would be lost also.

Losing is not an option.

He was going to have to come up with a better plan...and soon. Halloween would be fast upon them. Time was running short...

CHAPTER 42

Melissa detested seeing Brad so emotionally beaten down, defeated. This investigation was taking a huge toll on him. He'd lost weight. He couldn't eat well, he seemed jittery and nervous all the time, and he rarely, if ever, was in the mood for any kind of bedroom affection in the last few weeks. It was as if he'd become a totally different person.

A stranger sharing my bed.

She knew that he was worried. He hadn't been having the nightmares any longer. Not since he began wearing the silver crucifix around his neck. She wore a matching one around her own neck, Brad having insisted upon it. In fact, he'd adamantly argued with her that she was not to take the crucifix off for any reason. *Not even to bathe*, he'd told her. While she thought it was odd that he took this superstition so seriously, she knew that he believed in what he was saying, so she would honor his request.

She believed in The Pumpkin Man, at least she believed that something profound happened here in the past with The Pumpkin Man, and the town of Summer's Cove, she just wasn't ready to buy into the notion that

Brad may have accidentally set him free upon the town again. In every account Brad had shared with her previously, he'd made it sound like death and mayhem on a widespread level had accompanied, and signaled, the arrival of The Pumpkin Man on the scene.

As far as she knew, life within the confines of Summer's Cove didn't seem any less normal than on any previous day. No one was acting oddly, and the town seemed perfectly normal. Outside of a suicide, a murder of a teenage girl by a jealous ex-boyfriend, the killing of that same boy in a shootout with police, and a quadruple murder-suicide by a depressed, racist cop in a neighboring city, things seemed very, very normal. Nothing screamed "there's a demon on the loose" to her.

Still, she trusted in Brad, trusting in his judgment to the fullest. He knew what he was doing, and she knew that if something evil really was brewing, he'd find a way to get to the bottom of it.

She was going to ask Brad to be included in an investigation, for the first time in many years, when he awakes this morning. While she knew that he would be reluctant at first, she knew that he'd agree to include her. She wanted to know everything. *She needed to know everything.* If this case was making her husband this nervous, this stressed, this distraught, then she wanted to be dialed in.

■■■

Just as she'd expected, Brad wasn't too excited about sharing everything with her. He'd put up more of a fight that she'd anticipated. When he'd finally broken down, agreeing to share everything with her, including her on the team, he'd done so with tears in his eyes; something she'd never seen before in all his years of investigations into the paranormal.

He told her everything. He told her about his dreams. About his past. All of it. All the pain, the memories, the things he'd buried; kept from her about his childhood. It all came out. He also told her about how The Pumpkin Man invaded his dreams, switching her out in place of his sister. Forcing him to watch as it was *her* who was violated repeatedly. She listened in horror as he detailed what happened to her in his dreams, as he was forced to watch. He explained to her that the silver crucifixes were a barrier between The Pumpkin Man's mental corruption and their minds.

She was amazed that he'd managed to keep these details from her for so long. It did explain why he was so stressed out. She listened in horror as he detailed the woman's horrific death by drain cleaner. When he got to the part about the teenage girl, and the mock crucifixion, she couldn't take much more. She knew that only a true monster who wasn't human could have done such a thing. She listened as he detailed how he thought that the kid with the shotgun was probably just an innocent pawn in the demon's game.

Most frightening of all was Brad's assurance that Halloween would bring certain death and destruction if The Pumpkin Man wasn't stopped. Brad detailed his belief that The Pumpkin Man would kill hundreds, if not thousands more people if they couldn't stop him. To hear Brad tell it, they town faced certain annihilation if they didn't find and defeat him before it was too late.

The prospect of Brad so harried and troubled worried her more than she cared to admit. If he was this upset, it was bad. It was really, really bad. Soon, she'd find out just how bad things could really become...

CHAPTER 43
OCTOBER 31ST, 2032

Halloween.

It was Halloween today, and still they were no closer to finding The Pumpkin Man. No closer to stopping him; or even possessing a concrete plan to do so. By all outward appearances, there was nothing amiss. The average Summer's Cove residents would feel and detect nothing out of place. The tension that permeated the air seventeen years prior did not exist. People were smiling, happy, and genuinely clueless that many of them stood the chance of dying within the next few hours.

Ever since the last attack of The Pumpkin Man, the town celebrated Halloween again, albeit in an understated manner. There would be trick-or-treating and celebrating, but it wouldn't come even close to the partying that some cities and towns did on Halloween. No, there's more of a somber tone in Summer's Cove each year on this day. Still, as time marched on, even those who witnessed the prior tragedies allowed their memories to fade with age.

Elton Crosby knew there could be no quarter given to the enemy. They needed to attack him head on, a full-scale assault, if they were to win. Nothing less would do. He could not allow the team to give up, and he could tell that many of them were ready to do so.

No, we have to see this through. Failure isn't an option.

Brad was speaking to the group, frustration obvious in his voice, while Elton stood by his side, ready to interject as necessary.

"I don't know where we go from here. The Sheriff's office will be no help. We have a suspect who we believe is the person possessed by The Pumpkin Man. We know that he's planning something, but we have no idea, not even the slightest clue where, or what, he's going to attack. Or even when." Frustrated, he ran his hands through down his face. He was exhausted; worn down by worry and stress.

"But do we really know he's here?" Chris asked. "Are we chasing a ghost? A phantom that doesn't exist?"

"I'm with Chris," Jane spoke up. "So far, we have a lot of circumstantial evidence, and a good ghost story to tell around a campfire. Not much different from hundreds of cases we've tackled before."

"Is it even worth it to continue at this point?" Marty asked. "Should we all just go home and enjoy Halloween with our families? I mean come on, Brad. All we have here is a brutal murder suicide, a missing teen, and a suicide. Not a lot of "there" there. We've declined cases that have more substance than this."

Brad listened to some of his most loyal team members, people who were on the verge of giving up. He had to admit it; he'd had doubts of his own. Now, hearing them voice their own doubts, it was beginning to wear down his resolve. Maybe, just maybe, he'd been too close to the story, too heavily invested in hoping that it was true.

Had he become one of his typical clients? Had he gotten so invested in the legends, hoping they were true, that he let himself get carried away? Had he, in his eagerness to find truth, let himself see things that weren't there? Had he become one of "those" people?

"Maybe you're right. Maybe this is all just a fool's game," he began.

A loud boom sounded, startling everyone in the room, rattling the conference table.

"No!" Elton yelled as he slammed his palm down on the conference table. "We are not giving up! Do you want the blood of all those innocent lives on your hands if you're wrong?" he asked the group. Turning to Brad, he continued. "Because I can tell you from experience, it's not an easy thing to live with." Juanita Tanner-Crosby stepped up to Elton, putting a comforting arm around her man. She gave his hand a reassuring squeeze. Having stood in the shadows, allowing Brad and Elton to lead the team, she spoke up for the first time.

"Listen to what he's saying, folks. Years ago, myself and others spent a lot of time trying to convince Elton that the threat was real. That something needed to be done. We failed. People died. It wasn't all his fault." Squeezing his hand again firmly, she continued, "Perhaps we should have tried harder. Don't repeat our mistakes of the past." She stressed the word "our".

Taking a cue from Elton's spouse, Melissa also spoke up, having previously watch the proceedings in silence, she addressing the group for the first time.

"Listen, you have all known Brad for a long time. You know he's the real deal. You know he has disproved more paranormal claims than he's verified. You know that he approaches every case with a healthy dose of skepticism. You know that he always errs on the side of caution, and that's he's made a lot of people mad by debunking their hauntings." She looked around the table, meeting every person's eyes for a moment, imploring them silently to hear her words, and know the truth in them. "You know he wouldn't have assembled you all here, if he didn't believe that there was a real threat to this community."

The first to break the silence was Marty.

"So, what do we do now? We have no clue where he is, or where he might emerge. If he holds to his prior patterns, won't he attack sometime tonight, and in spectacular fashion?"

"Yes. That's always been his prior MO," Juanita spoke up. "But he seems to be operating differently now. Instead of blatantly attacking people, letting everyone know that he is behind the attacks, he seems to have adopted a new tactic. What better way to avoid arousing suspicions, than to provoke people to commit murder, then have them kill themselves before they can be questioned?"

"But how we can stop a demon that we can't even find?" Abdullah Akkad asked. "We can't hit a moving target."

"I think I have a solution to that," Brad stated. "I have a group of locaters on the way. They should be arriving here in about an hour."

"Locators?" Elton asked.

"People possessing special abilities that allow them to locate persons or lost objects, by focusing on an item they've either owned, or come in recent contact with," Brad explained. "Akkad has the ability, although his talent is not as fully developed as these three individuals. They are the top in their field."

"But what do we have in our possession that would allow us to locate The Pumpkin Man?" Marty asked.

"This," Brad said, pulling the thin silver chain from his pocket. "I'd say that this should do the trick."

"It'd better do the trick," Elton said. "We're running out of time here."...

JACK BEAUMONT

CHAPTER 44

Yes, The Pumpkin Man thought. *These fools have just handed me the keys to victory, and they don't even know it yet. I'll use their own abilities against them, leading them to right into a trap...and their ultimate destruction.*

As he formulated the final plans that would lead to the demise of the group, allowing him to take down Summer's Cove without resistance, he almost merrily laughed out loud. He knew now that he'd be successful. For the first time ever, victory was well within his grasp. He could already taste its sweet savor.

For now, he'd enjoy one last sweet treat, before unleashing hell upon the unsuspecting inhabitants of this community of unsuspecting prey. He turned towards the young lady who was tied to the bed, her eyes were frozen on him, wide with shock and fear. He'd been enjoying the ambrosia of her emotional turmoil for the last hour, as he gave the final mental commands to his unwitting minions.

Now, it was time to finish the girl, so that he ventured into this special night riding high on a wave of death, power, and destruction...

JACK BEAUMONT

CHAPTER 45

Abdullah Akkad entered barn with trepidation. He didn't know why he'd been drawn here so strongly, but he knew he had a purpose for being here. It was as if Allah himself had drawn him to this place. Maybe Allah wanted him to have the glory of being the one to finally discover the whereabouts of The Pumpkin Man. Maybe he would be the one to receive the fame and glory once this adventure was over.

I'll be the hero who saves this town. The glory of Allah while shine through me.

He envisioned the book deals, the movie deals, and the speaking engagements he might receive if he pulled this off. He knew that he should have called this information in to Brad and the team, waiting on their arrival, per protocol, but he wanted to verify that this was indeed where the final battle with The Pumpkin Man would take place.

His talent told him that The Pumpkin Man wasn't here. Not right now. But he would be. Of that there could be no doubt. This was his lair.

He's not here now. Oh, but he's been here, Akkad thought. The decaying bodies he'd found in the house were evidence enough of that. Now, where was he being led to? A strong pull lured him towards the large metal structure that stood out in the field, behind the house. It appeared to be a huge steel barn. He made his way toward it with caution, using his talent, feeling his way forward. He knew The Pumpkin Man wasn't inside the building either. He couldn't feel his evil presence at this location at all.

As he pulled one of the double doors open, he saw the structure *was* indeed a large barn. Inside were several stalls on the left-hand side, in which cattle or horses could be housed. All manner of farm tools and farming equipment hung from the walls. Along the right-hand side of the barn were three large tractors used for working the farm. Hanging from the ceiling rafters were long wooden stakes, each filled with the large, brown and green, drying leaves of tobacco plants.

As he drew deeper into depths of the barn, he felt drawn toward one of the horse stalls. He pushed the stall door open cautiously, blinking, hardly believing his eyes. There was no doubt in his mind as to who led him here, and who stood before him now, radiating glory and power. *Allah.* Allah in the flesh, waiting to bestow his glorious blessings upon him. He stood inside the stall, peace and love, and a warm inner light seeming to flow from his body. In his right hand, he held out what looked like a heavy fabric vest. Wires exited from a small electronic device on the side of the it, the other ends of the wires disappearing into a thick clay-like substance that wrapped around the vest itself in small packets.

As he walked forward with eagerness to accept the mission presented him, he knew that Allah had chosen him, above all others. It was a deep honor. He would get the glory for this mission. He walked into his God's loving embrace, feeling the sense that his life had just achieved deep meaning, meaning well above that of most mortal men.

As his pawn walked forward, believing the delusions that he cruelly fed into his mind, The Pumpkin Man let out a hearty peal of laughter.

This is almost too easy…

JACK BEAUMONT

CHAPTER 46

Brad glanced at his watch, eagerly awaiting the arrival of the final member of his team. The paranormal locators had all arrived on schedule and were ready to go. The team would be split into three groups, each with their own locator in the lead. Should they receive a "hit" on the location of The Pumpkin Man, they would alert the rest of the team. Then, they would all converge as a group, attempting to put The Pumpkin Man down for good.

It was nearing 6pm. They didn't have much more time. They needed to find The Pumpkin Man, and they needed to find him quickly. From the historical accounts, and the personal stories he'd read, The Pumpkin Man would likely strike just as darkness descended upon the town. That gave them roughly an hour before time ran out. As of now, no one had reported anything amiss. Whatever terrible plans he had for the town; The Pumpkin Man was keeping it well under wraps. He wasn't foreshadowing his actions as he'd always done in the past. While this made it infinitely harder to try to stop him, Brad held out hope that they would still come out on top. Deviating from one's usual patterns usually led to mistakes. If they could find a mistake, and capitalize on it, they might come out victorious in this all-important battle.

At least, that's what I hope.

As the clocked continued to tick past 6pm, Brad knew they had to move on. Akkad would have to catch up to them sometime later. Brad called the team together in his driveway, beginning to go over the details of their assignments one last time, including the plan for dealing with The Pumpkin Man when they found him.

"I don't have to tell you that this investigation is unlike anything we've done in the past," Brad started. "If we fail tonight, if we falter, there likely won't be another investigation...for any of us."...

∎∎

Ten minutes later, Brad finished the briefing, and they loaded up in three separate vehicles, setting out. Brad and his team would head to the southern point of Summer's Cove. The second team would focus on the center of town, with the third team taking the northern third of town. Brad hoped that with the locators helping guide them, this approach would allow them to more quickly ascertain the whereabouts of The Pumpkin Man. He'd learned from what Elton told him, and historical accounts of The Pumpkin Man, that if they took him down, all his plans would fail, all his devotees would immediately cease to be enthralled. Like a machine with the plug yanked from a wall, the things he set in motion would all be halted the moment he was defeated.

As they pulled away, Brad couldn't help but wonder what had become of Akkad, and where the man might be...

JACK BEAUMONT

CHAPTER 47

The cab of Brad's truck was deathly silent with apprehension. He and his team members didn't want to distract Wilson, the locator assigned to them, from his job. The man's brow was furrowed, sweat beading across his forehead, concentrating deeply as he gripped a section of the silver crucifix in one hand. Eyes shut, if Brad didn't know better, the man would appear to be in the midst of a silent, fervent, desperate prayer.

Cutting through the deep silence like an explosion, Brad's cellphone began jangling. He knew from the ringtone that it was none other than his missing team member, Abdullah Akkad. Snatching up his phone, and silencing the noise, he spoke into it, exasperation and annoyance clearly evident in his voice.

"Where the hell are you?" he asked without offering a greeting.

"Boss," Akkad began exuberantly, "I know where he is!"

Brad could hear the excitement in Akkad's words, yet it took him a moment to process what the man was saying.

"What? What do you mean?"

"I know where he is! I know where The Pumpkin Man is!" Akkad exclaimed breathlessly in Brad's ear. "I've found his lair!"

"What? How?" Brad asked in confusion.

"I'm sending you the coordinates now. Get the team here, and hurry!"

"Wait!" Brad said. "You need to back off. Get away from there. Now! Don't give us away before we can get out there to help!"

No reply came.

Brad pulled the phone away from his ear, looking at the screen. Akkad had already hung up. No longer caring if he interrupted the locator's concentration, Brad sent the coordinates, that Akkad texted over to the rest of the team, accompanied with an urgent command to converge at that location. He changed course, heading for the route that the GPS app showed on his phone...

CHAPTER 48

Elton was more than a little pissed that he and Juanita weren't being allowed to accompany the team on their final quest to locate The Pumpkin Man. He'd been floored, literally blindsided, when Brad had given him a side task, instead of allowing him to join the rest of the team on the hunt.

"You know that we're being sent on a wild goose chase, just to get us out of the way, don't you?" he asked Juanita.

"Yes, dear," she replied. "But, that's okay. I wasn't really all that excited about seeing that nightmare creature up close, and in person again, anyway." She gave Elton's right knee a gentle squeeze. "Coming face to face with a demon once in a lifetime should be enough for anyone."

"I can't argue with that. Still, I think I could have been helpful to the cause." He reached down, gently squeezing the loving hand that still rested on his knee.

"You *have* been helpful, dear."

"Yeah, without me, The Pumpkin Man wouldn't have risen again…"

"No, without you, the elite team of paranormal experts who are searching for, and are preparing to defeat him now, wouldn't even be here. It would likely be just you and I, against an immortal demon, with nothing but our wits and our faith to help us. I like the odds a lot better this way."

Elton stopped their vehicle in front of the Sheriff's department, sighing deeply. He wasn't looking forward to undertaking the mission that Brad assigned to them. He knew that this was likely not going to go any better than the last time they'd tried to persuade the Sheriff to help them. In fact, he'd be lucky if the Sheriff didn't throw him in jail, just for bothering him about this matter again.

Still, Brad had felt that it was worth one last attempt, hoping to get the Sheriff to dedicate *any* resources to their search. Even a deputy or two would have been a huge help. At this point, without knowing where The Pumpkin Man was hiding, every person that they could find to help with the search would be an asset. That's why it still bothered him that he and Juanita had been sent away on this doomed mission in the first place, instead of being allowed to help with the search.

"Well, let's go do this," Elton said, with reservation.

Juanita gave his knee another squeeze before removing her hand to unbuckle her seatbelt. "It'll be okay, no matter what happens, Elton. It'll be alright in the end."

"I know it will, my love," he said, as he exited the vehicle. "With you by my side, everything will always be okay."

■■■

Fifteen minutes later Elton and Juanita exited the Sheriff's department feeling dejected, having failed in their mission to sway the Sheriff.

Not that I had expected anything else, Elton thought.

As they got back into their awaiting vehicle, Elton wondered what their next move should be. He briefly considered catching up with the team and rejoining the hunt for The Pumpkin Man. He wasn't sure.

"What should we do now?" he asked Juanita.

"Go home. I think we should go home, Elton. We've done what was asked of us. If the team needed us, they would have kept us on. Let's go home, turn down the lights, lock the doors, and pray like we've never prayed before."

"That sounds like a good idea, dear. We're going to need some divine help to survive this night."…

JACK BEAUMONT

CHAPTER 49

Good, good! thought The Pumpkin Man. *My little lambs are on the way to the slaughterhouse, and they don't even realize they are on the way to meet oblivion!*

He glanced over at Abdullah Akkad, where the pawn stood still and waiting, ready to carry out his orders with eager anticipation. He still basked in the awe that his God had reached out to him personally, willing that he, Abdullah Akkad, receive the glory for helping Allah with this important task.

Imbecile, The Pumpkin Man thought dismissively. *If you weren't going to die very soon, I'd gut you right now, just to see you suffer. But no, it's better this way,* he thought, getting his emotions under control. *Soon, your entire team of ghost hunters will be nothing more than a few scattered bloody remains; and no one will be left to stand in the way of my reign of terror.*

As he thought of the ingenious trap that he'd laid for those who would stand in his way, he let loose with a raucous peal of inhuman laughter yet again. It was an especially ironic fate that he had in store for them. Killed by one of their own, in one of the most stereotypical methods and scenarios possible. Now, it was time to cloak himself, before the team arrived on scene. He couldn't give away his location too quickly, lest they escape his grasp.

Within a few hours, this town will be completely under my thumb…

CHAPTER 50

As Brad pulled up to the large farmhouse, he saw that Akkad's car was parked in the driveway. *Not very subtle there, Abdullah.* He still wasn't sure how Akkad had managed to find The Pumpkin Man, when no one else could, but possibly his skills at locating were stronger than anyone had initially thought. It was unlike the man to break protocol by pursuing a lead by himself though.

The locater riding with Brad's group had confirmed that this area held a strong connection to The Pumpkin Man. While he did not appear to be onsite at the moment, he was nearby. At least, close enough that the locater could faintly sense his aura. He could possibly be a few miles away, but not much farther.

Definitely not closer than that, thankfully.

Brad was becoming more and more worried that time was running short for the town, and the team.

*We have to end this. We must end this **now,** today. Before things spiral out of control. We must be victorious in this battle, because any other outcome would lead to massive losses of life.*

These thoughts repeated themselves constantly, in Brad's mind, just like they had for the last several days.

I must end what I started when I removed the crucifix that held this monster at bay.

Before he exited the truck, Melissa, who was sitting behind him in the rear passenger seat, reached forward, giving his shoulder a small, reassuring squeeze. They'd shared such nonverbal communications thousands of times over the last several years. It was their way of saying "It's going to be okay" without having to actually say a word. He reached up, holding the hand that rested on his shoulder for a moment. "I know it will", his return gesture said. As one, they broke contact, exiting the vehicle.

As the rest of the team pulled up to the house, they exited their vehicles, before briefly huddling, discussing strategy in the driveway. Then they headed, as a group, for the large, metal barn-like structure. That's where the locaters all agreed that Akkad would be found. When they got to the steel structure, Brad was thankful for the lack of the oppressiveness and thick heaviness in the air that signaled The Pumpkin Man's presence.

That means he's not here yet, Brad thought. *With any luck, maybe we can be in place, ready to attack, before he arrives.*

He was convinced that The Pumpkin Man intended on causing as much havoc in town as possible, probably from his base here on this farm, before heading into town to "clean up", claiming his disciples in the aftermath. That meant he'd be likely be directing things from this location and might be distracted. He might also be overconfident. If they could have the team set, and ready to go before he returned, they could take him by surprise, possibly getting a jump on him. When dealing with an enemy who was stronger than yourself, the element of surprise could often be the difference between success, and failure, in combat.

Brad and Melissa led the way to the oversized steel barn. As they did, Brad couldn't help but feel a sense of apprehension. Dread at the coming confrontation made his stomach queasy. He supposed it was normal to feel this way. After all, they were soon to take on a real, live, in-the-flesh demon who had killed dozens, maybe even hundreds, of people in the past. He reached the massive double doors to the barn, quietly easing one side open.

Inside, the building was well-lit and well organized. It was obvious that whoever lived here or *had* lived here before The Pumpkin Man likely killed them, was someone who had valued their property, taking good care of their possessions. Brad saw a few large tractors used for farming inside, and the usual farm equipment hanging from the walls and rafters. He smelled, as well as saw, the drying tobacco hanging from the ceiling above, impaled on large wooden stakes.

What he didn't see was Abdullah Akkad.

Brad's sense of dread suddenly grew as he began realizing that something wasn't right. Something was off, but he couldn't quite put his finger on it. He didn't have much in the way of paranormal senses to speak of, but he did know that his gut feelings were rarely wrong. Suddenly, his stomach seemed to knot tighter, and he knew that trouble was coming. Without a word, he put a firm hand on Melissa's shoulder, turning her slightly toward the open door.

It was at that same time that Brad saw the missing Akkad emerging from the middle stall, on the left-hand side of the building. Brad noticed immediately that something about Akkad seemed off, different somehow.

An almost glazed over, shiny look was in his eyes. He also seemed to be swollen around the midsection. Almost looking severely bloated. It looked as if he'd gained twenty pounds since he'd last been seen. Brad eyes lit on Akkad's neck momentarily, and that's what saved his life.

The silver chain's gone!

Brad's mind screamed at him silently. *He's under the control of The Pumpkin Man!* Suddenly the oppressive weight of the thick air threatened to suffocate Brad.

Oh, God! He's here. It's a trap!

Sudden realization of what caused Akkad to look so swollen hitting Brad like a freight train, causing him to throw himself bodily into Melissa, at the same time he yelled over his shoulder, "Everyone! Hit the deck!"

The force of impact drove Melissa out through the open steel door, and to the ground, with Brad landing on top of her. A split-second later, all hell broke loose as the sky, which had just completed its transition from daylight to dark, roared into searing brightness with the heat, fury, and noise of a violently erupting volcano.

Brad lost consciousness as the concussive shockwave of the blast that leveled the building smacked him like a heavy concrete cinder block…

CHAPTER 51

The Pumpkin Man towered over Melissa where she lay naked, and bleeding, upon the floor. With a small wave of his hand, she was jerked upright, into standing position by unseen bands of air. Her arms were held out, as if by invisible hands, stretched straight out to her sides. As she stood naked, and immobilized, in front of her nightmarish captor, Melissa fainted again. Her head lolled forward on her neck, her chin nearly touching her chest.

As he stood before her, appraising his prey, The Pumpkin Man waved his hand again, and Melissa's neck was lifted off her chest and held in place, straight up, as if she was looking straight ahead. She would have almost appeared to be sleeping while standing, had her arms not been stretched out wide, as if wanting to embrace a long-awaited lover.

Brad watched all of this transpiring in abject horror, fear for his beloved wife tearing him apart. His nightmares were coming true before his very eyes. Had he not been immobilized by the same invisible forces that held Melissa upright, he knew that his emotions may have rendered him just as useless to her. He was going to have to watch as the love of his life was violently assaulted, and likely murdered, in front of him, and there was nothing he could do about it.

His heart hammered in his chest; tears spilling quietly from the corners of his eyes. Despair threatened to overwhelm him. Helplessness had thrown his very soul into the abyss, and his mind threatened to shut down in protest of his raging emotions. Intense hatred, helplessness, fear, despair, heartbreak, and rage all conflicted within his mind, making it hard for him to think straight. He knew he had to save Melissa; he also knew that he couldn't save Melissa. He was incapable of doing anything, save watching her impending demise in growing horror. He only hoped that he could find a way of turning The Pumpkin Man's wrath upon himself. If he couldn't save Melissa, at least maybe he could die first, and thus be spared the agony of watching her suffer. Without him to watch her torture, perhaps the demon would finish Melissa off quicker, without extending her suffering.

∎∎

As Brad considered his very limited options from the corner of the room, The Pumpkin Man continued his appraisal of Melissa; the way a man would appraise a shiny new car before buying it. He walked around her, as she stood frozen in place, arms stretched to the sides, and still unconscious. He gave another wave of his hand and her long brown hair was swept back from her face, giving him a clearer view of her facial features. With yet another small motion, her legs were parted further, with her feet about two feet apart. Issuing a small laugh, he gesticulated again, making her arms and legs move up and down, in and out.

Just like Da Vinci's Vitruvian Man, he thought to himself, with another chuckle. *Oh, Da Vinci! Now there was a man who knew darkness; pretending to serve the very church he despised. He was truly one of the few humans I could at least tolerate.*

He looked over his shoulder, where the husband of this very nice specimen of a woman sat unmoving, held against the wall.

"So, Ghost Hunter, now that you've discovered real evil, what're you going to do about it?" he sneered. "You've made a nice living chasing things that go bump in the night, and things that scare others. Now that you've 'caught' me, what can you do to stop me?"

He loosened his grip on the chains of air that held Brad for just a moment. As, he suspected that he would, Brad took the bait as soon as he felt his restraints loosened. With a fierce yell, Brad bolted upright, rushing toward him…only to crash face first into the solid wall of air that The Pumpkin Man had erected between them. Brad's nose crumpled with a sickening crunch, blood starting to flow from his left nostril, immediately upon impact.

With a dismissive flick of his wrist, The Pumpkin Man sent Brad flying backward until he hit the sheetrock wall of the room hard. Instead of sagging, and falling into a heap on the floor, he was held upright by the same forces that had thrown him into the wall.

"You silly little man. Did you really think I was just going to stand still while you attacked me?" The Pumpkin Man taunted him with a chuckle. "I'll gut you like a fish…just as soon as I'm done with her!" he said, turning his attention back to Melissa's still unconscious, naked form.

■■

Brad's head was spinning, from the excruciating pain coming from his broken nose, the pain in his brain from the concussion he'd sustained from the force of the explosion, and from his ever-deepening despair. His raw emotions threatening to overwhelm his ability to think or act rationally. He was very close to becoming sobbing, gibbering mess.

I have to hold it together, he thought. *If Melissa is to have any hope at all, I have to hold it together for her sake.*

He vowed not to allow The Pumpkin Man to take his sanity…or the life of his wife. He must clear his head in order to think of a solution to get them, or at the very least, Melissa out of this mess. He was to blame for allowing this menace to escape; he would have to make sure to put him back where he belonged. As The Pumpkin Man turned his attention toward Melissa, Brad racked his brain for ideas. He searched his memory for any sort of weaknesses that he could remember, especially those regarding demons, that might help them in their plight.

■■

The Pumpkin Man walked over to where Melissa stood upright, held by chains of air. With the slightest flicker of his wrist, Melissa's legs parted even further, as if she were frozen in the middle of performing a set of jumping jacks. He walked around her once more, evaluating his prize once again. He smiled, the effect of which was his jack o' lantern face twisting into a grimacing snarl, eerie orange light spilling from within. It was quite a frightening sight to behold, and Melissa happened to open her eyes at that very moment.

Her screaming echoed through the room; her eyes becoming as wide as saucers. Abruptly her screams were cut short, as The Pumpkin Man used a thin band of air as an effective muzzle over her mouth. Quiet sobs racked her body as she struggled vainly to free herself from his restraints.

"Now, now," The Pumpkin Man said in his deep, gravelly, slightly otherworldly voice, "There's no need for all of that," he laughed. "At least not yet. We're going to have ourselves a little pleasure, before the pain begins in earnest." He chortled, a low rumbling laugh that was devoid of any real mirth.

Turning toward Brad again, The Pumpkin Man flashed him another one of his frightening, grimacing smirks.

"You've done well for yourself, Brad. She's quite a catch...and spirited too. I'm going to really enjoy this. I don't know if she will, and I *seriously* doubt that you will. But me? I'm going to *love* this!"

As Brad witnessed his wife being taunted, taking in the meaning of the cruel intentions behind The Pumpkin Man's awful words, he knew he must do something. He needed a plan, and he needed it quickly.

I have to kill him now. Before he has a chance to rape Melissa.

■ ■

The Pumpkin Man had started turning back toward Melissa, when Brad's thoughts flashed through his mind. With lightning-fast speed, he whipped back toward Brad, strode over to where he stood, yanking him forward by the throat, violently choking him.

"Listen here, Ghost Hunter, you will *never* kill me! I can't be killed!" He screamed into Brad's face, as flames licked outward from his hellish jack o' lantern mouth opening. Brad winced, trying to pull back from the searing flames, and the nauseating breath of The Pumpkin Man. His eyebrows and eyelashes all curling from the heat issuing from the gaping maw.

"Don't you get it, boy? I am ETERNAL!" The Pumpkin Man threatened to crush Brad's windpipe in his blinding rage. Brad's face was rapidly turning crimson, as his air was cut off; his body crying out for oxygen. "I can read your mind, so you can forget any hopes you have of defeating me." He flung Brad back against the wall again; the chains of air once again holding him in place.

"Now, you'll watch as I first enjoy your wife, in every way possible. Then, you'll watch as I *carve* her…in every way possible. And lastly, you'll watch as she dies in the most painful way possible." He laughed, one of his rumbling, echoing chuckles of pure malevolence again. "Soon, you'll pray for her to die; then you'll pray for death for yourself!"

Brad's remaining resolve died in that instant.

He knew that if The Pumpkin Man could read his mind, knowing his thoughts as soon as he did, and it appeared that he could, there would be no gaps, no lapses in concentration, no distractions that would afford him the chance to save Melissa's life. The only thing left to try was something that he hadn't done in years…and he didn't have any real faith in…prayer.

He closed his eyes, silently saying what was possibly the most heartfelt prayer that he had ever offered;

to a God that he still wasn't sure even existed. He had little faith that his prayers would be heard.

He momentarily closed his eyes, while he was beseeching God for deliverance; and when he opened them, he was shocked to see that The Pumpkin Man was standing directly in front of him. Brad's head jerked hard to left as The Pumpkin Man rocked it with a jarring backhand. The blow left his face stinging, his eyes watering, and his vision cloudy.

"I can hear you, even when you pray to your pathetic God silently in your head," he hissed, the flames inside his mouth flickering out of the sides of his hideous grin. "He won't hear your prayers...but I will." He growled, stabbing a finger toward Melissa. "And, if I hear another one, I'll gut her like a deer, and eat her beating heart right in front of you!"

He once again slammed Brad tightly against the wall, holding him there with invisible bonds. The back of Brad's head hit the wall hard, and once again he felt a wave of pain rush through his skull, his mind threatening to go dark. He could feel the blood continuing to pour from his shattered nose, but he was powerless to wipe it away. As the blood dripped unabated from his ruined nose, he felt it mingling with the warm flow from his split, swollen, and bleeding lips. Both of his eyes seemed to be swelling shut, his left eye was already half closed, probably the side effects of his broken nose.

Brad tried his best not to think; but even the very effort of trying not to think required thought. It was very unsettling to know that the monster, who was now moving back toward his wife, could hear even his most intimate, private thoughts. He found himself rapidly sinking into the deepest depths of despair; yet again nearly immobilized by helplessness, as his hopes for saving Melissa dwindled. How could he come up with a plan to foil The Pumpkin Man when his enemy could hear his very thoughts?

. . . .

"Oh, I'm going to enjoy this," The Pumpkin Man teased, with another sneering glance at Brad. "She's a fine piece indeed. Yes sir, I'm going to enjoy this immensely." He again gave Brad an evil, lascivious smile. He was enjoying taunting the man, feeding on his fear, savoring his dread, tasting his hate, relishing in his pain; both emotional and physical.

"I think she'll look even better after I decorate her a little," he goaded Brad further.

. . . .

As Brad took in the demon's words, he tried desperately to keep control of his intense, raw emotions. Without thinking about it, he began praying once more. He feared that The Pumpkin Man would lash out at him again, or worse, at Melissa, so he stopped himself immediately.

. . . .

Now it's time to wake the girl and let the real feast of fear begin, The Pumpkin Man thought, hearing at the same time, the faintest of prayers coming from the Ghost Hunter's mind. *Little good that will do you*, he snickered inwardly. *Go ahead and pray to your impotent God. Beseech him all you wish. He hasn't been answering human prayers in a long time.*

Still, just for fun, he caused Brad's right hand to be momentarily released from its bonds. Then he entered Brad's mind, causing that same hand to fly upward, brutally slapping himself several times across his already bloodied lips and face.

I think he gets the picture now, The Pumpkin Man thought, hearing Brad's mind go silent again, except for the stinging pain, and some mindless gibbering.

"Wakie, Wakie," he said, almost gently, to Melissa, caressing her lips with a pointed finger. "Come on, darling. Wake up now." He gently tapped her right cheek with his index finger.

"We're gonna get started now, and it'll be so much more fun if you're awake."

■■

Melissa moved her head away from his finger, slowly opening her eyes. As her vision came into focus, her eyes widened again in horror. She beheld the nightmarish creature who stood in front of her. The being that she and Brad had moved to this town to pursue. The mythical Pumpkin Man in the flesh. The head of a lit jack o' lantern sat atop the body of a man, but a man who possessed powers that were not of this world. Unfortunately for Brad and Melissa, they had found exactly who, and what, they had sought…and now they had absolutely no idea how to deal with it.

Worse than the horror which stood right in front of her, was the horror that she could see over his shoulders. Brad stood behind The Pumpkin Man, pinned against the wall. His face bloody; blood oozing in a continuous flow from his battered lips and his broken nose. His eyes were bruised and darkening; the left sealed nearly shut, the right also severely swollen. She couldn't even tell whether he was asleep, or if his eyes were open. In fact, the only indication that gave her any hope at all was that she could tell by the rhythmic rise and fall of his chest that he was still alive and breathing.

For now.

"Hello, dear," The horror spoke to her. "Are you ready to begin our fun?"

Her heart hammered with his words, as she looking down, realized she was stark naked. After the blast leveled the barn, both she and Brad had been knocked out cold. The monster must have stripped her of her clothes while she was out. She'd heard about what The Pumpkin Man had done to many of his victims, and here she stood naked and unable to move, with the demon standing just inches in front of her. Her heart threatened to beat its way out of her chest. She struggled to breathe. Panic was starting to set in, and she knew that if she allowed it to fully take hold, she'd die here tonight, and so would Brad. She had to maintain control of her senses so that if any chance of escape were to present itself, she'd be prepared to take it.

Suddenly, the monster in front of her regarded her with a slight sneer as he spoke, "There will be no chance of escape," he said with a menacing smile. "You will die. Whether you maintain control of your emotions, or not," he said with a laugh.

Oh, God! It's true! He can read my thoughts!

Melissa was shocked. She couldn't see what possible hope existed for herself and her husband now.

How can you defeat a monster who can read your thoughts?

If she weren't being held upright, immobilized by some mysterious force, her legs would have collapsed under her, as despair and dismay settled in.

"You can't defeat me!" The Pumpkin Man roared in her face. "I am eternal! I will exist long after your flesh has rotted from your bones, and even longer, after your bones have crumbled and turned to dust. I've been with mankind since the dawn of the earth, and I will be with mankind until I help end the humans' existence, forever."

Melissa would have recoiled from his breath if she could have. The heat issuing from his mouth curled the fine hairs of her eyebrows, and the odor of his breath was like that of rotting flesh. She felt her gorge rising as her eyes watered from the stench. She fought the urge to vomit, just barely winning the battle.

....

"Enough of this. Time to start the fun," He turned halfway back toward Brad, "Are you watching this lover-boy?" He felt the hate and fear rolling off of Brad like giant waves breaking on a beach. It was like a jolt of energy to him.

"Good, let's get to it."

He turned back toward Melissa and, holding up his right hand, pointed his index finger at her face; and he savored the horror written on her face, as the nail grew to about an inch and a half in length, gleaming along its razor-sharp point at the end. He walked forward, teasing Melissa with his nail, enjoying her fear as it slowly started to grow. He traced lines on her cheeks ever so lightly. Then, moved to her forehead, tracing a line from her head down the bridge of her nose, to the tip.

"So perfect in many ways," he said. "Beautiful bone structure. Perfect nose. Glorious eyes." As he said the word "eyes" he let his finger hover directly over her right eye. "In fact, those eyes look almost edible!"

Melissa and Brad both screamed as he jabbed his finger toward her right eye. Melissa waited for the gut-wrenching pain that was sure to come. Instead, The Pumpkin Man let out another deep, rumbling laugh.

"No, not yet. I think I have a craving for something a little juicier." He placed his finger on Melissa's chin, drawing it straight down. Down her throat, hovering for a moment near her voice box; then down the rest of her neck; down the valley of her breasts, finally stopping just over her heart. He started to apply slight pressure, savoring her fear as it continued ramping up. He savored Brad's waves of fear crashing against his back as well.

Time to draw some blood!...

CHAPTER 52

Brad watched in horror stricken as The Pumpkin Man taunted Melissa, moving his unnatural, razor-sharp, elongated fingernail down her naked form. He nearly lost it when he thought that The Pumpkin Man was going to take Melissa's right eye. Instead of relief, he felt dread when he moved elsewhere, because he knew that the fiend had something much, much worse in mind. He feared that the demon would make the nightmares that he showed Brad a reality. Brad's horror only increased tenfold when he heard the next chilling words from The Pumpkin Man's mouth.

"Such beauty. Such form. Nearly perfect." He said moving his finger downward, to Melissa's navel. He made little circles around it as he spoke. The light pressure from his nail leaving a thin red mark in her unbroken skin, tracing where it had been. "But, we can improve upon it a little. Time to decorate my prize."

As soon as he spoke the word prize, Brad saw Melissa wincing in pain as The Pumpkin Man dug his nail into the soft flesh above Melissa's tender navel. Her screams echoed through the room a moment later, as the demon sliced through the skin of her abdomen in a curving upward motion, continuing around until he had completed a full circle. Brad watched this happening, feeling more desperate, and more helpless, than he'd ever felt in his entire life. This was even worse than what he'd endured as a child, when he'd been forced to watch his younger sister being raped. Worse yet was the fact that Brad knew that this was just the beginning of the torture that Melissa would suffer at the hands of this animal.

To his horror, as The Pumpkin Man continued his grisly work, he realized what it was that he was carving in Melissa's flesh…it was his signature. A jack o' lantern, complete with eye holes, a triangular nose, jagged teeth, and even a stem. Before he'd finished his work, Melissa once again passed out. Like an artist examining a completed work for anything that needed touching up, he stepped back, viewing his creation.

Momentarily, Brad's vision was blocked by The Pumpkin Man, as he stood before Melissa. When the demon took a step backward, turning toward Brad, he was even more shocked to see that the demon had added to his ghastly handiwork, on his gruesome canvas of flesh.

"So, whatcha think lover-boy? Is it a masterpiece, or what?"

Brad fought back tears as he saw the damage that had been done to his precious wife. Her once flawless, flat abdomen was a gory mess of dripping blood. Still, even with all the blood, Brad could make out the "drawing" that had been done in her flesh. Added to the jack o' lantern was a bat in the night sky, accompanied by a large full moon. In the background, the demon had expertly carved a tree in Melissa's flesh. Blood wept from all of the cuts. It had started flowing in thin streaks down her abdomen, dripping off her pubic area in slow, steady beads. A small pool was beginning to form under her, between her spread feet.

Reading his thoughts, The Pumpkin Man again let out a peal of evil laughter. "So, you don't like all the blood, huh? Okay, we can fix that."

He moved back in front of Melissa, kneeling. Brad watched in captive horror as The Pumpkin Man put his lips to the wounds, licking the blood where it flowed down Melissa's abdomen. He made sick slurping sounds as he cleaned the blood from her body with his tongue. As Brad watched his wife being defiled by this spawn of the devil, his anger rose. He wished he could break free and kill this bastard. It didn't even matter if he was killed in the process, as long as he could stop the assault on his precious wife.

Brad was even more outraged when a new sound replaced the disgusting slurping sounds of moments prior: a hissing, sizzling sound arose from where The Pumpkin Man's mouth and tongue touched Melissa's body. Suddenly, her eyes snapped open, and she let out a piercing scream...."aaaaaaaiiiiiieeeeeeeeee!" An acrid, thin trail of smoke rose from her abdomen, as the gut-wrenching realization hit Brad that The Pumpkin Man was cauterizing the wounds by whatever unholy fire burned inside his evil jack o' lantern face.

As she screamed in pain, Melissa's eyes bugged out in her head, her body thrashing in violent protest, straining against the unseen bonds holding her captive. Brad wept silent tears, watching in horrified helplessness.

The Pumpkin Man abruptly stood, turning toward Brad. Stepping aside, so that Brad could view his handiwork, in a mocking tone he asked, "There, is that better? I got rid of the blood for you, and stopped the bleeding." With another raucous laugh he added, "Too bad she'll be bleeding from other places soon enough."

Brad couldn't take much more. He was afraid his heart was going to explode from the conflicting emotions. On the one hand he felt defeated, depressed, hopeless, and a deep despair. He felt fear, apprehension, anxiety, and dread. On the other hand, he felt a love for Melissa that grew more intense than ever before. He wanted to save her. He *had* to save her. To make it all better, to hold her in his arms, never letting her go. To make the hurt go away. To shield her from ever being harmed again.

He also felt an intense, deeply burning rage. For the first time in his life, he felt the true desire to kill a living being, and he knew it for what it was: bloodlust. Pure and unadulterated hatred with the desire to kill the monster who had Melissa helpless, and at his mercy. He wanted to make The Pumpkin Man pay, he wanted to make him bleed. He wanted to spill an ounce of The Pumpkin Man's blood, for every drop of Melissa's precious blood that had been shed at his hands.

As these feelings raged inside himself, Brad noticed The Pumpkin Man, standing still for several moments. Almost in a deep, trance-like state. He had a satisfied expression frozen upon his grisly face. It was an almost pleasant expression, for such a hideous creature.

That's when the truth hit Brad like a speeding car. *The bastard is feeding off of my emotions!*

With trepidation mounting, Brad also realized what this meant for Melissa. *He's like a psychic vampire. He's using my emotions as an all-you-can-eat-buffet. The more I hate, the more I hurt, the more satisfaction he derives from my feelings.* Brad knew then that Melissa was in very profound trouble, if he couldn't save her soon. The Pumpkin Man would continue to torture her, so that he could feed off not only her emotions and pain, but off Brad's as well. Without a doubt, Brad knew that far, far worse things were in store for his beloved wife...

JACK BEAUMONT

CHAPTER 53

Aaahh! The Pumpkin Man thought. *The sweet ambrosia!*

The emotional turmoil pouring from both Brad and Melissa, with him standing in the middle, was like a "surround sound" system for his psychic pleasures. The rich mixture of raw emotions like that first jolt of heroin entering a junkie's system; or the first strong drink for a recovering alcoholic. It invigorated him; recharging him, making him feel more alive than ever before. He felt as if he were almost glowing. In the next few minutes, as he ramped up his brutal game of "tease and torture", the emotions were only going to get rawer; more intense. More delectable. More fulfilling. His power increased with each new wave of emotion from the couple.

He truly felt unstoppable.

He basked in the glory of his newfound rush of power for several more seconds, before becoming aware of Brad's wayward thoughts again. He sensed the recognition of his endgame in Brad's musings. He knew that Brad recognized full well what he was doing; how and why he was drawing this out. Knowing however wouldn't save either himself, or his wife. In fact, The

Pumpkin Man thought it was better this way. As Brad sought to control his emotions, he would ramp up the terror even more, and he knew just what buttons to push.

He taunted Brad yet again.

"Tell me Brad, would you like to revisit your childhood? Would you like to see those things you witnessed with your sister, reenacted with Melissa playing the starring role?"

■■

Brad felt new levels of hatred burning through his being. Every fiber and cell in his body felt alive with hatred. Tingling with the desire to kill this monster, he warred with the frustration of knowing that he couldn't move. He was impotent to do anything to stop him.

■■

Suddenly, it seemed an earthquake shook the house, as Brad heard the echoing report of several explosions in the far distance, a few seconds after the ground trembled violently. It was at that moment that the true cost of his and his team's failures truly hit home.

Most of the blame he put on himself.

My failures led to the deaths of my entire team and now, by the sounds of it, the assault on the town has begun as well...

CHAPTER 54

Little Tommy Turberville *loved* Halloween, he just loved everything about it! The costumes, the trick-or-treating, the make believe, and don't forget the candy! Starting around his birthday, in late September each year, he'd start planning, searching for the perfect costume for Halloween. This year, he was going out trick-or-treating as a scary werewolf. His parents had allowed him to go all-out with his costume. They even purchased him the werewolf's clawed hands/paws to go with his expensive, life-like mask, which also featured a cool, hinged jaw attachment. The jaw of the mask moved when *his* jaw moved, making the werewolf mask appear even more realistic, and life-like.

He looked positively ferocious this year. He got a little bit of a thrill as the younger kids that he encountered moved out of his way, as if they couldn't decide whether his costume was real, or simply a fantasy, like their own outfits. His snarling visage scared some of them to the point that they hid as he passed by.

Like most nine year-old boys, he thought of Halloween as a magical night of make-believe and wonder. Visions of his favorite candies paraded through his head as he went door-to-door with his parents in tow. Already, by his count, he'd received several dozen of his favorite candies in his large Halloween bag. People seemed to be very generous with their offerings this year, and if he made it through his entire neighborhood before his parents decided that they were done, he'd have the largest haul he'd ever brought in on a single Halloween night.

As he was waiting for his neighbors, the Smith's, to answer their door, he heard several really loud noises, explosions that sounded almost like thunder, nearby. It appeared that the echoing reports came from the mountain top, up near the lake that formed the expansive reservoir. That's where he and his dad went fishing several times each summer. He liked fishing near the dam up there, because he and his father always caught the largest fish, right by the spillway.

His parents stood waiting for him at the edge of the street. As he heard the commotion, he turned back toward them, seeing his parents looking in the direction of the reservoir as well. Suddenly, he heard a loud rushing noise, growing in intensity by the second. He briefly saw his parents standing at the edge of the street, frozen with horror, before they were swept away in a raging torrent of water; a split second before that same wall of water crushed him, pinning him against the side of the Smith's car.

His last thought before he drowned was that he'd lost his bag of candy when the water crashed into him…

CHAPTER 55

Deputy James Smith of the Summer's Cove Sheriff's Department smiled, carefully loading his sawed-off shotgun. He had two others that he'd taken from a couple of the other deputies' cars, already fully loaded, and ready to go. He had taken the other two deputies' service handguns as well. All six guns were now fully loaded, and ready for action.

The daily pre-shift briefing was about to take place in the department's conference room, and that's where he'd find most of his fellow deputies, as well as the Sheriff. They would all be assembled together, ready to change shifts; waiting to be briefed on the priorities and assignments for the night shift. Standard procedure. He'd give them a few minutes to get started, before making his appearance.

Tonight's briefing would be anything but standard procedure...

■■

Having waited roughly ten minutes after the briefing was underway, he knew that all but the deputy who was manning the front desk and the telephone system, would be gathered inside the conference room. He strode down the long hallway toward the crowded briefing room with confidence, one handgun nestled in his holster, two more shoved in his waistband. He cradled all three shotguns in his arms.

As he turned the doorknob, entering the conference room, the Sheriff, who was standing behind the podium at the front of the room, greeted him with his usual surly, wisecracking manner.

He hadn't even noticed Smith's unusual cargo.

"Nice of you to join us, Smith. Next time how about..."

That's as far as he got with his sarcasm, before the first shotgun blast removed most of his face. Quickly turning the gun on the assembled, seated deputies, firing off blast after blast, from the shotguns. As soon as he emptied one gun, he dropped it to the floor, immediately beginning to fire the next. By the time he'd emptied all three shotguns, twelve deputies were down.

He managed to take out three more men, before the first shots were returned in his direction. He was hit twice in the arm, and once in a leg, never feeling the pain, as he continued firing into the crowded room. He made sure to make clean headshots now that he was down to using the handguns. Before the sixth, and fatal bullet hit him, all but two deputies were down.

Inexplicably, these two remaining deputies, instead of offering aid to the wounded and dying, turned their guns on each other, simultaneously firing off fatal headshots toward one another. Both fell dead as their bullets found their marks in the other man's forehead.

Hearing the sounds of all-out warfare coming from the briefing room, Deputy Fred Nocito, who had been manning the front desk, came rushing into the briefing room, gun drawn, ready for seldom seen action. When he burst through the door, ready to take on the unknown assailants, he found a mass of dead, and severely wounded deputies. The coppery smell of blood and the acrid odor of cordite hung thick in air, making him want to gag. Bluish smoke filled the room, casting it in a surreal light.

Horrified at the massacre inside the conference room, he knew that he had to do something...so he went around the room, seeking to find each and every deputy who was not already dead or dying. When he came across a deputy who was still alive, and possibly able to be saved, he aimed his handgun at the man's head, finishing the job. He went around the room, repeating the process. In all, he took out six other deputies. Not bad for a rookie cop who'd never had cause to even draw his weapon before. He was proud of the work he'd done. He checked the bodies of the dead, and mortally wounded once again, just to be sure.

Uh, oh. Deputy Mason seems like he's a fighter.

Despite having taken a grazing shot to the head, and a shotgun blast that had exposed most of his left shoulder, clear down to the bone, Mason was trying to rise.

Can't have that.

Deputy Nocito placed his gun against Mason's forehead, pulling the trigger. Mason went down, a warm spray of blood and brain matter blowing back onto Nocito's firearm and right hand.

That's gross, he thought, cringing at the gore.

He wiped his gun and right hand carefully on a handkerchief that he kept in his left pocket. Then he placed the same barrel, of the same gun, firmly against his temple, squeezing the trigger.

And in a space of five minutes, the Summer's Cove Sheriff's Department was no more...

CHAPTER 56

Laquon Johnson returned the smile of the teenage girl who he'd just checked in at the Cosmic Bowling Alley. She was quite a delicious little hottie, with a cute smile, and a rocking body. She either was a very, very friendly person by nature, or she was interested in him as well. He'd have to get her phone number when she came back to return her rented shoes.

Man, she's hot, he thought, as she turned back toward the counter, favoring him with another warm smile. *But, she's not the only fish in the sea,* he thought, as he spied several more girls about the same age looking his way, giggling amongst themselves.

Man, what am I thinking? he asked himself inwardly. *None of these girls will be available after this night.*

The bowling alley was packed with people tonight, as the owners had offered a two-for-one special, exclusively for Halloween night. Most of the customers at the alley tonight were older teens, about the same age as himself, those who were too old for trick-or-treating. He hadn't seen the alley this busy before, and he'd worked here for nearly two years.

As soon as his coworker Jeff, came in, he would be taking his lunch break. He had an important task that he urgently needed to finish. Over the last two days, he'd carefully placed the explosive charges where they'd be sure to have the biggest impact: all in preparation for tonight's celebration.

His prior studies to be an explosives and demolitions expert coming in handy for this special assignment. In fact, his knowledge in the field was why the master had picked him, instead of someone else, for this important task. Now, all he had to do was set the detonators in place, lock the front doors, and push a tiny red button. If he'd done his job correctly, the rest would simply be a matter of watching the fireworks from afar, while waiting for his master to arrive on the scene. He'd already taken the garbage out an hour earlier, using that as an excuse to chain lock the back doors shut, ensuring that no one would escape out the back entrance of the building.

As Jeff came in, relieving him for his lunch break, he retrieved the heavy duffle bag that he'd previously stored under the front counter. Inside the bag was another heavy chain, the six detonators, the ignition device, and a thick padlock. As soon as he had the detonators set in place, he'd chain the front doors, and then it would almost be all over.

A simple push of a button and his first mission, for his new master, would be complete…

■■

Ten minutes later, the detonators were all in place, and he had just finished looping the chain through the handles of the front doors. With a resounding click, he snapped the industrial strength padlock in place. No one would be exiting the building.

At least not in one piece, he thought, amusing himself with his wry sense of humor.

Now, to make sure that he got back, far enough away to be safe from the massive blast and flying debris, while still allowing for a good view of the fireworks. He drove his car out to the furthest area of the parking lot, getting out and sitting on the hood, holding the ignition device in his hands. He hesitated for an instant, wanting to savor this fateful moment. He didn't want to hit the small red button too soon; that'd spoil the fun.

As he observed the front of the building, a family of six pulled up in their van, parking near the front entrance. He saw another couple get out of their car, walking toward the entrance as well, holding hands; clueless as to what was about to happen. The couple arrived at the front doors first, examining the chains that secured the doors, curious as to what was going on. The family arrived at the doors a minute later, the father gesturing to the chained doors, engaging the man from the couple in conversation.

Here we go! Laquon thought, pushing the red detonate button.

For a brief moment, he thought that maybe he'd messed up somehow, nothing seemed to be happening. Then, he was rewarded with six nearly simultaneous, muffled *whumps!,* as the detonators did their jobs. Barely half a second later, the front doors and windows of the facility blew violently outward, instantly shredding the eight people who had been standing just in front of them a second before. The building itself seemed to expand outward, almost as if it were a living, breathing creature taking a deep breath, right before it collapsed in on itself in a fiery mass.

He'd done his job well.

There would be no survivors inside, and he'd managed to score an additional eight victims on the outside of the alley. Not bad work at all... for a novice. He knew that his new master would be well pleased with him and would be eager to reward him for his faithful actions. He'd sit right here, watching the blaze, as he awaited further instructions from his master...

CHAPTER 57

As he felt the new waves of conflicting emotions rolling off Brad's mind, The Pumpkin Man suppressed a desire to clap his hands in joyous celebration. The Ghost Hunter now knew that he'd failed miserably in his quest to be the hero of the day. His friends were dead, he and his wife captured and at his mercy, and the sounds of destruction reaching their ears representing a resounding emphasis that the town was under full assault from his minions.

"Ah, the sweet sounds of chaos!" he exclaimed as he soaked up the psychic emanations of the death and destruction that flowed his way. "You want to know what's happening right now, Ghost Hunter?"

Brad remained silent, so he turned around, facing Melissa, posing the same question to her.

"What about you? Hmmm? ... No?"

She remained silent as well. Not that he'd really expected them to respond, or even cared if either of them gave a response. He was going to rub their noses in their colossal failures regardless.

"Well, I'll tell you anyway. One of my minions blew the dam at the reservoir on a few minutes ago. That was the first set of explosions that you heard. Just now, several billion gallons of water wiped out about eighty-five homes, and almost two hundred men, women, and children; many of whom were out trick-or-treating, or just sitting at home minding their own business. How's that epic failure feel now?"

Letting that thought marinate for a minute, he basked in the emotional turmoil roiling beneath the surface of the pair's calm outer façade. He'd break that façade soon enough.

"And, don't go counting on Summer's Cove's finest to help out. The Sheriff's Department no longer exists." He felt this new information hit Brad even harder. Without law officers, he knew that the chaos in town would likely go unchecked; it also crushed any remaining hope that they might somehow be saved by the authorities. He knew that no help would be coming from town now.

"That second set of explosions? Now that was a real beauty! The Cosmic Bowling Alley is no more. Probably a few hundred people died there tonight, the entire building is now little more than a pile of smoldering rubble. And, things are just getting warmed up! What'dya think of that Ghost Hunter?"

Brad remained silent. His soul crushed to the point that he couldn't have come up with much of a retort had he wished to.

It's gonna get a whole lot worse before the night's over Brad, The Pumpkin Man thought with glee.

"Man, Brad, when you mess up, you mess up big time, don't you? Here you were, thinking that you had it all under control, and yet, you didn't have *anything* under control, now did you? Your failure has already cost this town nearly five hundred lives! How do you come back from that, Brad? What do you do for an encore?"

He continued to hammer home the stake of failure, deep into Brad's heart, driving him further and further into despair.

"Did you know that the Summer's Cove Ravens had a football game scheduled for tonight over in Silver Springs? Too bad! Seems like they're gonna have to forfeit the game. Something just possessed the team's bus drivers to drive straight off the road, near the steep drop-off on Hanson Road. All three buses just went over the cliff like huge, yellow lemmings."

He was enjoying taunting Brad; the man taking his defeat very personally, and very, very hard. He wasn't done with him yet.

"Oh, don't worry. I'll make sure that there are no survivors from the crashes. Before this night is through, the only survivors will be the ones who follow me, as my new disciples. Even as we speak, townsfolk are killing townsfolk. Family members are raising weapons against family members. Lovers are hacking each other to death, with reckless abandon, and don't even know why. The death count is now nearing seven hundred, and it's rising quickly, Brad. What're you going to do about it?"

He waited for thirty seconds for an answer that he knew wasn't forthcoming. Then prepared to unleash his best mockery yet upon his helpless victim. One that he knew would be the death knell to his broken spirit.

"See, Brad? You've failed them all. Just like you failed your own sister as a child. And now, you've failed your precious wife too. It's your failure that will lead to her suffering the exact same fate of your sister, although I think I'm going to be just a tad rougher with Melissa than your neighbor was with your sister. After I'm done, then you'll get to watch her slowly die."

He had indeed hit a sore spot with Brad. The only thing that he feared worse than Melissa being raped, was Melissa being brutally gutted in front of him. Little did he know, but the Pumpkin Man intended to make both of these nightmare scenarios a reality.

He turned back toward Melissa, speaking to Brad, as he put both hands on her naked body. He traced the outline of the pumpkin carving he'd made with the fingers of his left hand, as he walked around, standing behind Melissa, running his right hand down her smooth right thigh in a gentle, caressing motion of a familiar lover.

"Are you going to enjoy watching this, Brad?" He chuckled with the words, giving him a lascivious wink. "Which way do you want me to take her first?"

. . . .

Brad closed his eyes. There was no way that his mind or his spirit could take what was about to happen to Melissa. At least he wouldn't have to witness what was happening to her, if he kept his eyes closed tightly. He felt sure that The Pumpkin Man would ensure that he *heard* enough of what was happening.

At least he can't force me to watch it, Brad thought.

"Oh, but I can, Brad," The Pumpkin Man said in response to Brad's thoughts. "Open your eyes now, or I'll gut her this very second!" he roared. "I want you to see every moment of this!"

Brad quickly opened his eyes.

The Pumpkin Man still stood behind Melissa, but his hands were now in new positions. His left hand now cupping Melissa's left breast, in a mocking, soft caress, like that of a willing lover. His right hand hovered directly before her face. As Brad watched, transfixed in horror, the already unnaturally long, razor-sharp fingernail of his index finger began elongating even more. In the blink of an eye, it extended to about eight inches in total length. As it lengthened, it also grew thicker and sharper. When it was finished growing, The Pumpkin Man touched it gently to Melissa's right cheek, drawing it downward. Immediately blood began flowing from her cheek in a thin streak, where the nail had left a deep scratch with the precision of a surgical scalpel.

"If close your eyes for a moment, even to blink, the next thing that you'll see is your beloved wife's intestines spilling to the floor," he said with a sinister grin. "Now, let's get this party started!"

He retracted his fingernail, sliding his right hand down toward Melissa's pubic area. As the demon's hand slid across her naked body like a deadly serpent, Brad made a final silent, desperate, beseeching prayer.

God, please end this, or let me die now, he prayed...

JACK BEAUMONT

CHAPTER 58

The Pumpkin Man moved his hand downward, toward Melissa's most tender private parts, savoring the moment, taking his time, making his rapacious intentions known. He was enjoying the sweet torture of both of his victims. Melissa and Brad threw off enough raw emotion to fuel his psychic needs for quite some time to come. Now, it was about to get even sweeter. Since her screams had died when he sealed the wounds on his carving, Melissa hadn't uttered the slightest sound; or even twitched a muscle. If he couldn't read her thoughts, sense her fear, her pain, her panic, he would have thought she'd gone catatonic.

We'll fix that, he thought. *I'll make sure to get plenty of screams out of her starting right now...*

■ ■

Just as The Pumpkin Man was about to violate Melissa, in the worst possible way, Brad saw a faint flicker of movement behind him. A ghostly figure appeared behind, and slightly to the left, of the nightmarish figure, who was too busy groping Melissa to notice. Brad couldn't quite make out what it was that he was seeing at first. It appeared to be the spectral form of a raven-haired beauty. A translucent figure of a girl, appearing to glow with internal radiance. She was clothed in what appeared to be a simple, yet somehow elegant, white robe. She was strikingly beautiful; one of the most beautiful women who Brad had ever laid eyes on. With a glance directly, knowingly toward Brad, she raised a finger to her lips in an unspoken gesture of silence. Brad did the best that he could to shield his mind, from the demon. He wasn't sure what was going, but he didn't want to alert the demon.

Just before The Pumpkin Man's hand reached her sex, about to roughly penetrate her, Brad saw the demon's eyes widen in stark confusion. He removed his hands from Melissa's body, starting to turn, just as a melodic voice rang out loudly, reverberating in the large room.

"Titus Anastas! Stop this now!" the figure standing behind him demanded with authority.

The Pumpkin Man whirled around, facing the phantom figure, clearly shocked at this intrusion. He wasn't happy about unwanted interruption of his games. As The Pumpkin Man turned toward the phantom, Brad saw a couple of very curious things. The first was The Pumpkin Man's head. Where before it had consistently appeared as that of an oversized pumpkin, complete with sneering jack o' lantern features, for just a brief second, Brad saw it morph into a regular human head; that of a regular boy, who would be in his late teens. Brad watched with detached fascination, as he had no clue what was going on, or what this unexpected confrontation meant. The second thing that caught Brad's eye, immediately following the first, was that a second spectral figure now stood behind Melissa, barely visible to him over her other shoulder. Unlike the first apparition, this one was decidedly male. He too, wore a simple, yet elegant, robe of the purest white. He was unlike anyone that Brad had ever seen before. He smiled, nodding to Brad with a wink, then suddenly disappearing from the room! Inexplicably, Brad felt his tensions and fears beginning to abate, despite their still dire circumstances.

"R-Rose?" The Pumpkin Man spoke for the first time, with a voice that was unlike the one that he had used before. This voice sounded like that of a scared, teenage boy. Once again, the large, orange pumpkin disappeared from the boy's shoulders for the briefest of moments, replaced by a normal teenage boy's head.

"Stop this now, Titus. You must fight him," the girl pleaded.

As Brad looked on in awe, conflict and deep confusion seemed to be written on The Pumpkin Man's *normal* face. He seemed torn, by some inner conflict that only he, and the apparition of this girl knew the meaning of.

Suddenly the demeanor of The Pumpkin Man morphed into one of rage; the normal head disappearing, the jack 'o lantern back in its place again. He lashed out violently at the woman's ghostly form, to no avail. The razor-sharp fingernail passed through her ghostly form, as if through empty air.

"I wish you weren't already dead; I'd kill you all over again!" he screamed, flames escaping his mouth like spittle from an enraged man. "You can't save them," he said, gesturing toward Brad and Melissa, "and you can't stop me!" he screamed in her face.

"Titus, fight him!" She pleaded. "You were never meant to be with him. You were supposed to be with *me*. Forever. Fight him. Fight back," Rose stated calmly, in response to the monster's raging.

The Pumpkin Man again lashed out at her, this time with a fireball that seemed to come directly from his right hand. It passed right through her flickering image, striking the wall behind her, immediately setting it ablaze. Brad watched with rapt attention at what seemed to be a conflict from a time past, as The Pumpkin Man, a boy named Titus, and a beautiful and mysterious girl named Rose sparred in an emotional battle.

"He can't fight me! He's a part of me now!" The Pumpkin Man roared, flames licking his lips. "You're nothing more than a ghost from the past. You mean nothing to us!" he spat viscously.

Brad's hopes began to rise further, as he watched this drama being played out in real time. At the very least, it was a welcome diversion. One that had bought Melissa more time. Time that Brad was using diligently, trying to discover a way he might save Melissa. He knew that he still had the silver crucifix in his pocket; the one that had been used to restrain The Pumpkin Man before, but it was of no use to him in his current immobilized state. He needed to get free and save his wife from the clutches of this demon.

As the flames continued to lick at the walls of the room behind him, suddenly, The Pumpkin Man turned his attention back toward Brad... and Melissa.

"Don't think you're anywhere near saved by this distraction, Ghost Hunter! She's still going to die!" He turned his deadly attention back to Melissa.

"Titus, stop him. Do not allow this!" Rose pleaded. "This is what those monsters did to me. Remember that Titus. Remember what was done to me, and don't allow this. Come back to me. Come home."

Again, Brad saw The Pumpkin Man's visage change back to that of a regular kid. What he saw was a confused, torn teen, caught between two worlds. If the situation had been different, it would have broken his heart for what was obviously two young lovers, who'd been separated by evil circumstances.

"Rose, help me," the youth spoke. "Help me."

"You have to free yourself Titus, *you* have to take control back from *him*," she replied.

Brad continued watching with rapt attention, as the youth's visage remained in place of the jack o' lantern, this time for a longer period. He could see the boy was struggling, fighting an inner battle; one that he seemed to be winning at the moment.

"Samuel, help him. You have to help him fight the demon," Rose said, watching the epic struggle with obvious hope and anticipation. "Fight the evil inside! Both of you, work together and drive him out."

"Noooo!" roared The Pumpkin Man. "There is *no* Titus anymore! There is *no* Samuel anymore! They are dead!"

Turning toward Brad, he raged, flames spewing from the openings in his face, licking the sides of his pumpkin head, causing the pumpkin shell to turn sooty.

"And there is no salvation for you, or your bride!" he screamed at Brad.

With those words, he turned his attention back toward Melissa, raking his clawed hand violently down her chest and abdomen. Brad saw what happened, immediately crying out "Noooooooo!" from the depths of his soul. A deep gouge appeared in her torso, running from her sternum, all the way to her pubic bone. Blood immediately gushing from the mortal wound, Melissa's eyes going wide with pain and shock, before once again losing consciousness.

Brad's mind was screaming, although he couldn't seem to draw enough breath in to make another sound. Pain shot through his heart and soul, as he realized that Melissa would soon die of blood loss. Already, the floor beneath her feet contained a circle of blood that grew wider and deeper by the second. Brad thought he could see her breastbone, where the skin of her chest had been parted; cleaved wide open. He was afraid to look closer for fear of what he'd see. He knew enough already to know that her wounds were mortal. With nothing else he could do to help her; he broke down in tears.

God, help her, please! He called out frantically, with all of his mind and spirit.

The Pumpkin Man turned back toward Ruth, as Melissa's life slowly slipped away. She looked horrified, absolutely stricken, by what he'd done. She again spoke to the boy, trapped inside with the demon.

"Titus, you have to fight back! You have to stop this! This is what they did to me, Titus. You're allowing him to do to this couple the very same thing that was done to us. Fight back. Don't let this happen again!" she pleaded desperately.

Again, the boy's head and tortured face reappeared, where the pumpkin had been before.

"Ruth?" he asked, clearly confused. "Ruth, help me."

"You can do it, Titus. You have to separate yourself from him," she pleaded. "Please come home, with me, where you belong."

"Ruth," he said, holding an outstretched hand toward her. She moved toward his reaching hand, love and translucent tears gleaming in her eyes. A split second before their fingers would've touched, the jack o' lantern once again reasserted itself in place of the human head, and the outstretched hand was brutally snatched back.

"You pathetic creature," The Pumpkin Man said, derision dripping from the words. "You can't defeat me!" Again, he turned his attention toward Melissa, who had now lost so much blood that she'd turned a ghostly shade of pale gray.

"Don't go dying on me yet," he told her. "We have much more fun still to come, right Brad?" he asked, with another lascivious wink at Brad. He pointed his left index finger at Melissa, and Brad saw a small flame as it appeared at the tip. The Pumpkin Man drew the flaming finger downward, tracing the wound that he'd previously made; the wound closed, cauterized by fire, leaving the reeking odor of burning flesh to fill the room.

Ruth once again spoke to The Pumpkin Man, as Brad watched in unmitigated horror. He knew now that The Pumpkin Man would bring Melissa to the brink of death many times before this night was over, but he wouldn't allow her to die... not until he'd filled his dark need for causing torture, pain, and finally death. Brad didn't know how much more of this torture he could take himself, before his mind would snap, leaving him a gibbering, incoherent mess, unable to help himself, much less Melissa...

CHAPTER 59

"Titus, Samuel, you have to fight him. You can do it! You can escape his grasp, Titus. You can come back with me, to be with me, where we belong. Forever," Ruth pleaded.

Once again, Brad saw the pumpkin on top of the boy's shoulders flickering rapidly between that of a normal human head, and the hideous jack o' lantern visage, before finally once again settling as that of a normal teen boy.

"Ruth," the boy said. "Ruth, help me. Please help me!" the boy sounded desperate in his pleas. His voice was joined, this time by a different voice; this one that of a second frightened, and confused, teenage boy.

"What's happening? Help us!"

"Fight. Fight him now! Both of you fight him for control! Together you can defeat him," Ruth yelled.

At that exact moment, something very strange happened. The mysterious, white-robed man appeared again. This time, standing right in front of Brad. He looked deeply into Brad's eyes, speaking directly to his mind, without uttering a word, or even opening his mouth.

"Trust me," he told Brad.

Two simple words.

Two words from this man, and where Brad had once been on the verge of a nervous breakdown, just seconds before, his mind immediately calmed, like a tornado suddenly dissipating into nothingness. The chaos was there in his mind one moment… only to be replaced with a quiet, relaxing calm the next. A sense of wellbeing, hard to explain under the current circumstances, flooded his spirit. Immediately following these comforting words, spoken inside his mind, the man stepped forward, disappearing…into Brad's own body.

Peace, and a happiness beyond description, flooded throughout his being. His every cell seeming to sing with unspeakable joy. Even in these most indescribable moments of terror, Brad found himself in a deeply tranquil mood. He had never felt such a state of calm euphoria before. He felt no pain. No panic. No fear. It was as if such emotions had never existed for him. As he experienced all this, in just a fraction of a second, Brad heard the man speak to him again.

"Trust me. You will live."

Multiple things then happened at once. As Ruth encouraged the innocent boys to fight back against their demonic captor, The Pumpkin Man fought back just as hard, regaining control over the body he now possessed.

"They're mine!" he roared, as the pumpkin flickered back into existence above the boy's shoulders. "You have no right to interfere," he raged. "The power over this dominion belongs to my master, and his principalities!"

Ruth responded calmly in response to him. "This world may belong to you; but the people in it do *not*. Let them go!"

While this was happening, Brad suddenly felt the invisible chains that held him broken, by a stronger, unseen force. While Melissa still seemed to be hanging in place, immobilized by invisible restraints, he was now free of his bonds. He felt a sense of weightlessness, and the euphoria of having the other inside his body. He felt free. Not just free of his bonds, but truly free. Like floating on a cloud, free from the laws of gravity and physics.

"I'm taking control now. Don't be scared," the warm, gentle voice told him. "It's only temporary."

He caused Brad to walk forward slowly, taking advantage of the distraction presented by The Pumpkin Man's argument with Ruth. Brad had no idea what was happening, or what was about to happen. He placed his trust fully in the man who now controlled his every movement. His body moved through no effort of his own. It was as if he were a passenger, hitching a ride inside of his own head. Or, as if he were watching a movie that was filmed with POV camera angles.

He continued walking forward, until he stood directly behind The Pumpkin Man. When he was within arm's length from the demon, The Pumpkin Man, seemingly having won the internal battle with the boys, once again regained control of the body he possessed.

That meant that he also regained control of his supernatural abilities as well. He picked up on the thoughts of Melissa, who'd been watching the strange events taking place behind him, while maintaining eye contact with Brad. The Pumpkin Man whirled around, suddenly realizing that Brad was standing directly behind him, and almost beside of Melissa.

"You're not saving anyone today, Loverboy," He shouted, taking a lightning-fast swipe at Melissa's tender neck. With the sound of a sharp knife parting a ripe apple, The Pumpkin Man's razor-sharp nail pierced the soft skin of Melissa's neck; her blood immediately began spurting into the air.

"No one can save her now!" The Pumpkin Man raged.

Brad saw what happened to Melissa, his brain screaming against what his eyes told him, and his heart feeling like it was about to explode. Seconds later, the other spoke in his mind again.

"It'll be okay. Have faith, Brad."

Despite the fear, the heartache, and the obvious mortal nature of Melissa's wound, Brad felt his sense of wellbeing and peace returning with the stranger's words. It was near incomprehensible that you could feel such profound peace, especially as your beloved wife was literally dying in front of your very eyes. Still, Brad trusted the voice, as it told him to remain calm.

The Pumpkin Man took a menacing step toward Brad. As he did so, he taunted him yet again. "I'm going to make you cut your dying wife into little pieces for trying to stop me! You'll be forced to eat her heart!"

Without him knowing that it was about to happen, Brad's right arm shot forward, striking The Pumpkin Man square in the chest with a closed fist. At the same time, Brad spoke in a deep, commanding voice that was not his own. A voice that rang with authority, demanding to be heeded.

"Anamalech, come forth out of this child!"

Brad was amazed, not only by the voice issuing from his mouth, but also by the fact that his arm seemed to protrude from The Pumpkin Man's chest, buried up to his wrist. His hand was literally inside of the demon's chest, although no blood or gore issued forth. With a rapid pulling motion, the stranger directing his movements, drew his arm straight back. Brad was further amazed to see that no hole, and no mark was left in the boy's chest, or clothes, when his arm was removed from it.

As he watched with rapt, dumbfounded attention, a dark silhouette was pulled away from, and out of the young boy. As soon as the entity was free from the teen, the jack o' lantern head that had been resting on the boy's shoulders split into two halves, falling to the floor. It began to rot immediately, forming a puddle of putrefying, foul-smelling waste. The boy collapsed to the hardwood floor, as if a marionette with strings that were suddenly severed. At the same time, Melissa folded nearly in half, falling to the floor as well.

To Brad's wonderment, yet another ghostly figure appeared on the scene; a handsome boy, of late teen years, now stood before Ruth, gripping her in a fierce, yet loving, embrace. This must be the person she'd been addressing as Titus. He too glowed, a translucent glow of a spectral being.

The dark, shadowy figure still struggling in Brad's firm grasp; it was truly a sight to behold. It struggled, twisting and turning, in a vain attempt to free itself from the stranglehold that Brad maintained on its writhing neck.

The creature itself was the stuff of pure nightmares. It had two large, spikey horns protruding from an oversized, lumpy, scaly head. Its ears were absurdly large, resembling those of an oversized bat. Its eyes were glowing, oval-shaped, burning red orbs in an otherwise completely obsidian body. Its snout was like that of a grotesque pig, mucus dripping from both nostrils in thick trails. Steam rose from its gaping mouth, where a double row of sharp teeth, resembling those of a shark, were bared, in a grimace of deep pain, and anguished frustration.

The stranger inside of Brad, used his free hand, reaching into his pocket, removing the silver crucifix. With a commanding shout, the stranger spoke an order through Brad's mouth.

"Anamelach, I command you to leave this world and return to hell, where you belong. Never bother these children of mine again!"

With the last word, he shoved the crucifix into the mouth of the demon. With a blowing whirlwind of heat, and the strong, nauseating odor of sulfur and brimstone, all those watching saw the demon seemingly blink out of existence. At the same time, the growing flames that had been devouring the wall of the house behind them, as well as all of the smoke the fire had caused, disappeared without a trace as well.

Brad felt a sudden slight pressure upon his body. As soon as the sensation passed, so did the euphoria that he'd been experiencing. The pain from his injuries came crashing back down upon him, as he saw the mysterious stranger standing in front of him once again. Finally free to move of his own volition again, Brad turned, finding Melissa lying curled on her side next to him, on the floor. He sat down beside her, cradling her head in his hands.

Her eyes fluttered open briefly, and she gave him a weak smile.

"I love you," she murmured.

Brad knew that her condition was bad. He could tell he was beginning to lose her. Fighting back stinging tears, he gave her his trademark response, "I love you more, sugarplum."

With a shuddering breath, Melissa passed from life into death. Brad felt her body rapidly growing cold; his desire to live beginning to grow cold with it. He turned, looking helplessly at the others, a forlorn expression upon his face; warm, salty tears stinging his eyes, and streaming down like rain. He saw Ruth and Titus, still standing next to where he sat, holding hands, deep sympathy and compassion written on their faces. The other boy still lay where he'd collapsed in a heap; breathing, but unconscious. The stranger who'd defeated The Pumpkin Man wept as he took in Brad's pained, lost face. He reached down, placing a hand upon Brad's heaving shoulder, leaning down next to him. This time, he spoke aloud, with words that Brad saw coming from his mouth, and heard with his physical ears.

"I told you that it would all be okay," the man said soothingly. "I always keep my promises."

With that, he laid a gentle hand on Melissa's forehead, speaking something in a language that Brad didn't comprehend. Then, he took Melissa's hand, and simply said "arise."

To Brad's utter disbelief, Melissa, who he knew had been dead just a moment before, opened her eyes, allowing the stranger to help her to her feet. Brad leapt to his own feet, embracing Melissa in a massive bear hug. All he could say was "I love you!" over, and over, and over again; hardly giving her a chance to respond. When he finally quieted, he turned back toward the stranger. As he did so, he noticed that Ruth and Titus were no longer in the room with them.

"They've gone on, to where they belong," the stranger said, obviously reading Brad's thoughts. Following Brad's line of sight to the crumpled boy upon the floor, he spoke again. "He'll be alright. When he wakes, he'll remember little to nothing about this event, or his life prior to this. He'll need new caretakers."

Brad and Melissa shared a look, and an unspoken thought. Before either could utter a comment, the stranger spoke again.

"Woman, behold your new son," He said to Melissa with a broad smile. Brad and Melissa nodded their heads in unspoken agreement.

"Now, I have something to tell you, and you *must* heed my words very carefully," he said, with a more serious expression. "Take the child and disappear. Go far, far from this place, and never come back. Do not stop by your home. Do not pack any belongings."

Brad started to ask a question, but the stranger cut him off.

"You have sufficient provisions in your car to get you where you need to go, and you will know when you arrive there. Leave this place and leave it immediately. Take no thought for the need of anything. If you tarry until morning, you'll surely perish."

Brad and Melissa thanked him, and taking his command seriously, Brad squatted down, scooping the boy up in his arms. As he did so, he suddenly noticed that his head, his nose, and the rest of his battered body didn't hurt as much as they had before. He also noticed that, by some unknown means, Melissa was now fully clothed again, although she hadn't moved from his side the entire time the stranger had spoken to them. Upon collecting the boy, Brad noticed that the stranger had disappeared, just like Ruth and Titus had. No fanfare, no goodbyes.

They were on their own now.

Brad carried the boy outside, putting the child in the back seat of his SUV. A glance into the rear cargo area showed that the vehicle had been miraculously stocked with all manner of food, and clothing items. Without even checking, somehow they knew that the clothes would all be a perfect fit. Brad and Melissa climbed into the front seats, buckled up, making ready to begin their new life.

Inside the glovebox, Melissa discovered enough cash to easily reestablish themselves, comfortably, in a new location. Without another word to each other, Brad started the car, and they drove out of town as fast as they could, trying not to see the carnage that had been visited upon the town itself, as they headed for I-20 Westbound...

JACK BEAUMONT

CHAPTER 60
NOVEMBER 1ˢᵀ, 2032
WHITE HOUSE-1600 PENNSYLVANIA AVENUE

Hillary Clinton reached over Huma Abendin's still, sleeping form snatching the jangling private cellphone off the nightstand. When she picked up the phone, she saw that the clock read 6am.

It's only 6am. This had better be good, she thought. *Or someone's going to go home today jobless, and with ringing in their ears, from the tongue lashing I'll give them before they're shown the door.*

"Hello," she croaked into the phone, still half asleep.

"Madame President," General Xavier greeted her formally. "It's happened again."

No further explanation was forthcoming, no further explanation was necessary. This was a call that she'd half expected for the last several years. It was one of many such calls that she'd fielded in her lengthy time in office. Since the trouble that she'd stirred up while she was Secretary of State under Obama, and the trouble that she'd fomented worldwide after her stunning election losses to a reality television star in 2016, and the bumbling idiot's election in 2020, had come to a head in the third year of year of *her* Presidency, she'd convinced Congress to grant her emergency war powers, convincing them to sign a resolution allowing her to stay in office until the extreme threats against America had been dealt with. So, here she was...still president even after her first term ended, and she hadn't had to run for a second. Her third term would continue well after her second should officially end, in January.

She'd dealt with all of the other situations the same way that she'd deal with the current one. And, there had been many, many such "hotspots" of *activity* in this country, although none even remotely as bad as that of Summer's Cove. This was fortunate though. She could use it. The American public had begun to tire of her leadership, and she was sure that Congress would try to remove her very soon. That was part of the reason that she began taking interest in these paranormal hotspots in the first place. She'd long ago vowed that she'd harness the power of even Satan himself...if it allowed her stay in office.

Events like those in Summer's Cove were a threat to her power, even if they temporarily had their uses. She didn't like competition very much.

She sat up in bed, throwing her legs over the side, and stumbling towards the bathroom. She gave General Xavier, who waited for her instructions on the other end of the line, the words that he'd been waiting for.

"Execute Directive 67," she said into the phone.

"Yes, Ma'am," came the curt, professional reply, before the line went dead.

She placed the phone on the large, double vanity before regarding herself in the mirror. She'd figured out a way to kill two birds with one stone. First, she'd use the events in Summer's Cove to accomplish her goal: strict gun control by Executive Order. Secondly, and most importantly, she'd ensure that Anamalech would never rise again.

"I don't like competition," she reminded herself with a malicious grin at her own reflection. For just a moment her icy blue eyes morphed into fiery red orbs, before hiding behind their false cover again. "No, I don't like competition at all."

A few minutes later, Huma joined her in the bathroom. She put an arm around Hillary's waist, resting her head on her lover's shoulder.

"What is it?" she asked. She could tell something was bothering Hillary.

"A group of white men, probably a neo-Nazi, white supremacist group, armed with assault rifles, RPG's, and possibly stolen military hardware, just wiped out an entire small town in Alabama," Hillary lied…

CHAPTER 61

Elton Crosby and his wife Juanita were awakened by a loud, insistent banging on their front door. Fearing the worst, Elton removed his gun from inside his nightstand drawer, tucking it in his waistband of his pajamas, and went downstairs to the living room. He peered through the keyhole, expecting to see the worst. Instead, he was greeted with a much welcome sight. It looked like the night of horrors was over, and the Calvary was here to help with the cleanup. A pair of US Army soldiers stood on their front porch.

Elton and Juanita had hunkered down in their home the previous night, praying throughout the long night before eventually falling asleep. Their prayers seemed to have been answered. Throughout the seemingly never-ending night they'd heard gunshots, multiple explosions, and more screams than they could count. It looked like the rising dawn had seen them surviving their second brush with The Pumpkin Man.

Elton pulled the gun from his waistband, setting in on the crescent table in the hallway, and opened the front door. Over, the shoulders of the two armed soldiers, Elton was surprised to see the devastation that had been wrought to his neighborhood. Three of his neighbor's houses were in various stages of burning to the ground. Mr. Pentash's house looked like it had been leveled by a bomb blast. His stunned survey of the neighborhood was interrupted by one of the soldiers.

"Excuse me, sir," the soldier said. "We are under orders to move all survivors to the movie theater downtown. Is there anyone else in the home?"

"Y-yes," Elton said. "My wife is inside." Turning toward the inside of the house, he called for Juanita.

"Yes, dear?" she asked, entering the living room from the kitchen.

"It appears that we are being moved to the movie theater, while they clear the town," he responded.

"Okay, let me grab some things, and then we can go."

Stepping forward quickly, the second soldier said, "That won't be necessary ma'am. There'll be more than enough food and supplies where we're going."

"We have to clear the rest of the town. We need to go, now," the first soldier prodded.

Elton allowed himself and Juanita to be hurried toward the awaiting transport. He was relieved to see some familiar faces among those already in the back of the large transport truck. It seems that at least some of those he knew had survived the nightmare of the previous night. Some of those waiting in the truck had blank, vacant stares fixed upon their faces. Others were covered in blood, whether their own, or someone else's, Elton didn't know. Nor did he care to ask. He was sure that all things would be sorted out once they got to the movie theater...

CHAPTER 62

The theater was packed full of people. Each of the three auditoriums held about two hundred people. All were filled nearly to full capacity. Still, by Elton's count that was only about six hundred people.

Is this all that survived this time? Elton wondered with horror.

The thought of so much death and destruction weighed very heavily on his heart. He felt the terrible weight of all those deaths upon his tired and weary soul. He didn't think he'd ever feel right again. Especially knowing that he was partially to blame for The Pumpkin Man rising again.

Slowly, it began to dawn on Elton that things didn't seem to be right here. First of all, the survivors had been sheltering in the movie theater for nearly three hours now. During all that time, Elton had seen no one attempting to treat the wounded and badly injured. Secondly, no one had offered the survivors food, drink, blankets, or any other comforting items that would be normally handed out in this kind of dire situation.

No kind words were spoken to the shaken and confused residents of this town. No presence of doctors or nurses could be detected anywhere he looked. No attempts to communicate what was happening on the outside of these walls was made. No one attempted to explain to the survivors what would happen next.

People were beginning to get restless with all of the waiting without food, comfort, or communication. Soon, the need to eat, drink, and even use the restrooms, would have to be addressed by those in charge. The auditoriums all featured emergency exits near each corner of the movie screens. Each emergency exit was flanked by a pair of armed soldiers. Another pair of armed soldiers were stationed by each side of the doors at the front of the auditoriums. Elton had noticed that a couple of attempts by others to leave the auditorium were rebuffed, with little to no explanation.

Just as Elton was beginning to become more and more anxious about what was going on, he saw another soldier enter from the emergency exit, briefly speaking to one of the armed men by the door, nearest the right-hand side of the movie screen. Being only a few feet away from the men, Elton was able to hear a snippet of the conversation, relieved to know that something was finally about to happen here.

"It's time to go," the Captain told the soldier. The soldier nodded his head in acknowledgement, then walked over to his counterpart on the other side of the room, relaying the same information to him.

Finally, Elton thought. *We're going to get somewhere.*

He was glad. Juanita badly needed her insulin shots that she'd been forced to leave behind at their house. She also needed to eat pretty soon, to keep her blood sugar steady. Otherwise, she was likely to pass out.

He watched as the soldiers at the front of the auditorium exited the room. Other survivors had seemed to notice that something had changed, that something was about to happen, too. The auditorium began to fall silent, in anticipation of what was to come.

In the absence of hundreds of voices speaking at once, Elton heard a small sound that chilled him to the bone. He could hear what sounded like heavy iron chains being pulled through the door handles of the double doors, on each side at the front of auditorium. At the same moment, the emergency exit doors on each side of the movie screen opened, and eight more armed soldiers entered; four on each side.

The soldier, who the Captain had previously spoken with, issued a silent signal and the soldiers raised their guns. The chatter of automatic gunfire filled the room, as screams competed to be heard over the explosions of hundreds of rounds being fired in rapid succession.

Elton's last thought before going down in a hailstorm of bullets was, *I guess Juanita won't be needing that insulin now...*

JACK BEAUMONT

CHAPTER 63

WHITE HOUSE- 1600 PENNSYLVANIA AVENUE
1200 HOURS

"Yes?" Hillary spoke into the phone, setting her fork down on her napkin, sighing impatiently. Her displeasure at being interrupted was written across her face in an impatient scowl.

"Madame President," the General said. "It's done."

"Good. And we got them all?" she asked.

"Yes Ma'am," He replied. "The ones who didn't die during the event, were taken care of as per Directive 67."

"Great. Well done," she said, clicking off the phone. She favored Huma with a small smile. Then she ordered her, "Let's get that press release, and my statement on this out. Immediately after lunch, I expect to address the media in the Rose Garden." Shaking, her head in mock sadness, she continued, "This is a terrible tragedy that must never, ever be allowed to happen again."

She picked up her fork and resumed eating.

"I'm on it." Huma, the ever-faithful servant, jumped up, leaving her plate untouched, and went about handling the President's business.

Such a loyal one. Naïve it's true, but loyal to fault. Mission accomplished. Gun control on a scale of epic proportions is shortly to become a new reality. No one could argue after hearing that an entire town of people were wiped from the face of the earth, by armed domestic terrorists, that guns needed to be banned for the greater good of the people.

This new development would allow her master plan, her endgame, to be implemented without the voting citizens being able to put up very much resistance. Her plans...oh yes, indeed. "She" had plans.

As the demon named Tanit continued eating with a smile, she thought about just how great her plans were, and how much more she'd be able achieve in the very near future. Gaining more and more power, and stripping more and more freedoms from the people, would afford her greater ability to purge her "brothers and sisters" from her domain. Her power would only grow stronger as events sped up.

She picked her phone up again, hit a key, and Huma answered immediately.

"Please have Ap---I mean Donald...please have Donald call me immediately."

She'd almost called Donald J. Trump, her Secretary of Defense, by his true name, Appolyan. That would have required some explaining. More explaining than she'd prefer to do. No one, except for herself, knew his secret...or her own.

She believed in keeping her enemies close...

CHAPTER 64
SUMMER'S COVE, ALABAMA

Silence now encamped about a once bustling, small, middle class American town. A town that was once plagued by a demonic entity, and recurring events of epic tragedies. In the last week, more Americans had died in this quant town than had died in the infamous attacks of September 11th, 2001. It was nearly unbelievable that this small rural Alabama town was the location of such wholesale slaughter.

The lone soldier, posted at the barricade leading into town, watched the buzzards circling overhead. Even after all of the bodies had been burned in a massive bonfire that had stayed lit for four days, the large birds that feasted upon the flesh of the dead, still circled the skies about town. At times as many as two dozen could be seen making their lazy, spiraling vigil in the skies above his head. They could still detect the copious amounts of blood that had been spilled here.

I'll be glad when this assignment is finished, the soldier thought to himself with small shudder.

To be honest, this assignment had spooked him far more than any in Iraq or Afghanistan. While he hadn't understood exactly what had taken place here, he knew it was a far cry from what he'd witnessed overseas. This wasn't fighting an enemy without uniforms, who couldn't be distinguished from a friendly civilian, no this was way off. Different. This was the slaughter of unarmed, and innocent American civilians.

The official line that the Army grunts, such as himself, were given was that this town had been infected with a super-deadly virus. One that had replicated, spreading rapidly among the people. What was done here had been said to have been done for the greater good of the American people. The official cover story in the media, supposedly to stave off public panic about a pandemic disease that was purportedly worse than Covid-19, was that a group of white supremacists had attacked the town, taking hostages, and then killing every man, woman, and child that they could find still alive.

Yet, he couldn't bring himself to believe either of these scenarios. He knew the latter to be false, and he seriously doubted the veracity of the former. Why? Well, for starters, the lack of hazmat suits or preparations that usually accompanied such an event sent up several red flags.

Wouldn't we all be required to wear protective equipment and gear if risk of a deadly viral contamination existed? How could we be allowed to walk around unprotected, if the disease was as viral as they claimed?

As he continued to ponder and question what the truth behind this massacre *really* was, he heard a rustling in the woods to the right hand side of the road. As he watched, a ragged, unshaven, unkempt, middle-aged man made his way through the thick underbrush, and onto the deserted road. He was bloodied, with torn clothes, and had deep scratches covering his arms, and a face that had been battered and bruised. As he saw the soldier standing there, his eyes shown with relief.

"Thank God! Please help me! I've been wandering the woods for six days..."

"Stop where you are."

"What? Wait, I need your help," the man pleaded as he continued to stumble forward. "My wife suddenly attacked me with a baseball bat. She nearly killed me before I escaped. This whole town seems to have gone nuts..."

"I said stop right there!" the soldier shouted now, raising his rifle toward the man.

"But, please, I need help," the man pleaded again. He continued, towards the soldier. "I need medical attention. I've got a broken..."

Ka-blam!

The soldier's reply came in the form of a single shot, dead center in the civilian's forehead. The man dropped like a rock, dead before his body hit the ground.

Man, I hate his assignment! the soldier thought with regret.

Still, he couldn't be one hundred percent certain that these people *weren't* carrying the virus that his superiors claimed that they were. His orders had been clear: shoot, on sight, any civilians that he encountered. No one was to be allowed to leave this place alive, unless they were with the military, or civilian authorities.

Thank God, this assignment ends in the morning.

Tomorrow, they were pulling out. Once all military personnel and equipment were pulled out, the Air Force would be doing its part in this cleanup. They would be dropping six strategically placed FOAB's on this town, which would wipe out virtually everything for nearly two miles. Then the dozers would come in, and within a few days, it'd be like this town never existed in the first place.

The FOAB, nicknamed the Father Of All Bombs, had nearly double the blast radius and power of the MOAB, or Mother Of All Bombs, which was first used by the US military on the border between Afghanistan and Pakistan in 2017. Basically, the FOAB was the non-radioactive equivalent of a small tactical nuke. Designed to detonate in the air above the target zone, the majority of the damage caused by a FOAB came from the intense heat generated, and the concussive power of the massive shockwave following the detonation.

All the damage, without all the radiation. There probably won't be much left of anything to clean up, even when it comes to trees and plant life. One thing was sure: whatever the truth was behind the events in this town, Uncle Sam was intent on performing a "full sanitation" at this location.

No one would ever be able to discover any "hidden truth" about what occurred here, by this time tomorrow. Within ten years, unless the town was allowed to be resettled, no one would even know it ever existed, or even be able to locate it. Any remaining signs of civilized life would be erased by nature.

Morning can't come soon enough, thought the soldier, as he began the tedious process of moving the heavy corpse to the burn site…

EPILOGUE

HUNTER'S GLEN

Five years later...

Hunter's Glen.

The site of so much violence and trouble. A large meadow on the far outskirts of a small town in rural Alabama. You'd never know about, nor believe, the things that had occurred here years before, had you not lived through it.

You'd be hard pressed to find a more serene or beautiful wilderness setting. Once a place that was mysteriously devoid of life, the quiet meadow now flourished with all manner of plant and animal life. Deer fed in the grassy fields, squirrels played in the trees, and birds sang in the skies overhead.

Overlooking the meadow, situated as if it were a giant sentry perched on top of a steep hill, grew a massive oak tree. Nearly three hundred years old, the tree had seen a lot of life...and death, during its time overseeing the meadow. It still stood, silent and waiting, watching time continue to unfold before it, as it always had in the past.

The town that had once stood just a short drive away, had been decimated and destroyed. Razed to the ground after the third coming of an evil demon named

The Pumpkin Man. The roads, the only remaining evidence that a town had ever once stood near these parts, had been reclaimed by nature; the asphalt cracked and broken over time, weeds growing through it. In some places, small trees now grew where yellow lines had once marked the separation of travel lanes.

No one had stepped foot in Hunter's Glen for five long years. That is, until today. Deer scattered as a lone vehicle traveled down the now barely visible entrance road to the meadow. As the man pulled his car up to the base of the hill, stopped, and exited the vehicle, birds scattered from the branches of the great and towering oak.

The man climbed the steep hill, surveying the meadow from the vantage point at the top, under the protective branches of the old oak tree. The tranquil scenery put a big smile on his face. Huge open meadow, a rushing stream on the border, wooded backdrop, and a massive oak tree atop a hill as a focal point.

This will be the ideal place to build the retreat, the man thought with a smile.

Its secluded, serene, wilderness setting would serve his needs well, its location far from any towns or main roads, ensuring that the land could be had for a song and dance. He would make the offer when the banks opened on Monday.

As he walked back down the hill to his car, the sun was suddenly blotted out. For a moment, the glen appeared as dark as dusk. Then, almost as suddenly as the darkness fell, the blazing sun returned, banishing darkness once again.

The man was so lost in his own thoughts that he hadn't noticed a change of atmosphere in the meadow. As if cut off by a closed window, the sounds of teeming wildlife suddenly disappeared. The birds that had once roosted in the great oak, now safely waited across the stream. Gnats, flies, and other insects no longer buzzed and hummed in the midday sun. The deer that had been grazing close by, now sprang for the woods.

Had he noticed these things, he might have found them oddly curious, but not worrisome. Had he seen what had pushed through the soft earth underneath the oak tree in the short time since he'd left, he would have likely not known the significance thereof. Instead, the man continued onward to his car, unaware of the subtle changes all around him. Visions of an expansive retreat, a resort for rich folks swirled in his head.

■■■

Atop the hill, the lone pumpkin vine stood two inches high above the soil, despite having just broken through the soft ground a moment before. Under the tree, it would watch and wait, looking to seize the perfect opportunity once again.

Patience. Must have patience…

JACK BEAUMONT

ABOUT THE AUTHOR

Jack Beaumont is the author of three other novels, *Night of the Pumpkin Man*, *Dawn of the Pumpkin Man*, and *The Park* (soon to be released by King's Way Press) as well as three novellas, *Santa Claus Comes Tonight!*, *Santa Claus Comes Tonight Too!* and *The Green-Eyed Monster*. Jack has several more writing projects in the works, with another novel due to be released before the end of fall.

When he's not writing, he spends most of his time with his wife, and wonderful children, in their western North Carolina home. He enjoys the great outdoors, football, time with family, and a good book, by a warm fire, with a hot cup of coffee, on a cold day.

If you enjoyed this book, please be sure to drop Jack a line on his private email, or visit his Facebook author page: pumpkinmanjb@gmail.com